# My Wife's Boyfriend

## & Our Feud with the Highlands Ranch Homeowners Association

# REGGIE RIVERS

To Trisha
Best Wishes
Reggie Rivers

SCA Publishing
16 Inverness Place East, Suite E-200
Englewood, CO 80112
Copyright © 2006 Reggie Rivers
www.reggierivers.net

Cover design and interior layout by MacGraphics Services
Cover Illustration: Fred Eyer

This book is a novel. References to real people, events,
establishments, organizations, or locales are intended only to
provide a sense of authenticity, and are used fictitiously All other
characters, and all incidents and dialogue, are drawn from the
author's imagination and are not to be construed as real.

Published by
SCA Publishing
16 Inverness Place East, Suite E-200
Englewood, CO 80112
(303) 790-2020
www.sharoncooper.com

Library of Congress Cataloging-in-Publication Data
Rivers, Reggie.
My Wife's Boyfriend & Our Feud with the Highlands Ranch
Homeowners Association / by Reggie Rivers
p. cm
ISBN 0-9704542-1-X
LCCN: 2006908407

A portion of the proceeds of this book will be donated to the HOPE Scholarship Program run by Minority Enterprise & Educational Development in Denver. HOPE is an acronym which stands for Helping Other People Emerge. The program awards scholarships to middle school students who have achieved academic excellence or who have shown significant improvement in their studies. Each student's prize money is invested in an interest-bearing account, and when he or she graduates from high school and enrolls in a university, college, or trade school, the money is distributed to pay for tuition and fees. The program's goal is to reach students at an age when many of them are just beginning to think about dropping out and encourage them to continue their education. Reggie Rivers has been the spokesman for the HOPE Scholarship program since 2001.

Also by Reggie Rivers

*The Vance: The Beginning & The End*

*Power Shift*

*4th and Fixed: When the Mob Tackles Football It's No Longer Just a Game*

# Acknowledgements

Many people helped me during the long process of researching and writing this book, but none had a bigger impact than my editor, Peggy Cole. She has read and re-read the various editions of the manuscript more than a dozen times, always applying her keen sense of word-choice and story development. She was my private English professor, continually challenging me to become a better writer. Thank you, Peggy! Her husband, Jim, provided a fresh perspective that reminded me of the overall focus of the book. My siblings, Darryl, Mike, Jackie and Gwen helped with the final copyediting. However, despite all of this guidance, I made a few style and storytelling choices that defied the recommendations of my editors. So if you notice anything that strikes you as a mistake—it's entirely my fault. Karen Saunders at MacGraphics, Ann Marie Gordon at United Graphics and Fred Eyer all helped transform my manuscript into the bound book that you're holding in your hands. As always, Sharon and Steve Cooper have been my constant business partners and friends. And I owe a special thank you to my wonderful wife, Stephanie, who has supported and encouraged me throughout the development of this story. Stephanie gave her approval for the title of this novel even though she knew that people would constantly ask, "Is this about *you*?" No, it's not about her. This is a work of fiction.

In loving memory of
Aunt Sue

**Boop boopy doop**

# prologue

A woman laughed in a corner booth—eyes closed, mouth open, face rising toward the ceiling as her lover nuzzled her neck. The few patrons in Panzano Italian restaurant at 1:30 a.m. turned to smile at her. She was a pretty blonde, probably mid-thirties, in a conservative blue skirt-suit snug against her trim frame. She was getting louder with each drink. The man sitting with her tried to unbutton her silk shirt, but she giggled and brushed his hands away. Her black Enzo heels were askew under the table, and her stocking feet arched out sensuously every time he kissed her.

Her companion wore tattered jeans, a black turtleneck with the sleeves pushed up to his elbows and paint-splattered black boots. He was sitting with his back to the room, his auburn hair flowing over his shoulders. Whenever he turned to sip his cocktail, patrons saw a handsome profile—full lips, a strong, prow-like nose, long eyelashes, and sculpted sideburns. His right forearm boasted an ornate tattoo of a Christian cross with a huge nail through its center, as if Christ had been crucified through his abdomen, like an insect.

He whispered something into her ear and she laughed again, flashing straight white teeth. When the waiter brought their check, the long-haired man reached for it halfheartedly, but the blonde woman snatched it up.

"Are you sure, Shorty?" he asked perfunctorily.

She pulled the tab closer and studied it—appetizers, salads, entrees, desserts, several glasses of wine for her and rum and Cokes for him. The bill was just over a hundred dollars.

"Yo, can I at least get the tip?" he offered.

She shushed him and slipped an American Express gold card into the bill folder. "Dinner is on me." She stared at him somewhat aggressively and said, "We're staying here tonight."

"In the restaurant?" he asked facetiously, again reaching for the front of her shirt.

She slapped his hand away. "In the hotel." The restaurant was on the ground floor of the Hotel Monaco.

He glanced at his watch—a stainless steel TAG Heuer Carrera Chronograph—it was nearly two in the morning. They'd worked late at the gallery, had drinks at Club Purple on Market Street, and then had cruised over to Panzano.

The waiter returned with her card, and she added a large tip. When they walked out of the restaurant, she swayed in her heels, but she walked with determination as if she could overcome the effects of the alcohol through sheer will power. Her lover's arm was wrapped around her waist. The cross tattoo fluttered in the light as his fingers danced on her hip.

They crossed the lobby to the front desk, where she asked the clerk to put them in room 1034. Her lover cuddled her from behind, burying his face in her hair.

"Let me check to see if that suite is available," the clerk said, discreetly noting that she wore a gleaming diamond wedding band but her companion had nothing on his ring finger. It was a Tuesday night—Wednesday morning actually—and they had no bags with them. "Ah, yes, we can accommodate that request."

He made two keys and directed them to the elevator.

They groped each other as the lift ascended. On the tenth floor, they crab-walked down the hall, kissing passionately. They stumbled into a radically decorated suite; each ultramodern piece of furniture looked like a one-of-a-kind work of art.

He tried to lead her toward the bed, but she shook her head and pulled him back to the door.

"Right here," she purred, letting her jacket slip off her shoulders.

He ran his hands up the outside of her legs, caressing the lacy bands of her thigh-high stockings, and then tracing the thin straps of her garter as he raised the hem of her skirt up over her hips.

"Naughty girl!" he said, grinning slyly. "No panties."

She threw her legs around him, gasping as he pressed her against the hotel door.

"Right here," she moaned.

# one

Howard Marshall was sinking. He looked down and saw his black, Kenneth Cole dress shoes disappearing into a strange substance, thick and sticky as fresh concrete. He tried to lift one foot, but he could not escape.

"This is ridiculous," he said, laughing nervously as the cuffs of his navy Brooks Brothers slacks descended into the bog. He looked around for something to grab onto, but everything around him was completely black. He squinted, turning his head from side to side, but he couldn't make out any shapes.

He called out, "Is anyone there?" He heard no response.

Despite the surrounding darkness, he was somehow bathed in light. When he looked down at his left hand, he could see the black briefcase his wife had given him for his birthday four months ago. It was quickly swallowed by the bog. As he sank up to his abdomen, the hem of his suit jacket spread out and floated on the surface. His hands touched the substance; it was neither cool nor warm, and it didn't seem to have an odor.

"What the heck is this?" he asked. But there was no panic in his voice. He sounded like a man who thought he was the victim of a prank, as if he expected someone to pop out at any moment, laughing. Soon the substance was up to his neck, and, still, no one had jumped out to say "Gotcha!" When he tilted his head back to keep his mouth clear, his wife, Sophia, suddenly appeared in front of him.

"Bassiff!" Howard called to her. "I'm stuck!"

She watched impassively as he sank. Howard took a deep breath and closed his eyes. His nose filled with gunk, and he tried to raise his hand, but his arms were immobilized. He waited, certain that Sophia would rescue him. Though his eyes were closed, he sensed light below him. It was warm and inviting, and his fear started to fade away. But after half a minute, he hadn't reached the light and his lungs were burning. Panic set in.

He opened his mouth ... and awoke with a jolt.

He sat up in bed, breathing hard in the darkness. He looked at the digital clock. It was 3:42 a.m. This was at least the tenth time he'd had this sinking dream in the past month.

Slowly, Howard regained his bearings. He recognized the honey oak four-poster bed his wife had purchased at the Park Meadows Mall a year earlier, the Sony flat-screen TV on the wall, the mauve sofa and oak coffee table in the sitting area of the spacious bedroom, and the long bourbon drapes on the windows. He realized that he was in his own bed, safely nestled in the bosom of the Highlands Ranch subdivision. But the feeling of being submerged persisted.

What had awakened him?

He looked across the room at the keypad of the security system. The illuminated red lights told him that the alarm was armed in AT-HOME mode, and no windows or doors were open.

He stared through the bedroom doorway into the darkness of the upstairs hall. He took a slow breath. He didn't hear any footsteps. No creaking, no bumping, no sinister sounds. There were no normal sounds either, like a flushing toilet, voices from the TV downstairs, or beeping from the microwave. Everything was quiet.

Howard turned toward the other side of the bed.

Sophia was gone.

Again.

He swallowed hard as the wet, concrete threatened to engulf him. He stared at her dented pillow for a long time, not wanting to accept the obvious answer.

He slid his legs off the bed and rubbed his head. His thick brown hair was matted and tangled, and when he wiped his face, stubble grazed his palm. At six-foot-two, two hundred and twenty pounds, Howard was a large man, and still fairly fit as he approached his fortieth birthday. He'd boxed Golden Gloves as a teenager and had played Division I football at the University of Tennessee. But that was a long time ago. Now he worked out when he could and had to suck in his gut to button the thirty-eight-inch waist on his slacks.

He turned on a lamp and studied the wedding photo on the bedside table. He and Sophia were running toward the camera as family and friends waved in the background. Sophia was holding up the skirt of her dress with one hand and clutching Howard's arm with the other. Her blonde hair was bound into swirling curls, and she was laughing rapturously, white teeth sparkling in the golden sunlight, green eyes looking right at the camera. She was perfectly posed, like a model who knew exactly how to find her light, and she looked a decade younger than the thirty-three years she'd actually been when they'd wed two years ago.

Gazing at the picture usually brought a contented smile to Howard's face. He felt lucky to have found a wife whom he loved passionately and who loved him with equal ardor. But tonight the picture didn't elicit the usual reaction. Howard picked it up and stared at it in confusion for several minutes, wondering what she was thinking behind those pretty eyes.

Long before he'd met Sophia, his married and recently divorced buddies had joked that Howard was lucky that he didn't have a wife, kids, a mortgage, and responsibilities to smother his spirit.

"Marriage will suck the life out of you," they'd warned. "Get married and have a couple of kids. You'll lose that lopsided grin."

Howard had laughed with them, confident that he'd been shrewd in avoiding the altar during his twenties and early thirties. He had always been suspicious of marriage—a life-long union seemed, to him, an exercise in futility.

Howard had always been a serial monogamist, working his way through girlfriends as if they were automobiles on lease—every three years he had a new one.

Then he met Sophia.

Amazingly, the more time he spent with her, the more time he wanted to spend with her. Howard discovered that Sophia was a catalyst who enriched every aspect of his life. His weekends were more relaxed when he was with Sophia. Meals tasted better when she was sitting across the table. Movies were more entertaining when she was holding his hand. Problems seemed more manageable, conversations were more interesting, and sex was more satisfying. Eventually, Howard started calling her Bassiff—a reference to the old TV commercials for B.A.S.F. *"We don't make the things you love. We just make the things you love better. We're B.A.S.F."*

His cynicism about long-term relationships melted away, and Howard suggested that they move in together—the first time he'd ever wanted to live with a girlfriend. But Sophia had rejected the idea immediately. In Highlands Ranch, she was surrounded by married couples with children, and she worried that her neighbors would disapprove.

"Since when do you care what they think?" Howard had asked.

"They're my customers," Sophia countered. She owned the art gallery *Anomalous*, near the Park Meadows Mall, and the bulk of her clients were women who lived in Highlands Ranch. "It's been tough enough fitting in around here as an unmarried woman with no kids. Most of the wives think I want to steal their husbands, and most of the moms only talk about their children. Since I don't have anything to contribute to that conversation, they're not sure what to say to me. A live-in boyfriend would just be another thing to set me apart."

Howard had argued that most of the women in the neighborhood probably envied Sophia. "You're gorgeous, you have a perfect body, you own your own business, you bought this big beautiful house by yourself, and you travel the country constantly looking for new art to bring to your gallery. For most of these women, you probably represent either a time in their life that they wish they could recapture, or you're the epitome of what they wish they could become."

Sophia had shaken her head. "All the smooth talk in the world isn't going to convince me on this, Howard. If you want to live with me, you should propose to me."

Three months later, Howard did just that on the conveyor belt in the middle of the B-Concourse at Denver International Airport. They were on their way to visit some friends in Miami. Howard slid his backpack off his shoulder and dropped to one knee. Hundreds of people waiting for their flights instantly recognized that a proposal was in progress, and they watched as Howard and Sophia floated past: He was gazing up at her; she was gazing at the ring. When Sophia said "yes," the crowd hooted and cheered.

A male voice screamed, "Watch out!" and Howard laughed, thinking this was a warning about the perils of marriage. But Howard wasn't worried. He no longer feared marriage;

Sophia was his Bassiff. He knew that everything in their lives would be better now that they were together. He hugged her tightly. Several people screamed "Watch out!" Howard and Sophia opened their eyes just as they reached the end of the conveyor belt. They tumbled onto the thinly carpeted floor. Her purse hit the ground and its contents exploded in every direction like a grenade. They looked at each other and burst out laughing. The crowd, which had initially gasped, laughed with them, and several good Samaritans stepped forward to help them gather up their belongings.

They got married a year later.

# *two*

In the wedding photo on the bedside table, Howard's hair was cut short, and his square jaw was shaved clean. He was handsome and rugged, like an actor in a pickup truck commercial. His blue eyes were turned toward Sophia, as if he were captivated by her beauty, as if he never wanted to stop looking at her, as if she held the answers to all of his problems. The day before the wedding, Howard's father had told him that the secret to a long marriage is to make his wife the center of his life and, in the picture, Howard seemed to be doing just that. A familiar grin spread across his face, and a feeling of ease began to replace the anxiety of the sinking nightmare. Looking at their wedding picture always made him remember the best moments of their marriage. Howard started to rise from the bed, but stopped, his smile frozen in place, as a long-buried memory rose to the top of his mind. He looked closely at his expression in the wedding photo and realized, for the first time, that it wasn't just affection that had locked his eyes on his bride's face. Now, seeing his slightly off-balance pose, the odd tilt of his head, his free arm arching across his body, and the way his eyes were turned slightly more than his head—as if they had darted to the side—he remembered that Sophia had stumbled as they'd exited the reception hall. It had been a subtle misstep. Howard doubted that anyone watching them had sucked in a breath, fearful that the bride was about to fall in her beautiful gown. But he recalled that her grip on his arm had suddenly tightened, and he had reacted instantly, turning to catch her.

He picked up the photograph and held it at an angle to study it more closely under the light. Though he was smiling in the picture, he also saw strain around his eyes, urgency in his neck muscles, and fear at the corners of his mouth. His reaction to her near fall now seemed so obvious that he wondered why he had never noticed it.

Part of it, he realized, was the way Sophia had presented the photo.

"This is the one!" she'd said, after sifting through nearly two hundred pictures trying to find an image that best captured the emotion of their wedding day. "I love the way you're looking at me! Like you can't take your eyes off me!"

"Not until I die," Howard had promised. She'd handed him the photo, and he'd seen what she'd seen. "I'm captivated!" he'd agreed.

They'd printed hundreds of wallet-sized photos and sent them to their families and friends along with thank-you cards. Howard had put a framed eight-by-ten copy on his bedside table and one on his desk at work. For two years, he had looked at the photo daily, and he had always been buoyed by the loving memory of their wedding.

But now it was clear that the photo had actually captured the anxious split-second of Sophia's stumble. When he looked closely, he could see her right hand digging into his forearm like a talon, but her other hand hadn't moved. She hadn't averted her eyes from the camera or changed her expression. Aside from the slightly awkward position of her left foot, there was little evidence that anything was wrong. Howard thought uncomfortably that perhaps this *was* the best picture of their marriage. The photographer had inadvertently captured Sophia acting as if nothing were wrong, while Howard adjusted to handle the problems.

"No, no, no," Howard said to himself in the darkened bedroom. They had a good marriage. They were trusting, considerate, and faithful. If Howard ever had even the slightest doubt about Sophia's honesty, he needed only recall their first date five years ago.

# *three*

The night of their first date was the first time Howard had ever entered Highlands Ranch, and, naturally, he got lost. He'd taken the Lincoln exit off I-25 and had turned west through the town of Lone Tree. But within a mile, the sameness of the architecture, the subtly curved roads, the straight streets that changed names, and the absence of distinctive landmarks left him confused and disoriented like a man trying to navigate through an endless desert with only shifting sand dunes to guide him.

Howard had thought that he was driving west on Lincoln, but he failed to notice that the road curved north. When he looked up at a street sign, he saw that he had somehow ended up on University Boulevard. He took a left on Venneford Ranch Road, thinking that it would take him west again, but it subtly curved to the south. For half an hour, Howard drove in circles, never traveling in the direction that he believed he was moving and, therefore, never regaining his equilibrium. He turned down long residential streets that ended in cul-de-sacs, retreated and turned down roads that spiraled deeper into the neighborhood. He had directions, but he couldn't get back to where he'd started to pick them up again. Finally, he called Sophia and confessed that he was hopelessly lost.

"Trust me," she said, gently, "you're not the first victim of the neighborhood. Where are you?"

Howard laughed and looked around at the endless rows of homes. "I'm pretty sure I'm still in Colorado."

"Are you parked in front of a house?" she said.

The question confused Howard. "A house? Yes, I'm parked in front of a bunch of houses." How could he not be? "But I don't think one of them is yours."

"Just go knock on someone's door and tell them that you're looking for Sophia Andreasson."

Howard laughed again, but when Sophia didn't laugh with him, he realized that she was serious. "I can pick *any* house and they'll know where you live?"

"Yes."

"Are you famous or something?"

"I'm the only one in the book."

This wasn't making much sense to Howard. "In the phone book?"

"No, in the Directory. Listen Howard, you've got to hurry or we'll miss our reservations."

Confused, Howard hung up the phone and climbed out of his car. He looked up and down the block. *Any house?* He decided on a beige two-story home with two Ford Explorers parked in the driveway. The man who answered the door was mid-forties in a white dress shirt and slacks with his tie loosened at the neck. His mouth was full of food.

"Excuse me for bothering you," Howard said. "You're not going to believe this, but—"

A little boy exclaimed, "Who is it, Daddy?"

"Yeah, who's there?" another little boy asked.

Two kids suddenly appeared in the doorway. They were probably five and seven. Dark-haired boys with surprisingly light eyes, staring up at the stranger on their doorstep without a hint of fear.

"Aiden and Ethan, go back to the table," their father said.

"But who's this man?" the older boy demanded.

Howard smiled and was about to explain that he just needed a little help.

"He's lost," the father said, still chewing.

Howard stared at him. "How do you know that?"

"Everyone gets lost!" the boys said, in unison.

"We got lost one time," the younger boy said.

"Go back to the table," the father said, but the boys didn't budge. To Howard, he said, "Who are you looking for?"

Howard said, "Sophia Andreasson."

"Any other identifiers?" the man asked.

"Any other whats?"

"Identifiers!" the older boy repeated, shaking his head as though he thought Howard might be a little slow.

The father clarified. "Spouse, pets, type of car?"

That didn't clear things up at all for Howard. He scowled and shook his head.

"Hang on," the father said, pulling his boys back from the doorway. He disappeared into the house for several minutes. When he returned, he handed Howard a sheet of paper, and said, "Just follow the line. It'll take you right there."

Howard thanked him dully and studied the page as the man closed the door. The paper was an aerial diagram of Highlands Ranch, and from that vantage point, the neighborhood looked like a huge maze. The man had used red ink to draw a line through the twists and turns of the subdivision. Howard got back into his car and traced the route. Amazingly, it took him straight to Sophia's front door.

He walked up to her porch and was about to ring the bell when the door swung open. "You made it!"she exclaimed, smiling at him with flushed cheeks. Her hair was swept up in a bunch, with a few sexy strands framing her face.

"Yep," Howard said simply, dumbstruck by her beauty.

"We'd better hurry," she said, closing the door and taking his elbow.

Howard opened the passenger door and waited to close it behind her. Then he walked around the car and fell into the driver's seat.

Immediately, Sophia said, "Uh ... Howard." Her good humor seemed to have dissipated.

"Yes?" he asked cautiously.

"Would you please roll down the windows?" she said quietly. "I just shot a bunny."

Howard had never heard that particular euphemism for farting, but he knew exactly what she meant. He resisted the urge to laugh, and marveled at the comfortable honesty in her voice. He nearly fired off one of his father's standard lines when a family member passed gas: *You smell like someone who wants to be alone!*"

"Or," Howard suggested, as the windows descended with electronic efficiency, "I could shoot a bunny too. Then we could roll up the windows, turn on the heater and marinate in our collective funk." He pulled away from the curb.

Sophia laughed, her face open and relaxed. She didn't seem embarrassed at all. "I think you'd shoot something bigger than a bunny."

"A bear maybe."

"More like a rotten hyena," she said, poking him in the leg. Howard looked over at her and decided that she was the most beautiful flatulent woman he had ever met.

"So what do you think?" he asked. "Should we take a chance?"

"I don't know, Howard. A bunny, a hyena, *and* the heater? I don't think we're ready for that much intimacy."

But they were already intimate. The simple candor of

her confession had revealed something important about her. Throughout their relationship, Howard would hear her confess mistakes and omissions in her personal and professional life with a child-like honesty that made her easy to trust and even easier to forgive. Until recently, nothing that she'd ever said or done had seemed deliberately hurtful.

After dinner, they'd returned to her house, and Sophia had effortlessly guided him through identical twists and turns of the neighborhood despite the darkness and her slightly inebriated brain.

"Hey," Howard said, "when I got lost earlier, you told me to knock on *any* door because they could look you up in the Directory. What is that?"

Sophia giggled. "It's the Homefinder Directory to help lost souls."

"So all I have to do is tell someone your name—"

"And they'll look me up."

They sat next to each other in the dim living room. Candles flickered on the mantle, and light music danced in the air. Howard laid his hand on her knee; they both looked down for a moment, then she put her hand on top of his. He wondered if she could feel his heartbeat in his fingertips. Her free hand occasionally massaged the back of her delicate neck as she told Howard about her trip to Hawaii with three girlfriends. She described the sights and sounds of the islands, the wild nights, the sedate mornings, the nude beach where they discovered a voyeuristic snorkeler pretending to look at fish, and the difficulty of holding a serious conversation with a naked stranger.

"In a situation like that," Howard remarked, "conversation is probably overrated."

Again, her hand rose to her graceful, long neck, and once

again, Howard was tempted to give her a shoulder massage.

"I like your shoes," he said, aiming the compliment as far from her alluring neck as he could.

She looked at her thick-soled sandals and wiggled her painted red toes. "Thanks. You know," she said with a sly look, "these are the shoes I'll wear if I go back to that nude beach."

Oh, how Howard envied that snorkeler!

# four

Now, for the second time in a week, Howard had awakened to discover that Sophia was not in bed. The first time, he'd simply rolled over and returned to sleep, but now she was gone again, and Howard *knew* that she was in the basement.

Their basement was an opulent guest suite with a sitting area, a big-screen TV, a private laundry room, a small gym, an art studio, a large bedroom, and a bathroom with marble floors, granite counter tops, a Jacuzzi tub, and a steam shower. Howard had designed the suite especially for out-of-town artists whose work was on display at *Anomalous*.

Their current guest was Davis Delaney, a long-haired, thirty-year-old painter from Arizona. Though he was white and from the suburbs, he dressed, spoke, and acted like a black hip-hop artist from the inner city. He called every woman, "Shorty," every man, "Money" or "Dog," and punctuated every second or third sentence with a "yo."

Sophia chose artists who were uniquely (maniacally, Howard thought) focused on a single image or type of images. A year ago, she'd hosted Cynthia Mason, a fifty-three-year-old woman from Florida, who had lost her sight at age four. She claimed that each of her oil-over-acrylic paintings featured seahorses—the only image she recalled from her youth. Howard didn't want to be uncharitable to a blind woman, but he thought the best that could be said of her work was that it was consistent—like wallpaper. Every painting was the same perfect square (five feet by five feet), same background (cobalt blue) and same design (quarter-inch, squiggly, pea-green lines arranged in uniform rows). He had initially assumed that the green squiggles were supposed to be the seahorses, but he'd learned from observing Cynthia's fans, that the paintings apparently contained hidden images.

The twenty-four canvases on display in the gallery looked identical to Howard, but each one had a different name—*Hollering Gypsy, Guppies on the Move, Waterlogged, Cantaloupe Delight, Seahorse Rodeo*—and admirers of her work would stare at each bland image for several minutes and then say "Ahh," before moving onto the next one.

Howard never saw anything.

During the exhibit, a forty-something woman had exclaimed, "I see it! Oh my God! I see it!"

Howard and half a dozen other people had rushed to her side and stared at *Whoa, Nellie!*, hoping to see *it*, too.

"Right there by the seashell," she said, pointing at the left side of the painting. "It's rearing back on its tail, pointing its snout toward the surface."

*Seashell?* Howard thought. The flaw in Cynthia's back-story was that she professed to remember only one image from her childhood, yet her paintings allegedly contained all manner of other objects that she couldn't possibly have seen before losing her sight.

"Where do you see a seashell?" Howard asked.

"It's just to the left of the iPod," the woman replied.

"An *iPod*?" Howard said, mystified.

"Right next to Bill Clinton. Oh my! This is wonderful!"

Fittingly, after the blind woman, Sophia hosted a fifteen-year-old boy from Nebraska, who'd arrived with his mother and dozens of canvasses filled with eyes.

"Andrew is fascinated by vision," said his mother, Melissa Metcalf.

Andrew Metcalf's signature piece was a face with no nose, no mouth and no ears. A pair of eyes with dark black irises and bloodshot corneas was surrounded by dozens of other eyes embedded where the cheeks, forehead, nose, mouth, ears, and hair should have been. Surrounding the head were disembodied eyes with multicolored irises, droopy lids, and long, lustrous lashes. Some of the eyes were wet with tears, some leaked blood, some writhed with maggots, but each eye stared intently at the two eyes in the center. Whenever Howard looked at the picture, he got the eerie feeling that the center eyes were staring at him and, if they gave the order, all the other eyes would turn to stare at him, too.

Six months ago, the gallery had featured Wade Simpson, a handsome forty-two-year old from Wisconsin, who took close-up photos of the corns and warts on people's feet.

"When you put a toe against a black background and use the right type of lens and magnification," Wade explained, "the corns have the rounded appearance of other-worldly landscapes."

Each photograph had an alliterative name like *Donna's Diamond Belt*, *Laser Show Leslie*, *Gravitational Gertrude* and *E=MC²Elaine*, and Howard had to confess that the images *did* look like planets as seen from space. They appeared to be spheres with snowcapped mountains, dark valleys and swirling clouds in the atmosphere.

"How do you find your models?" Howard had asked.

Wade said, "I'm a podiatrist."

Howard thought about that for a moment. "So you say, 'Hey, Donna, before I freeze this thing off, do you mind if I take a picture of it for my art collection?'"

"Exactly!" Wade said.

"Do they know that you're going to name their warts?"

"They get a big kick out of the names."

"Even Gertrude?"

"Well," Wade admitted, "she doesn't like it, but I don't see why."

"'Gravitational Gertrude' isn't the most flattering name for a woman."

"Gravity is one of the most powerful forces in the universe."

"Only *big* things have gravity, right?" Howard asked.

"That's right! Things with lots of mass!" Wade said enthusiastically.

This guy, Howard thought, lives in outer space.

After Wade, Martha Ambrose from Pennsylvania, had a seven-day exhibit of pictures of umbilical cords—mostly from cows and sheep born on her family's farm, but there were a few human umbilicals, too.

The text under each of her photos was purely academic— "Jessie Ann's umbilical, one minute after birth. Jan. 21, 2004."

Now, Davis Delaney's work was on display, and he painted nothing but nails, hammers, and nail guns.

His work included a monstrous eight-foot-by-ten-foot canvas of a rusted, bent nail sticking out of what might have been Victorian molding around a window. The nail, slightly upturned and brushed with white paint near the bottom, was surrounded by deep fissures in the wood. The painting, titled *Survivor*, was a zoomed-in look at the nail, offering few contextual details about the room that housed it.

"Yo, that nail shouldn't be there," Davis said to prospective customers, though he never explained where *there* was. "It ain't holdin' nothin', and it's bent. But check it, yo, it wasn't bent by no load. It's bent upward, dog, like somebody tried to rip that mother out with a hammer. That nail represents everyone who said 'Hell no!' when the hammer of life told them it was time to go. That nail is a survivor, yo!"

Another of his paintings showed a box of nails dropped on the floor. The box was rebounding from its initial contact with the tiles, three or four inches off the ground, with nails scattered around it, and more leaping out of the open lid. It was titled *Opportunity Comes Knockin'*.

A painting of a hammer about to make contact with a nail was called *Headache*, while another, *Move Bitch!*, featured the gleaming, silver point of a nail coming through the splintered backside of a piece of wood.

In the lower right-hand corner of each piece was Davis' signature symbol—a cross with a nail through its center.

Usually the visiting artists stayed a single week—at most two—but Davis had been in residence for more than two months, and didn't seem to have any plan to leave soon.

He had arrived in Highlands Ranch in a peeling, blue 1973 Ford Econoline Van, towing a Harley Davidson V-Rod that was easily five times the value of the van. He shook every window on the block when he fired up the bike, and he shook up much more than that when he rode without a helmet, or strolled the neighborhood sidewalks without a shirt, openly flirting with the stay-at-home mothers.

"Yo, you wanna get nailed?" he would ask the women suggestively, waiting for shock to color their faces. Before they could say *no*, he would grin mischievously and say, "Don't get it twisted, Shorty. That's what I call it when someone buys one of my paintings—getting *nailed*."

The women always laughed and acted relieved, but their eyes made it clear that they were ready for Davis to make a more sincere offer.

"It's almost not fair bringing him here," Howard had said a few days after Davis first arrived. He and Sophia had watched the artist, shirtless in the driveway, washing his motorcycle. Three women had crossed the street to chat with him. Like smitten preteens, they'd giggled and played with their hair while he got soap and water all over himself.

Sophia had said, "*These* desperate housewives don't have a chance."

# *five*

In the darkened bedroom, Howard tried to recall if he had detected a hint of desperation in his own wife's voice.

Davis' van—emblazoned with the words *Hammer of Life Artistry* beneath a hammer rising out of the soil like a plant—was parked in the driveway. The homeowners association had issued three rulings against it, citing a prohibition on commercial vehicles as described in Article 2.18 of the Residential Improvement Guidelines.

Sophia had laughed angrily when she saw the first notice.

"These people are unbelievable!" she said, tearing the page into small pieces and throwing the shards into the trash can. Although Howard agreed with her assessment of the HOA board, he didn't think it wise to destroy a legal notice. He was a recent law school graduate, and he knew that if the HOA wanted the van removed they could force Howard and Sophia to comply. The letter, lying in bits at the bottom of the trash can, was merely the board's first salvo.

But, at the time, Howard hadn't worried. He had assumed that Davis, like the artists before him, would depart in a week or two and the van would go with him. However, a month later, Davis was still living in the basement, and the HOA board sent a second letter. This one was more forcefully worded, included a five-hundred-dollar assessment, and an order to remove the van within forty-eight hours, or face legal action.

"These goddamned micromanaging Nazis!" Sophia had

screamed. "They need to get a life!" She snatched a lighter out of her purse and held the flame to the corner of the letter.

"Sophia!" Howard exclaimed as the paper caught fire. She laughed as red-hot filaments rose into the air and drifted down to the carpet. Howard ran into the kitchen to get the fire extinguisher. When he returned to the living room, Sophia was no longer laughing. She was scowling fearfully, looking for a safe place to drop the flaming sheet.

"Close your eyes!" Howard yelled.

"What?" Sophia asked.

Howard squeezed the handle on the extinguisher and a thick clot of fire-suppression material shot out like a massive sneeze, smothering the flames. He turned the nozzle toward the floor and fired another blast at the sparks in the carpet.

Sophia coughed several times and dropped the tiny remainder of the letter onto an end table. The left side of her torso and face was covered with sodium bicarbonate; it looked as if she'd fallen into a vat of baking powder.

"Was *that* really necessary?" she asked, peevishly.

"You tell me," Howard countered, trying to contain his anger. He snapped the hose back into the clamp on the side of the extinguisher. "These are *legal* notices, Sophia. They tell us exactly what accusations the board has made against us and how we're supposed to respond. You tore up the first one, and now you've burned the second one. At some point you're going to have to stop attacking the pieces of paper and do something about the van."

They stared at each other for several moments. Finally, he said, "Maybe it's time for Davis to leave."

Sophia shook her head. "He's still selling two or three pieces a week."

Howard released a slow breath. He knew that Davis had

been the best selling artist who'd ever shown at *Anomalous*. He recalled the scene a couple of weeks ago, when Davis had been explaining his work to a group from a local Zonta Club.

"Yo, I call this one *Self-Inflicted*," he had said dramatically, pointing to a painting of a hammer missing the nail and hitting a man's hairy thumb.

"Ouch!" said a dark-haired woman in her forties.

Another woman, sounding breathy and seductive, said, "It's more violent than your other work—I like that!"

A third woman said, "You should have called it *Thumb-ta-dum-dum*." She sang it, like the theme from the old *Dragnet* detective show.

"Yo, that's dope, Shorty!" Davis said, tucking his hair behind his ears. "I might have to flip the script."

"Feel free to use it," she said proudly.

A day later, he did. A week later, a wealthy contractor's wife, who couldn't stop laughing, paid two thousand dollars for the painting. "*Thumb-ta-dum-dum*? My husband ...," she said, pausing between fits of laugher to lay down a MasterCard, "is gonna ... love ... this!"

The gray powder from the fire extinguisher had plastered Sophia's hair to the side of her face. She picked at it gingerly.

Howard said, "Why don't you ask him to move the van to the parking lot in front of your shop?" *Anomalous* was located in a strip mall. Howard thought the van might sit there for weeks without drawing any complaints.

He was wrong. After three nights, the property manager of the strip mall had threatened to tow the *Hammer of Life* van, so Davis had driven it back to the driveway.

"At least it's on a new clock, yo," Davis had said to Howard. "Since the van was AWOL for a few days, them association people gotta start over, give you thirty days notice, then another thirty days to do somethin' about it, you know what I'm sayin'?'"

Howard had simply shaken his head. He'd had a similar thought, but Section 2.46 of the RIGs included the line, "Periodic movement of the vehicle for the purpose of circumventing this standard shall not qualify the vehicle for exception from this standard." The clock would not start over.

A few days later, they received a third assessment letter, and Howard was careful to not let Sophia touch this one. He *read* it to her while she stood in the kitchen slicing a tomato into wedges with a butcher knife.

"They say that we're in default as defined in section 8.35 of the Community Declaration," Howard read. "We owe five hundred dollars, and we have thirty days to make the payment before interest and penalties kick in. If we don't pay, the board will exercise its legal options including putting a lien on the house and foreclosing."

Sophia chewed on her bottom lip, staring at the page as if she wanted rip it out of Howard's hands. "Couldn't we challenge it?" she asked.

Howard shrugged. "Of course, we *could*, but why would we?"

"You've beaten the HOA before," she said. "You could do it again."

"Sophia, I challenged the board because they wanted to control the *inside* of our home," Howard said. "We won that fight because the Fourth Amendment of the Constitution was on our side. This is not that type of fight."

"But it's *our* driveway," Sophia insisted. "Shouldn't we have the right to park whatever vehicle we like in *our* driveway?"

"It's not *our* van," Howard said. "We might have a case if the van belonged to us and we used it every day to make a living.

We might be able to argue that we were being discriminated against as self-employed, blue-collar workers who have to drive their work vehicles home. But this is a guest's van parked in our driveway, mostly without moving, for two months. We won't win."

But no matter what Howard said, Sophia would not surrender. She was not ready to tell Davis to leave, so eventually Howard had promised to attend the next board meeting to contest the assessment.

# six

Howard, still perched on the edge of the bed, looked at the clock. The fluorescent red numbers read: 4:10 a.m. He knew that his wife was in the basement getting nailed by Davis Delaney, but he couldn't understand why. He didn't think his wife would risk their marriage just for sex, so something else must have been motivating her.

"But if that's the case, why didn't she talk to me about it?" Howard wondered aloud.

*Maybe she tried and you didn't listen.* A voice in his head suggested.

"No," he said, pausing to think for a moment. "No, she's never said anything."

*Maybe she was afraid to tell you.*

Howard scowled. "Why would she be afraid?"

*You tell me.*

Howard wondered if he was overreacting. Just because Sophia wasn't in bed didn't mean that she was in the basement with Davis. Sneaking into the basement wouldn't be her style. Although her reaction to the assessment notices had been irrational, Sophia was generally very practical about logistical issues. She spent every workday with Davis. If she really wanted to have sex with him, she could do it at the gallery or go to a hotel. Why would she risk getting caught in the house.

The voice in Howard's head asked, *What if she wanted to get caught?*

"That's ridiculous."

*Maybe this is a passive-aggressive attempt to communicate with you.*

"About what?"

*You tell me.*

Howard wasn't sure that he should go looking for his wife. Even though he was suspicious, it didn't feel right to openly reveal that he distrusted her. Maybe he should turn on the TV and wait for her to return. If she wanted to talk, they'd talk.

No, Howard realized with a shake of his head. If he wanted to save his marriage, he had to act. He would go look for her. But what if she *was* in the basement? Would he knock at the top of the stairs and warn them that he was coming, or would he burst through the door and barrel down the steps, hoping to catch them mid-thrust?

Howard stood and walked slowly into the bathroom. He groaned as he stood at the toilet. Their house was an extension of Sophia's gallery; there were pictures everywhere, yet she owned only one original piece—a green squiggly painting titled *Hidden Treasure* mounted over the mantle in the living room.

"All the other originals are for sale," Sophia explained to guests. "So I keep them at *Anomalous*. I just have prints on my walls. As you walk around, you'll notice that I feature one artist per room."

The master bathroom was Andrew Metcalf's "eye" room. An eyeball with a snake climbing out of the pupil was mounted over the toilet, staring at Howard as he emptied his bladder. Howard had discovered that if he stood in the right spot— the mid-point between the two sinks—he could look in the mirror and see all eighty-seven eyes staring back at him.

When Sophia had first hung the pictures, Howard had joked, "We'll call this bathroom *Highlands Ranch*, because it feels like someone is always watching, even when you're in the most private room of the house."

Howard eventually discovered that the eyes had a remarkable empathetic quality—they tended to match his mood. When Howard was sad, the eyes seemed sad. When he was angry, they reflected his rage. When he was tired, the eyes were red and droopy. Although Howard still had trouble peeing in front so many witnesses, he had come to think of the eyes as his friends. Now, he couldn't help wondering what his "friends" might have seen during the past few weeks. Had Davis Delaney been in this room?

Howard sorted through his options. He could play it cool—walk into the basement and calmly ask Sophia what she was doing. Maybe ask her, "Are you having a good time?" with a hint of sarcasm. Or, say, "Sophia, can I speak with you when you're done?," saying it casually as if he were placing an order at a restaurant. He wouldn't address Davis at all. He wouldn't act angry. He'd just be cool.

Howard thought that dealing with his wife's affair shouldn't be a problem; after all, he handled difficult situations for a living. He was an organizer, a negotiator, and a broker, putting multi-million dollar deals together. He'd been working for Carson Technological Industries for seven years, and he planned to open his own brokerage firm in the near future.

"And broker what?" Sophia had asked derisively, two weeks ago. "You're basically a pimp-slash-valet, Mounds. You get strippers for Bob, make reservations, and pick up his laundry. That's not a business model. It's just a job." "Mounds" was a nickname she'd given him just before they got engaged.

Howard had been startled by the aggression in her voice. He said, "I can do a lot more than the penny ante shit that I do for Bob." In fact, Carson Technological Industries had paid for Howard's law degree, and as soon as he passed the bar exam, he planned to quit working for Bob Carson.

"Yeah? Like what?"

*Like what?* Before Davis Delaney came to Denver, Sophia would never have asked such a question. She had always encouraged Howard's dreams and supported his career, but now she acted as if she didn't have any confidence in him.

"Like all the things I've done for you," he said. It had been Howard's idea to invite niche artists to her gallery—though he'd left it to her to choose the actual people. It had been his idea to promise them exclusive display in the gallery, multiple cocktail parties, newspaper and radio advertising, and guaranteed sales. It had been his idea to create the basement suite, and he had overseen every step of its design, construction, and decoration. It had been his idea to host dinner parties at home once a month, inviting potential clients over to see the prints Sophia had hanging on every wall. Thanks, in part, to his efforts, Sophia ran one of the most successful art galleries in the Rocky Mountain region.

"I've helped you grow your business," Howard said, "and I could do the same for a lot of other companies."

Sophia had shrugged. "If it's such a good plan, get a loan from a bank. I'm not throwing my money away."

Howard had been too astounded to reply. Lately, Sophia's verbal "bunnies" had fouled nearly every conversation with him, but unlike her other farts, she never apologized for them. Yes, she earned much more than he did. Yes, she had owned the gallery for a decade, having started it with a one-hundred-thousand-dollar inheritance from her grandparents. Yes, she had purchased the house in Highlands Ranch long before she met Howard. But Howard's suggestions had increased the net revenue of the gallery from about seventy-five thousand dollars a year up to nearly two hundred thousand.

Until recently, she had never referred to it as *her* money.

# seven

Howard flushed the toilet.

*Flushed the goddamned toilet!*

He looked up—where six eyes arranged in a cluster stared back at him—and shook his head, disappointed. Whatever he did now, it would not be stealthy. The water would swoosh gently through the basement pipes, and Sophia and Davis would know that he was awake. Howard shrugged. That was okay, he decided. Trying to catch them in the act was undignified anyway. He was practically a lawyer, so he didn't need to spy. He could simply interrogate his wife and discover the truth. He took his time washing his hands, and drying them on a flowery towel. He selected a T-shirt from the dresser, slid into a pair of boxers, and walked downstairs.

The walls in the hallway and the stairwell were plastered with prints of stars.

"Not celebrities," Howard explained to friends who hadn't yet seen the upstairs hallway, "I mean stars as in celestial beings." Except for a swirling, circular painting of the United States flag with a spiral of fifty stars in the field of blue, none of the stars on the wall was a symmetrical five- or six-pointed figure. The artist was Geraldine Crawford, an angst-ridden seventeen-year-old from Mississippi, who believed that the round center of each star contained the spirit of a dead person.

"Every time a spirit tries to escape, his struggle pushes a point away from the center," Geraldine explained in a placard that was posted with the work. "It takes one million pounds of force to create each point, so the dead are very powerful! The more points a star has, the more angry and desperate the trapped spirit feels. I pray that I will never have to paint an exploded star."

A year ago, while studying a star with twenty-seven points, Howard had said to Sophia, "Promise me that you'll never invite this girl into our home."

"Oh, she's harmless," Sophia said.

"Trust me," Howard said. "No one being chased by this many angry spirits will stay harmless for long."

Howard reached the bottom of the stairs, where he passed the most recent of Geraldine's star paintings—a tiny orb with just one gigantic point extending all the way across the canvas.

The placard next to it read: "This spirit has decided to spend all of his energy trying to escape through a single point. This painting is not yet completed ...." In fact, the purchase agreement required that the owner of the original canvas return it to Geraldine once a year so that she could update the spirit's progress.

As he approached the kitchen, Howard saw Sophia's reflection in a large mirror in the living room. She was sitting at the breakfast table with a pint of Rocky Road ice cream and a book. She looked as if she'd been there for hours. Howard loved to watch her when she wasn't aware that she had an audience. There was something about the delicate way she moved that made him wonder what she was thinking. It was particularly interesting to watch her walk past a mirror, a plate glass window or any other reflective surface. She always stopped to study her reflection, but her body language seemed to indicate curiosity rather than vanity. Howard noticed that when most women looked into a mirror, they groomed themselves. They'd run their fingers through their hair, blot their mascara, re-apply lipstick, run their tongues over their teeth, or turn sideways to check their outfits. But in those quiet moments when Howard secretly watched Sophia, she would gaze at her reflection without fixing anything. It was as if she didn't see anything that she wanted to change about herself. Howard wasn't sure if that meant she was an egomaniac, or an exceptionally healthy individual.

He stepped into the kitchen. "You having a good time?" he asked automatically, because he had rehearsed it upstairs.

Sophia's light green eyes came up from the book. "What do you mean?" Her hair was hanging down loose, but untangled, as if she'd just brushed it. Her face was clouded with confusion.

"I mean ... couldn't sleep?"

She shook her head and gave him a weary smile. "A little insomnia I guess." She had pretty freckles on her pale cheeks, wonderful bone structure, eyes just the right distance apart, a petite aquiline nose, nicely-shaped lips and a gently squared chin. Howard thought again about the wedding photo on the bedside table and wondered if he had misread his expression in the picture. He could feel himself becoming captivated all over again.

"How long have you been up?" he asked gently, not at all like a prosecutor. She seemed genuinely tired.

"A couple of hours." A thick cotton robe was cinched around her waist. Howard wondered if she was wearing anything under it.

"Hot tea would probably help more than Ben and Jerry's," he suggested. He noted that the ice cream was still hard—frosty condensation coated the carton. But that didn't prove anything. She may have been sitting at the table for hours, but just pulled the ice cream out five minutes ago.

"I know," she said. "I just had an appetite for something sinful." She dug out a small wedge with her spoon and slipped it into her mouth, sucking sensuously. The possible double entendre felt like a dagger to Howard.

"What's wrong?" he asked.

"What do you mean?"

"You don't seem like yourself."

Sophia looked surprised. "How do you mean?" Her face was blank, not at all like a woman hiding a secret.

Howard felt that this was the moment to ask her point-blank if she was having an affair, but he didn't want to hurl an accusation at his wife without substantial evidence. He studied her for a moment and finally said, "If you ever want to talk, you know I'll listen."

"I know that, Mounds," she said quietly.

Upstairs, Howard had been certain that she was cheating, but now, standing in the kitchen looking at her, he wasn't sure.

She asked, "Why are you up?"

"Hungry," he lied, leaning down to kiss her forehead—it was warm. "Plus I've been worried about the bar exams coming up." He walked over to the cabinet next to the sink and grabbed a bowl and a spoon. He sat down next to Sophia, and said, "Let me get some," throwing a little double entendre back at her.

Sophia's eyes flitted briefly toward the basement door, but then came back to Howard, holding his gaze. She passed him the carton of ice cream. He looked down at her book—*The Amazing Adventures of Kavalier and Clay*, by Michael Chabon.

It lay open at pages 94 and 95. Howard had read the book last year, and he knew that Sophia had taken it from the bookshelf in the basement. It wasn't a title that his wife would normally pick up.

"So how's the book?" he asked.

# eight

"Howard, what's wrong with you today?" Bob Carson asked. It was nearly 6 o'clock Friday evening, and the sun was just below the ridgeline of the Rocky Mountains in the distance. A massive band of dark clouds rolling in from the north was snuffing out the final brilliant orange rays.

"Nothing, Chief," Howard Marshall said to his boss. He was sitting at the conference table in Bob's office, working on his laptop. His gray pinstriped jacket was slung over the seat next to him. His tie was cinched tight, and his powder blue shirt still had creases from the drycleaners.

"You don't seem like yourself," Bob said. He was in his mid-forties, balding, graying at the temples, with a chubby face and a bulbous stomach. A few years ago, he'd spent ten thousand dollars getting his crooked teeth covered with straight, white porcelain veneers. Now when his lips parted it looked as though he had a mouth full of Chicklets.

Howard shrugged. He was distracted by concern about Sophia, but he was surprised that Bob had noticed. His boss wasn't the empathetic type.

"Just personal stuff," Howard said. He was perusing the selection at the 1-800-flowers web site.

"Married life, huh?"

Howard chuckled without humor. "You know it." He had decided that confrontation wasn't the best way to encourage his wife to open up. Apparently, she wasn't ready to talk, so

Howard decided to show her that he loved her. Hopefully, she would reciprocate by sharing her thoughts with him.

"Wife stepping out on you?" Bob asked, looking amused.

That caught Howard's attention. He stopped typing and looked up. "What makes you say that?" he asked cautiously.

"Come on, Howard. I've survived three divorces and lots of affairs—mine and theirs—I know a little bit about wandering libidos."

Howard's eyes drifted across the room to a piece of art Bob had purchased from Sophia's gallery a couple of weeks earlier. It was a huge Davis Delaney oil painting titled *Say Something!* The image revealed the underside of a bright yellow nail gun with dozens of gleaming rounds poised for discharge. Davis had explained that this was how a nail gun looked to a frightened two-by four. Bob had purchased it because he imagined that everyone who faced him across a dock felt like that two-by-four.

Howard stared at the painting, wondering if his wife had seen the underside of Davis Delaney's nail gun. *Yo, Shorty, you wanna get nailed?*

"Tell me about it," Bob said. "Maybe I can help."

Very quietly Howard said, "Actually, I *am* a little concerned that—"

"Hey! What I oughta do," Bob said, snapping his fingers, "is sell my software in a country that doesn't recognize U.S. trademarks."

Howard stared at his boss blankly. Bob had two consistent qualities: He rarely talked about anything other than himself for more than a minute, and most of his stories started right in the middle of someone else's sentence.

"What do you think?" Bob asked, leaning back in his chair and grinning with his fingers laced behind his head.

From his desk on the 48<sup>th</sup> Floor of Republic Plaza, he overlooked everything in downtown Denver. When Bob had visitors, he'd show off saying, "That's Invesco Field over at ten o'clock, and at night when it's all lit up for a Broncos game, you can see the crowd rise to its feet and the whole place seems to sway from side to side. Over at eleven o'clock you can see the Pepsi Center and Six Flags Elitch Gardens, and at one o'clock you can just see Coors Field peeking over the roof tops. That big flat building that covers about four city blocks down at nine o'clock ... that's the Colorado Convention Center."

The lights of the city below popped on incrementally as dusk turned into night.

"I think you mean copyrights," Howard said. "Trademarks are a different issue." He returned his attention to the website, which had a special on teddy bears and Mylar balloons emblazoned with the message *I love you*! He ordered one of each.

"You know, like Taiwan, where they make fake Louis Vuitton," Bob said. "Over there, they don't worry about trademarks." That wasn't quite true, but Howard knew that explaining it to Bob would be pointless.

"What if Taiwan doesn't have any big software companies?" Howard asked.

"That's a detail," Bob said, waving him off. "Pick another country—I'm talking big picture here." He stood and paced in front of the window. The storm clouds were closing in on the city with surprising speed. Bob paced slowly, his arms crossed behind his back, like Lawrence Fishburne's character in *The Matrix*. Ever since he'd seen the movie, Bob had mimicked Morpheus' upright posture and gait because he thought it looked dignified, the way a CEO ought to look.

"I'm thinking," Bob said, "that this program might be

worth half a billion dollars to the right buyer." He stopped and stared at Howard, waiting for a reaction.

Howard was vacillating between roses and wildflowers. "If there's no protection for copyrights, why would a company invest a lot of money in the program? As soon as it hits the market, someone will start selling bootleg copies."

"That's a detail," Bob said.

"Okay," Howard said. "Here's a better answer. If you try to sell this program again you'll get sued, you'll probably have to give back the eighteen million Globalsoft paid you, and you'll probably get charged with fraud—that could mean prison time."

"But it's *my* software!" Bob whined.

The program was an innovative operating system created by CTI whiz kid, Rashid Punjab, whom Howard had persuaded to join the company despite the many offers Rashid had received from virtually every major software firm in the world.

When Bob's father, Earl was the CEO and President of Carson Technological Industries, Howard had suggested that CTI could promise Rashid something that none of the big software companies could ever deliver—autonomy.

Earl Carson said, "Have you forgotten that we're manufacturers of *hardware*, not *software*?"

"But what a way to break into the software industry!" Howard countered. "Every article I've read about this kid says that he's already developed and copyrighted the framework, and he wants the freedom to finish it the way he envisions it. But none of the big companies is willing to take that risk. They'll take the program away from him, throw him in a cubicle, and finish it however they see fit."

"That's not unreasonable," Earl shrugged. "The kid *is* only twenty-two years old."

"If the experts are right," Howard said, "this program will revolutionize operating systems and dominate the market the way Windows does now. If Rashid got it to this point on his own, then he can finish it on his own, and it'll make CTI an instant big player."

Eventually, Earl had been persuaded by Howard's logic. He'd offered Rashid the newly created position of Vice President of Programming, a $100,000 signing bonus, an annual salary of five-hundred grand, a room full of equipment, a staff of three, and a five percent equity stake in the company contingent upon the completion of the operating system.

Rashid had stunned the programming world by accepting an offer to work for CTI. Every business journal in the U.S. had praised the company for its cunning in winning the race for Rashid Punjab. Carson Technology Industries' stock price had increased by thirty-five percent that quarter, eighty percent by the end of the year, and it was expected to instantly triple or quadruple when the program was released.

To reward Howard for his initiative and creativity, Earl Carson had promoted him to Vice President of Sales, and urged him to go to law school.

"Brokering deals is what you do best," Earl had said. "A law degree will help you develop that part of your career."

"I don't have time," Howard said, "There's so much to do to get ready for—"

Earl said, "Rashid isn't going to be done with this program for another four or five years, so there's plenty of time. I'm paying for everything—tuition, books, fees, and whatever else—and I'm giving you one day a week off so you can study."

So Howard had enrolled at the University of Denver. Sadly, a year after hiring Rashid, Earl Carson died of a heart attack in the middle of his backswing on the tee box at the number three hole at the Cherry Creek Country Club. His estranged son, Bob Carson—who'd been living in San Diego on a monthly stipend from his father—inherited the company. Bob had immediately moved to Denver and, ignoring the recommendation of his father's advisory board, he appointed himself President and CEO of Carson Technological Industries. Fortunately, his defiant action hadn't disrupted the stock value, mostly because Rashid was still on staff developing his software.

Then, two years ago, Rashid crashed his Mercedes SLK500, suddenly accelerating into a bridge abutment at 120 miles per hour. Rashid, who was not wearing a seatbelt, was ejected through the windshield and tumbled nearly 600 feet before striking another bridge pillar. Accident investigators speculated that he must have been distracted by his girlfriend giving him a blowjob at the time of the crash. She had slipped out of her shoulder harness to lean across the center console, but was still belted in at the waist. She suffered a severe concussion and a broken pelvis, and likely would have survived the accident if not for Rashid's dick. The coroner's report revealed that on impact, she had clamped down on Rashid's penis, severing it at the base as his body flew out of the car. At the same moment, the steering wheel airbag had deployed, striking her in the side of the head and causing her to inhale sharply. She died of asphyxiation; Rashid's penis was lodged halfway down her esophagus.

None of the other programmers at CTI had possessed the talent to finish Rashid's work, so the incomplete operating system had languished for months, as useless to Bob Carson as a limp dick, while the stock price inched down a few points every day. Finally, Howard suggested that CTI sell the program to a big software firm, which was CTI's best hope of reaping a profit. A bidding war erupted, and Globalsoft eventually paid $18 million for the program. Less than a year later, Globalsoft launched the beta version of XP-3D, an operating system based on Rashid's platform, and sold nearly a billion dollars worth in the first three months.

Bob had watched Globalsoft's success sourly, dissatisfied with his multimillion-dollar payday, and secretly plotting schemes to reap more profits from Rashid's software.

"They can't put me in jail for selling my own program!" Bob insisted.

Howard chose to ignore him. "What do you think women like better," he asked, "traditional red roses or wildflowers?"

Bob eyed him suspiciously, his pudgy face pinching around an unlit cigar. "What woman?"

"My wife," Howard said.

"Birthday or anniversary?"

"A surprise. She's going to New York tomorrow. I want to have some flowers waiting at the hotel when she arrives."

"Why? Because she's cheating on you?"

So Bob *had* been listening a few minutes ago.

"Just to tell her that I love her," Howard said.

Bob shook his head solemnly. "What's her name?"

Howard gave him a curious look. "You know Sophia."

"I mean the girl you're sleeping with?"

Howard hesitated. "*I'm* not having an affair."

"Sophia's gonna think you are. Listen," Bob said, coming around his desk and running a hand over the downy hairs on top of his balding head. "You're feeling desperate because your wife is getting boned by some other dude." He pulled out a chair and sat across from Howard at the conference table. "You should probably just cut her loose. Don't ask any questions, don't get into any details, just call a lawyer and get a divorce."

"I love my—," Howard started.

"Yeah, yeah, love, schmove. You're not in love Howard, you're just prideful. You don't want to give her to the schmuck who's banging her. You want to win her back and then dump her. Leave on your own terms."

Howard shook his head.

"But I'm guessing that Sophia doesn't know that *you* know about the affair," Bob said. "So when she gets these flowers, she's not going to think that her husband is trying to win her back. She's gonna think you're apologizing for something."

"Come on," Howard said.

"Women aren't like us, Howard. They're practical, unromantic and suspicious creatures. They don't have any natural romantic instincts."

"That's a pretty broad generalization," Howard said. He selected roses and clicked Next.

"Well, we're talking about *broads* aren't we?" Bob winked. After three divorces and five kids he barely knew, Bob preferred purely transactional relationships with women.

"Actually, Bob," Howard said, with just a little edge in his voice, "we're talking about my *wife*."

"Whoa!" Bob raised his hands—big grin coming out to let Howard know he was joking. "Take it easy there, cowboy." He flattened his tie with his palm and said, "You think Sophia's gonna think it's romantic, you surprising her with flowers?"

"Yes, I do," Howard said, perfectly calm, the sudden flash of anger gone. He typed the address of the hotel in New York and hit Okay.

"Not a chance," Bob said.

"Hmm," Howard said, checking his watch.

"You hungry?" Bob asked.

Howard frowned. Bob was supposed to spend the weekend at his castle up in the mountains, so Howard had expected to have a rare Friday and Saturday night to himself.

"I thought you were going to Beaver Creek," he said.

"Later," Bob said. "First I want to pick up a couple of strippers."

"What happened to Angela?" She was a twenty-seven-year-old model who usually accompanied Bob on his out-of-town jaunts and in-town evenings at the symphony.

"She had to go to Florida," Bob said, waving her off. "Said her mother was sick."

Howard didn't say anything. He and Bob both knew that Angela was taking a weekend trip with another rich guy— probably an athlete. Despite his wealth, Bob was a B-list sugar daddy, because he wasn't famous. The computer prompted Howard to add a note to send with the card. He typed, "*Bassiff, have fun in New York! Mounds.*"

"Let's hit The Palm, get some surf and turf," Bob said.

Howard groaned inwardly, but he knew there was no avoiding a night out with the boss. He dialed The Palm Restaurant and reserved a table. They took the elevator down to the garage, where Edward, Bob's driver, was waiting at the backdoor of a stretched Range Rover limousine that seated twelve.

As they emerged from the garage onto Court Place, Bob said, "I'm serious about women and romance. Hey, Edward! How would you define *romance*?"

Edward shrugged, looking in the rearview mirror at his boss. Edward was a slightly built forty-five-year-old Ethiopian, who always had a smile on his face. "Candles, flowers, poetry, music—"

"No, no, no," Bob interrupted, "That's just a meaningless checklist of things. That's how *women* define romance—'He gets me flowers, he writes poetry, he opens my door; therefore, he's romantic.' But men know that, at its core, romance isn't a list of things. It's about mystery, excitement, uncertainty, anticipation, and surprises."

"That sounds like a list to me," Howard said.

"But not a list of *objects*," Bob said, raising one eyebrow. "Romance is a list of *emotions*." As if he knew anything about that subject. "Women have commandeered the language," Bob said. "They spend so much time defining romance their way that men have lost the ability to think about it objectively. But romance is really about mystery, and I bet you've never met a woman in your whole life who actually appreciated uncertainty and mystery."

Edward said, "My wife—"

"No, she doesn't!" Bob exclaimed, cutting him off, so that Howard never got to hear what Edward thought about his wife. But that was typical of Bob. No one around him ever really got to finish a thought. Bob turned to Howard and asked, "You want a drink?"

Howard shook his head.

"I'll take Scotch," Bob said.

Howard reached down to a shelf by his knees and poured an inch of amber liquid into a tumbler.

"Your wife is like every other woman," Bob said to Edward, though Bob had never met Edward's wife, Caroline, and had no desire to meet her. "Think back to your first date—you dropped her off at her house and you said, 'I'll call you.' What do you think she was thinking?"

Edward had met Caroline when they were in grade school in Ethiopia. Their families had lived in the same small town, and they'd spent nearly every day together in their youth. They'd rarely spoken to each other on the telephone; it was easier to simply walk outside and talk to each other. Edward and Caroline had gotten married when they were both seventeen, and in the twenty-eight years since then, they'd moved to the United States, raised three successful children, celebrated the arrival of two grandchildren, and had endured the unabated ignorance of people like Bob.

But Edward never lost his smile or his patience. Though he'd never had the type of first-date moment Bob was describing, he knew that his boss wasn't interested in the details.

"She was probably thinking, *when*," Edward suggested.

"That's right!" Bob exclaimed. "She immediately thought, '*When* is he going to call?'" Bob paused to take a sip. "She wanted to plan whether she would be home for your call or out with her friends. She wanted to decide what she would be wearing when you called, what music would be playing in the background and what she would say. Women are planners. They don't like mystery. They don't like not knowing what's going to happen."

During the ride over to The Palm, Howard called Sophia's cell phone twice, but she didn't answer. She was leaving for New York in the morning to attend a week-long art show, and Howard had hoped they could spend some time together on her last night in town. But he couldn't reach her—again. During the past few weeks, she'd been increasingly out of touch. She'd later claim that her cell phone had no signal, or that the battery had died or that she'd never heard it ring. Howard left a message saying that he was going to The Palm with Bob, but he'd get home as soon as he could.

Edward pulled the black Range Rover into the curved driveway of the Westin Hotel Tabor Center, and the valet opened the rear door. Bob and Howard climbed down and walked through the revolving door, past the Starbucks' kiosk, past the escalators leading to the Westin's front desk, and finally reached The Palm Restaurant, where the hostess greeted them warmly and welcomed them back. She knew that Howard would slip her one hundred dollars (of Bob's money) with instructions to seat all unaccompanied, attractive females near Bob's table.

The restaurant was half full, and Bob, doing his Fishburne walk, made quite an entrance, nodding to a dinner guest here and there as he strutted. Once they reached their table at the back, Bob picked up the conversation from the limo. "I know I'm right about this. Women just don't know romance."

Howard said, "Women might point to men's forgetfulness about Valentine's Day and anniversaries as counter examples of men's supposedly innate romantic instincts. Men are always—"

"Those examples prove my point," Bob said. The waiter came by, and they placed their drink orders—Scotch for Bob, Coors Light for Howard. "Valentine's Day is perfect for women, because they can look at the calendar and say, 'On this day I'm going to get flowers and candy.' When the flowers arrive at their office, they'll act surprised, and gush and call you and say, 'Honey, they're beautiful.' That's romance in a woman's world. They want to act surprised without actually *being* surprised."

"Sophia seems to like it when I surprise her."

"You send her flowers a lot?"

"Four or five times a year."

"Then she likes it because they're *extra*," Bob said.

Howard ordered an eighteen-ounce New York Strip prepared medium, with Au Gratin potatoes and broccoli. Bob got four pounds of Nova Scotia lobster with a twelve-ounce New York Strip cooked "until it's all the way dead," he said. "Don't bring me a bleeder." They both started with the Palm's signature Gigi salad and lobster bisque.

"Try this experiment," Bob continued. "Surprise Sophia with all sorts of fabulous gifts a couple of times a month, but don't buy her anything for her birthday, anniversary or Valentine's Day. I guarantee you she'll be pissed. Women only like surprises if they're *in addition* to the predictable stuff. If you gave her a steady diet of surprises with no predictable gifts, she'd complain to her girlfriends that you weren't romantic."

Halfway through the soup and salad Bob nudged Howard and nodded at a pair of brunettes following the hostess toward the back. The women had long, bronzed legs, short skirts, lean bodies and just enough cleavage to catch your eye. The woman in the lead looked Indian or Pakistani, with caramel-colored skin and brown eyes. She had sculpted black eyebrows, high cheekbones, and an indifferent expression as she glided through the restaurant.

The other woman looked part Asian. She was rounder in the face, eyes pulling flat at the corners, a softer nose, full lips, and gently rounded hips. Both women looked hyper-fit, like aerobics instructors. Everyone in the restaurant seemed transfixed by them as they settled into a table adjacent to Bob and Howard.

"Sales," Bob observed. "The hottest women are in sales." This comment seemed to sum up his view of *all* women—they all had something to sell, and Bob was convinced he could buy it. "I'm gonna get them a bottle." He started snapping his fingers at the waiter.

Howard laid a restraining hand on Bob's arm, and said, "Let me handle it." Howard knew that Bob would go overboard, ordering a $240 bottle of Dom Perignon, or worse, Cristal at $290. Howard thought it would be more discreet to send the women a couple of apple martinis.

Bob bellowed at the waiter, "Hey! I'm talking to you!" He gave the women an exasperated look, and then glared again at the waiter.

"I'm sorry," the waiter said, rushing over and bowing. "What can I get for you?"

"Not me!" Bob yelled. "Them! Don't they look thirsty to you? Don't they look like they need a bottle of Cristal?"

Howard groaned inwardly and sat back.

"Right away, sir," the waiter said, scurrying off to fill the order.

Howard noticed that up close, the Indian woman's eyes were hazel, not brown. "Really, we don't—" she started, but Bob cut her off.

"Of course you do," he smiled, raising his drink. "I'm Bob Carson."

She said, "We just want to have a quiet meal. That's not going to be a problem is it?" Her tone was that of a middle school teacher stopping a disruptive student before he got too wound up. Her cold gaze told Howard that Bob should ease back.

"It would be a lot quieter," Bob said, barreling ahead, "if we didn't have to yell across the aisle." He flashed his rich-guy smile—ten thousand dollars worth of porcelain Chicklets twinkling in the light. "Let me buy you dinner."

"No thanks," she said, smoothing the fabric of her blouse.

Bob said to Howard, "Who in their right mind would turn down a free meal?"

*With you?* Howard thought. He could have compiled a list.

"No offense," the woman said, "but we can pay for our own—"

"But when you look as good as you do, why should you?"

She was about to respond when the Asian woman nudged her. They put their heads together and talked for a moment. Bob gave Howard a thumbs-up.

"You win, Bob," the Indian woman said. They gathered their purses and stood up.

Bob was all smiles, pulling out their chairs, saying, "This is Howard Marshall, he's my assistant at Carson Technological Industries. I'm the president and CEO. You can call me, Chief."

"I'm Aziza," the Indian woman said, "and this is Keiko." Keiko kept a firm grip on Howard's hand until she was fully in her seat. The oversized cuffs of her black sweater gently caressed his wrist. She thanked him and brushed her straight black hair away from her face. In the warm light of the restaurant her skin had a golden glow.

"Ah-zee-za and Key-ko?" Bob nudged Howard. "Pretty ladies, but strange names."

Aziza smiled patiently. "Maybe *our* names are normal and yours are strange," she suggested.

"You can't get any more normal than *Bob*!" Bob said.

"Where are you ladies from?" Howard asked, trying to turn the conversation in a more productive direction.

"New York," Keiko said. "But we spend a lot of time on the road."

"He means *before* you came to America," Bob said.

Aziza studied Bob for a moment and saw that he was serious. She said, "I was born in Detroit, Bob. Keiko, weren't you born down South?"

"Austin, Texas."

Aziza said, "I think that means we're Americans, Chief."

Bob mimicked her sassy tone. "Then why don't you have American names, Ah-zee-za?"

Aziza said to Howard, "This is the CEO of an actual, profitable company?"

Score one for Aziza, though these days *profitable* was probably the wrong adjective. Howard sipped his beer.

"Don't mind, Howard," Bob said. "He's not too talkative tonight because his wife is cheating on him."

Howard stopped mid-sip and glared at Bob.

Keiko shook her pretty head. "I don't believe *any* woman would cheat on a man as handsome as Howard." She put her hand on his arm and smiled affectionately. He patted her hand twice before pulling away.

"How do you know she's having an affair?" Aziza asked.

Howard didn't speak for a moment, and then seemed to make up his mind. "I just have suspicions," he said finally

"Trust your instincts," Bob said. "If you think she's cheating, she probably is." Bob turned to the women. "You ladies must be in sales, huh?"

"Pharmaceuticals," Aziza said, "for Pfizer." She had a voice like a news anchor—perfect enunciation, perfect delivery, but without the syrupy warmth. To Howard, she said, "Why are you suspicious?"

"I knew it!" Bob said. "Didn't I say that the minute they walked in?" He slapped Howard's shoulder. "I said all the best looking women are in sales."

"You called it, Chief," Howard said. To Aziza he said, "I'd rather not talk about my wife."

"Of course," Aziza said, nodding respectfully.

"I think you should loosen up," Keiko said to Howard, tugging on his tie.

"I'm in sales, too," Bob said. "You know the new operating

system Globalsoft released this year? My company sold it to them." He explained the history of the program to the women, including the sordid details of Rashid's crash.

"That poor girl," Aziza after hearing about the death by asphyxiation.

Keiko said, "That's why I don't put those things in my mouth."

Bob said, "I'm thinking about selling it again overseas."

"Selling *what* overseas?" Aziza asked.

"The operating system."

"Doesn't sound like you own it any more," she said.

Howard tipped his beer at Aziza. Another point for her.

"It's *my* program," Bob insisted.

Aziza goaded him: "But you sold the rights to—"

"Just the *American* rights."

"Oh," she said doubtfully. "So what country are you—"

"I haven't decided yet," Bob said. "It's complicated."

"I'm sure it is." Aziza turned to her friend. "You need to use the restroom?" Keiko shook her head, and Aziza excused herself.

Bob stared at Aziza's ass as she sashayed toward the front of the restaurant. To Keiko he said, "You always let her do all the talking?"

Keiko shrugged. "She's good at it, and I don't have much to say."

"Oh, I'd bet you have plenty to say to the right guy," Bob said, winking.

She looked at Howard and said, "You always let *him* do all the talking?"

Howard smiled. "He's the boss." He liked Keiko. She was gentle, but savvy. He sensed that she knew exactly how to use her beauty to her advantage without letting men use it against her.

"You know," Bob said, "I'm thinking about branching out into drug sales myself."

"Yeah?" Keiko said.

"But I'll do it *freelance*." He laughed. "Freelance Pharmacology! How about that?" Keiko smiled politely and turned back to Howard.

Aziza returned, and Bob popped up to hold her chair. Aziza asked Howard, "So what kind of boss is the big chief, here?"

Howard shrugged. "He's a good guy. I enjoy—"

"What he enjoys," Bob interrupted, "is the shit-load of money I pay him just for running errands."

Howard sighed. Moments like these always made him miss Bob's father, who had valued and nurtured his employees.

Bob finished his Scotch with a gulp and rattled his ice cubes at the waiter. "Hello? Try to keep up here!" The waiter took the empty glass and rushed to the bar to get a fresh drink. "Howard didn't want to stay with the company after I took over, but I made such a monster offer that he couldn't refuse."

Howard managed not to laugh. He made seventy thousand dollars a year, a good salary, but hardly *monster*. He figured that both Aziza and Keiko earned six-figures.

"That's your style, huh?" Aziza asked. "See something you want and try to buy it."

"You got it, honey. Let me ask you a question. If you were dating a man who surprised you all the time with flowers and candy, would you get mad if he forgot your birthday?"

"Why did he forget?" Aziza asked.

"Doesn't matter."

"Sure it does," she said. "If he forgot because his mother was in the hospital, that's different than forgetting because—"

"Jesus Christ! Women get hung up on the details, don't they?" Bob said, nudging Howard. "Let's say he didn't forget at all. Let's say he just didn't think he needed to get you a present for your birthday because he buys you stuff all the time."

"I might get angry," Aziza said.

"See!" Bob exclaimed. "Women aren't innately romantic."

"I'd be angry," Aziza continued, "because he'd probably be a calculating dick like you, conducting some sort of experiment with our relationship."

"Pu-leeze," Bob said. "You'd be pissed because women don't know the first thing about romance. They don't understand that it's supposed to be about mystery and being unpredictable. You know why women love weddings?"

"I'm sure you're going to tell us," Aziza said.

Bob slammed back another drink and rattled his ice cubes at the waiter, who responded instantly with a new glass. "Because they can spend a whole year planning. They'll pick out a dress, choose bridesmaids, buy a cake, decide what kind of *paper* their invitations will be printed on, draw up a seating chart, and hire a photographer to take some corny staged photos! That's romance in a woman's world. No spontaneity. No surprises, just every little detail planned to the nth degree."

"Or," Aziza said calmly, "maybe women see a wedding as an important tradition, and they want to do things a certain way to reflect the solemnity of the occasion."

Bob rolled his eyes. "Honey, I've been married three times. You're not gonna sell me on solemnity."

"You like baseball?" Keiko asked quietly.

"Of course," Bob said. "America's pastime. You come back to Denver in the spring, I'll take you to a Rockies game. I've got a suite halfway down the first-base line."

"Baseball is just a big pre-planned ceremony," Keiko said. "It's full of rituals. The way the pitcher winds up; the way the batter digs his feet into the dirt, and the way an umpire dances when he calls someone out."

"And," Aziza added, "it wouldn't be a baseball game without peanuts, hot dogs and the seventh-inning stretch Without the rituals, it wouldn't be a baseball game, and without the rituals a wedding wouldn't be a wedding."

"Pu'leeeze," Bob said. "Listen, I gotta go drain the monster." He walked off with his arms folded behind him.

"How can you work for this jerk?" Aziza asked.

"Same reason you're sitting at this table," Howard said.

Aziza shook an admonishing finger at him. "Trust me. We're not for sale."

"I'm not saying one way or the other. I'm just pointing out that Bob tends to overcome people's resistance with money and sheer force of personality."

"Well, I'm paying for dinner."

Howard shook his head. "He won't let you. Picking up the tab is what he does best."

"Not tonight," Aziza said. "I gave my credit card to the manager."

Howard watched Aziza's pretty eyes. She stared back at him with a calculated innocence. "Bob's not going to like that."

"I know." Aziza said, taking a slow sip of her drink. "So is this his standard M.O.? Go to a nice restaurant, pick up a couple of women and start bragging about his money?"

Howard said, "After dinner he's going to offer you a ride in his Range Rover limo."

"That's him parked out front?"

Howard nodded. "He'll take you to Platinum Heels."

"Strip club?"

Howard gave her a thumb's up. "Then he's going to invite you to spend the weekend with him at his house in the mountains."

"I'm assuming it's a big ostentatious place."

"Ten-thousand square feet with every amenity."

"*Nearly* every amenity," Aziza corrected. "Sounds like he's trying to find a couple of *amenities* to take with him."

Howard said, "If you two are interested, it'll be you. If not, he'll hire a couple of strippers."

"Wow! How flattering!" Aziza said facetiously. She nudged Keiko. "It's either us or the strippers."

The interesting part, which Howard didn't mention, was that they wouldn't have to have sex with Bob. Once, Howard had asked the dancers at Platinum Heels if they were worried about getting in trouble for spending the night with Bob. He'd avoided the word *prostitution*, but they knew what he was saying.

"Don't worry, honey," said a stripper named Candi. She was a twenty-year-old former gymnast with a small face, blonde hair cut in a bob, tiny breasts, ripped abs, muscular legs, and so much flexibility that she could literally tie herself into a sexy knot. "None of us has ever had sex with Bob."

"Ever?" Howard asked, doubtfully.

"Ever," Candi said. "Bob talks a lot, but once he's alone with a couple of women, he doesn't know what to do. We dance for him, take his money, and leave him with a horrible case of blue balls."

A few other strippers blew up their cheeks as if they were about to burst. "Blue balls!" they screamed, laughing hysterically.

"We won't even let him masturbate in front of us," said a stripper named Raquel. She was a curvy, dark-haired Latina, with enormous fake breasts that looked like over-full beach balls. The skin in her cleavage was stretched so thin it was translucent—her veins glowed blue, and in bright light, the silicone implants showed up as opaque orbs under her skin.

"But he throws around so much money," Howard argued. "Surely, someone has given in to temptation."

The strippers all shook their heads.

"Bob is ...," Candi started, then paused to look around the table. "What's that word you used the other day?"

"Indiscreet?" Raquel suggested.

"Yes, he's indiscreet," Candi said. "If he just wanted to get laid, he could call a high-end escort service, get a couple of girls to come to his house and do whatever he wanted."

"But Bob's not into that," Raquel said. "Bob wants to stroll into a strip club, throw a lot of money around, and then impress all the guys by walking out with two or three dancers on his arm."

"While he's thinking about how cool he looks," Candi said, "we're thinking about how we look to our managers, the vice squad and anyone else watching."

"We're dancers, not prostitutes," Raquel said. "Trust me, we're not gonna get arrested going down on Bob."

Candi said, "Besides, we pay an off-duty cop to come with us whenever we leave the club with a client for security."

Howard had been stunned by this news, and it had taken an effort to keep a straight face the next time Bob said, "So ladies, let's talk about the naughty perversions we're going to get into tonight!"

# nine

"So let me get this straight," Aziza said. "Bob goes out, meets a couple of women, gives them a ride in his limo, takes them to a strip club, and then says let's go to my mountain mansion?"

"That's the script."

"Did he read a book on how to be a predictable rich jerk?"

Howard paused and said dramatically, "Does Bob look like a *reader* to you?"

Aziza laughed, and her face lit up with a warmth that had been absent until that moment. The indifferent prettiness was replaced by an approachable good humor, and Howard was instantly drawn to her. "You're right," she said, smiling prettily, "being a jerk must come natural to Bob."

Keiko seemed to sense Howard's attraction to Aziza. She laid her hand possessively on top of his wedding band, and asked, "How does your wife feel about her handsome husband going girl-hunting with the boss?"

Howard looked down at her hand for a moment, but didn't pull away. He wanted to say, *This is just my job*, but instead he said, "She knows Bob."

"So she feels sorry for you," Aziza said.

"Exactly."

"Yes, I *do* know, Bob," Sophia said, approaching the table with Davis Delaney following close behind. She watched Howard tear his hand away from Keiko's.

Howard stood up. "I've been trying to call you," he said

defensively. Why did he feel so guilty when *she* was the one having the affair?

Sophia looked stunning in a sheer black blouse over a black corset and tight black slacks. Her straight blond hair hung down past her shoulders, and she glided toward them like a model on a runway.

"I got your messages," Sophia said, stopping at the end of the runway, one hip cocked aggressively. Her eyes smoldered with an unspoken fury and her voice sounded choked off, as if she were barely constraining a torrent of words. To the saleswomen, she said, "I'm Howard's *wife*." She made no move to shake their hands.

Howard said, "This is Aziza and Keiko. They're friends of Bob's."

"Looks like they're friends of yours, too," Sophia said.

Davis stepped closer to the table. "What up, Money?" He raised a fist, black-power style and smiled. He looked like an early twenties club-hopper in his black Italian loafers, faded blue jeans, big silver watch, oversized Joe Namath throwback jersey and Kangol hat reversed and slightly askew.

"Davis Delaney," he said to the women, pouring on the charm. He bent down to take their hands, his long hair falling around his face as he smiled at them. "I'm an artist."

"Yeah?" Aziza asked. "What do you do?"

"Mainly nails."

Aziza scowled, confused. A manicurist wasn't exactly her idea of an *artist*.

Howard said. "I was getting ready to head home—"

"Then I'll see you later, Mounds," Sophia said. "I'm taking Davis to a party in Morrison."

"I'll go with you," Howard offered. He had never seen Sophia like this. She seemed on the verge of erupting.

Sophia shook her head and gestured toward Bob coming back to the table. "You stay here and kiss Bob's ass, and I'll go sell some paintings."

"What time is your flight tomorrow?"

She shrugged. "Late morning. I'll wake you up in plenty of time." She grabbed Davis' arm, and pivoted dramatically on one foot, her hair whipping around her head. Howard watched her march out of the restaurant and wondered what was happening to his wife.

Bob fell into his seat. "Whew! That was a close call!" Howard looked at him, confused for a moment, until he realized that Bob was talking about his trip to the restroom, not Sophia's visit.

"Wasn't that Sophia?" Bob asked.

"She's pretty," Aziza said.

"Her extensions are beautiful," Keiko said.

"Her what?" Howard asked.

"Hair extensions," Keiko said. "You can barely tell they're there."

"Why does she call you Mounds?" Aziza asked.

"It's a private nickname," Howard said.

"He won't even tell *me* what it means," Bob complained.

Aziza said, "It doesn't sound very affectionate."

"It's a long story," Howard said, still watching the door where Sophia had exited.

"And the guy with the hair," Bob explained, "is the lover."

"He does *nails*?" Aziza asked, confused.

"Paints them," Bob said, as if that cleared things up. "You should see the nail gun he did for me. It'll scare the life out of you."

Aziza looked completely baffled.

"Why didn't she stay?" Bob asked.

Good question. Howard knew Sophia had come to the restaurant because she'd received his messages, and he didn't believe her quick exit had anything to do with Aziza and Keiko—even though Keiko had been holding Howard's hand. Sophia knew that Bob often picked up women, but she had never been bothered by it, because she trusted Howard. It would have been more like her to pull up a chair and buy the women a drink.

"Where is she flying to?" Aziza asked.

"New York for a week," Bob said. "Art show or something like that, right Howard?"

Aziza said, "What a funny coincidence. We just came from New York."

"We'll be in Denver until next Wednesday," Keiko said. "Then we're heading down to Mexico to spend a week on the beach."

"I'm *so* ready for a break," Aziza said.

"Ooh," Bob said, rubbing his hands together. "If you're going to the beach next week, you should see the mountains while you're there. I've got a beautiful home up—"

Keiko leaned toward Howard and said, "Maybe *you* could show us the sights while we're in town."

Howard shook his head. "I don't do that."

"Do what?" Keiko asked, batting her eyes innocently. "Go sight-seeing?"

"Cheat," Aziza said. "You never cheat, Howard?"

He shook his head.

Aziza said, "Seems like it would be easy, given the situations you end up in, hanging out with the chief."

Howard supposed it must have been easy for Sophia, too.

"I'm a married man," he said. "So easy or hard isn't the issue, is it?"

Bob said, "Buck up, Howard. It's not your fault. Women in Highlands Ranch get bored and sleep around. You've seen the show *Desperate Housewives*."

"What's Highlands Ranch?" Aziza asked.

Bob laughed. "It's where Howard lives. They wouldn't like you down there."

"Why is that?"

Bob said, "Women down there come in one flavor—vanilla."

Howard rolled his eyes. "The *houses* are vanilla," he corrected, "not the people."

Dinner turned into one of the strangest outings in Howard's life. Usually, Howard picked up women, singly or in pairs, and handed them off to Bob, who dazzled them with talk about his money, cars, airplane, homes, and lavish vacations.

But tonight, Aziza challenged everything Bob said and changed the subject whenever he mentioned his wealth. Keiko flirted with Howard constantly, touching his arm and shoulder and asking, suggestively, if his meat was good, and whether he wanted to sample hers. Howard kept wondering why Sophia was upping the ante. She had gone from a secret affair with Davis Delaney, to sneaking downstairs in the middle of the night, to parading him into a restaurant so Howard could watch them leave together. Why was she pushing so hard? And why was *he* holding on? He recalled Bob's advice a few hours earlier, *You should probably just cut her loose. Don't ask any questions, don't get into any details, just call a lawyer and get a divorce.* Howard grunted and took another swig of beer.

After dessert, while Aziza was in the middle of a story about her job, Bob said, "You ladies want a ride in my pimped out Rover?"

Aziza laughed abruptly. "There it is!"

"There *what* is?" Bob asked, confused.

"The invitation."

"Have you ever noticed," Keiko asked quietly, "that you interrupt people a lot?"

Bob looked at her curiously. "What do you mean?"

"Someone will be talking, and you'll butt in and change the subject."

"Well, we can't sit here all night, darlin'. I'm just suggesting a change of venue. Ah-zee-za can finish her story in the car."

Keiko said, "Only if Howard is coming."

Howard held up both hands. "I've got to get—"

"Of course, he's coming," Bob said, clapping him on the shoulder. He signaled to the waiter, who responded immediately with his eyebrows raised. "Gimme the check," Bob said, reaching for his wallet.

The waiter scurried away and returned with a bill folder. Bob stared at the tab for a long moment. "This ain't enough," he said.

"That's just the bill for the Cristal," the waiter said. "Your meal has already been taken care of."

"Really?" Bob looked surprised but pleased. "Well," he preened, "tell the manager I said thank you." To the ladies he said, "I'm a good customer here."

"The manager didn't pick up the tab, numbnuts," Aziza said. "I did."

Bob's head bobbed back and forth between the waiter and Aziza. To the waiter he said, "You did this *behind my back*?"

The waiter apparently hadn't considered the possibility

that Bob would be angry about receiving a free meal. "Sir, your lady friend insisted."

"And you *let* her?" Bob growled.

Aziza said, "What's the problem, Chief?"

"*I* was going to buy *your* dinner," Bob groused.

"Oh well," she shrugged, innocently. "Now that we've paid for your food, we own you. Isn't that how it goes? You're beholden to us?"

Bob hesitated and then regained his footing. "I guess that depends on what you want to do to me now that you own me," he said with a wink.

Aziza stared at him with cold eyes. "We bought your freedom, Chief. Now get lost."

Bob looked genuinely shocked, as if this was his first rejection rather than the millionth.

"She's just playing," Keiko said quickly, leaning toward Howard. "Of course, we want to take a ride in the limo."

They climbed into the back of the Rover and headed off to Platinum Heels. Bob tried to slip his arm around Aziza, but she fought him off. Howard called the manager at the strip club and let him know they were coming. Then he put down his phone and watched as the city landscape floated past. Keiko kept talking to him, but Howard was oblivious to her.

# ten

Platinum Heels was the most upscale strip club in Denver, and Bob Carson was a regular. When they stepped out of the Range Rover, Pablo, the spiked-haired manager, was standing just inside the door with two strippers at each elbow. The scantily-clad dancers escorted the guests inside, one on each of Bob's arms, one each leading Aziza and Keiko, and none for Howard. He'd been to Platinum with Bob many times, and the dancers knew he was just the tour guide.

Pablo led Bob and his entourage past the tables and platforms in the main sitting area to a private room lined in red silk. Bob fell onto one of the soft, red couches and asked: "Has either of you drug dealers ever had a lap dance?"

Aziza said, "We've got to use the restroom." She took Keiko's hand and led her out of the room. Keiko blew a kiss to Howard, as they slipped away, and he knew they wouldn't come back. The strippers started dancing and Bob giggled like a little boy, stuffing twenty-dollar bills into their g-strings. The cocktail waitress came in with a bottle of Dom Perignon and tried to pour Howard a glass, but he declined. For the rest of the night, he would drink water.

After a while, a six-foot-tall African-American stripper named Natural leaned into Howard and asked, "You need anything, sugar?" She pronounced her name, Nat-cher-rawl, and her claim to fame was an enormous silicone-free bosom with silver-dollar sized areolas and half-inch nipples. Howard shook his head slowly, his eyes watery; her perfume was giving him a contact high. "You let me know when you're ready," she said, dragging her hand down his thigh as she backed away.

Twenty minutes later, Bob said, "Hey, where did the girls go?" He'd just noticed that Aziza and Keiko had departed, but by then it didn't matter. He was intoxicated by the attention of the dancers. They dripped baby oil on each other and rubbed it in. On top of whatever they earned in tips tonight, Bob would pay a couple of them four grand each to come up to the mountains with him—so they were auditioning. Howard gave his boss a thumb's up and told him to have a good weekend.

As Howard exited the club, a hard clap of thunder boomed overhead, and he ducked instinctively. "Damn that was loud," he said to the doorman, a thick-necked, three-hundred-pound body builder who hadn't flinched. The doorman shrugged as if to say that not even Mother Nature could impress him.

The rain was falling in thick sheets. Howard was about to hail a cab when Edward pulled forward in the Rover; Howard ran out from under the small canopy at the door and jumped into the front seat.

"You probably shouldn't take me," he said. "Bob could be ready to leave at any second."

Edward looked at the clock on the dash—it was 12:50 a.m.—and shook his head. Smiling, he said, "Mr. Bob will be there until closing. I will take you to your car and return for him."

Howard said. "Did you drive the women back to their hotel?"

"Yes, sir," Edward said. "They wanted a taxi, but I insisted."

"I appreciate your doing that."

"It was my pleasure."

"I felt bad for them, getting hijacked by Bob."

Edward shrugged, and his smile turned a little enigmatic. "They seemed to handle him okay."

That was the thing. Women always seemed to handle Bob *okay*. They either used him for his money or dismissed him as a rich boor. Yet Bob's confidence was not shaken. He still thought of himself as a ladies man.

Back at the office parking lot, Howard climbed into his BMW X5 and began the rain-drenched drive home to Highlands Ranch.

# eleven

The SUV seemed to know the route automatically, and before he knew it, Howard exited I-25 at Lincoln Avenue, turned right toward the mountains and cruised through the town of Lone Tree on his way to Colorado's largest subdivision.

Though his view was impeded by rain and obscured by darkness, Howard could still make out rows and rows of enormous homes arranged neatly all around him like Monopoly hotels. If there had been a little more light, he would have seen that every house was painted a pale, inoffensive tone, in keeping with a socialistic uniformity that outlawed overt individualism in the neighborhood. No home was permitted to draw attention to itself, because doing so might diminish the property values of the surrounding homes.

When Howard had first started dating Sophia, he'd been fascinated by the utopian appearance of the neighborhood. The homes were big and beautiful with pleasant colors and manicured lawns. The medians were perfectly maintained, the trees expertly trimmed, the fences straight and clean, and the cars and SUV's parked in the driveways were new, expensive, and shiny. The residents were friendly and life seemed perfectly orderly. It would take years before he would discover that dark secrets festered beneath this perfect veneer—some of those secrets were inside his own marriage.

The curvilinear streets of Highlands Ranch contained every amenity a family needed. There were parks, playgrounds, ball fields, tennis courts, skate parks, an in-line rink, hiking and biking trails, swimming pools, recreation centers, off-leash areas for dogs, movie theaters, restaurants, grocery stores, churches, schools, business offices, hotels, and the nearby Park Meadows shopping center, where a family could temporarily sate its thirst for consumption. While many suburbs were parasites that drew heavily on their host cities, Highlands Ranch was a mostly self-contained bubble in which homeowners could feed, clothe and entertain themselves without venturing into the high-crime, high-pollution, mixed-density areas north of County Line Road.

Howard had grown up in Chattanooga, Tennessee, in an old Victorian house with rotting shingles, peeling wallpaper and just a single bathroom for a family of seven. Though his family had always lived in lower middle-class neighborhoods, Howard had enjoyed a wonderful, rich childhood, and as an adult, he'd deliberately chosen neighborhoods that were middle-class, and filled with culture, history and diversity. His townhouse in the Park Hill area of Denver had been part of a six-unit, one-story building. All around him, homes of varying sizes, architectural styles and states of repair had stood proudly next to restaurants, automotive shops, groceries, veterinary clinics, bars, liquor stores, and other businesses. His block was home to married couples with and without children, one senior citizen couple who'd lived in their house for nearly sixty years, two senior women—one eighty-eight, the other seventy-three—who lived alone, single men and women in their twenties and thirties, and many unmarried couples cohabiting. The neighbors were black, white, Hispanic and Asian, Christian, Jewish, Muslim, gay, straight, and who knew what else. Some of the residents were obviously wealthy—it showed in the cars they drove, the clothing they wore, and the furniture and equipment that was visible when the drapes were open. Others were obviously poor, and Howard guessed that a few might have been receiving some form of government assistance. He'd always felt that the homes in his Park Hill neighborhood were comfortably imperfect, and it was those imperfections that gave the area its charming character.

By contrast, Highlands Ranch was aesthetically perfect, but it felt *uncomfortable*. The whole neighborhood reminded Howard of a five-year-old boy moping on a bench in his Sunday best while other kids—dressed more casually—ran, tumbled, and laughed on a busy playground. The boy's outfit was perfect, but he had to give up a lot to keep it that way.

Initially, Howard had felt strange every time he entered Highlands Ranch. But after a few months, he grew accustomed to the odd perfection. In fact, by the end of the first year, Howard concluded that Highlands Ranch was, by far, the most beautiful and the safest place he'd ever lived. There was no blight, no pockmarked streets, no dangerous blocks to avoid, no drug houses, no prostitutes prowling the sidewalks, no drunks stumbling out of nightclubs, and no homeless people panhandling on street corners.

Of course, that didn't mean that nothing bad ever happened in Highlands Ranch—it just usually wasn't obvious. Its wealthy residents occasionally got laid off, suffered ruinous divorces, or fell seriously ill, but if they started to stumble financially, they generally were out of the neighborhood before they finally hit the ground—without anyone much the wiser. Given the large mortgages, association dues, mandatory maintenance costs, and the other expenses, it simply was not possible to continue living in Highlands Ranch without a steady and substantial income, so even the recently impoverished could not stay.

The only obvious downside to life in Highlands Ranch was the overly strict homeowners association that demanded uniformity in the appearance of each cluster of homes—as if they were groups of row houses or condominiums rather than single-family dwellings.

"We keep your neighbor from painting his house fluorescent pink and dragging down the value of the neighborhood" was an oft-cited defense raised by the overzealous board. Irresponsible owners might have been the targets of the regulations, but Howard knew that the real victims were responsible homeowners who wanted to improve their properties by remodeling, painting exterior walls, building decks, landscaping, putting up fences, planting bird feeders, or raising flags. If they had been free to use their own discretion, most residents would have enhanced the appearance of their homes according to their own idiosyncratic tastes, and thereby enhanced the overall diversity and value of the neighborhood. But the board rejected even the mildest requests out of fear that any exception would set a precedent that might be used by some future resident to win approval for some more objectionable purpose.

Howard had become a minor celebrity in Highlands Ranch after he'd successfully defended himself against two assessments—a feat that no one else in the neighborhood had managed. Highlands Ranch used to be divided into four metro districts, each with its own five-member board, but a recent consolidation had brought the entire twenty-two-thousand-acre community under the control of a single seven-person board. The board had pursued Sophia and Howard for putting up maroon drapes in their windows and for hanging provocative pictures that were visible from the sidewalk when the drapes were open.

At the board meeting to challenge the assessments, Howard had argued, "The saying goes, 'A man's home is his castle.' All of us"—he paused to indicate the crowd of nearly one hundred residents—"know that if we choose to live here, then we surrender control over the external appearance of our homes. We give you that power, because we believe it serves our best interests. However, if we give you the authority to determine the color of our drapes or the content of our paintings, what will you do next? Will you tell us that we have to take down pictures of our family members, because they're visible through the windows? Will you make us repaint our living rooms to colors that you approve? Will you make us hide our children's trophy cases, remove religious symbols, or remove our china cabinets?"

The crowd had broken into applause and had chanted Howard's name as the board members huddled together for about a minute before rejecting his arguments. They ordered him to replace the drapes and remove the offensive pictures. Jennifer Meagert-Logan, chairperson of the seven-member board—who insisted that everyone refer to her as Chairperson Meagert-Logan—had banged her gavel for several minutes trying to regain control of the room after the crowd erupted in a chorus of boos and hisses. When the noise died down, Howard calmly stated that he intended to file a lawsuit against the association.

Chairperson Meagert-Logan smiled at him patiently. She was pretty, in her mid-thirties, with long dark hair, pale blue eyes, delicate features, and an immense bosom.

"Howard," she said, intimately. The tone caught everyone's attention and reminded them that she and Howard had dated several years earlier. "No one has ever successfully sued us."

Howard refused to refer to her by her title. Instead he shortened her name to Jenny, Jen, JML, and more recently, J-Lo.

"Well J-Lo, that's about to change," he promised.

She smacked her gavel on the desk and said, "My name is Chairperson—"

She was drowned out by the jubilant crowd. Howard marched out of the room as his neighbors cheered for him, and clapped his back.

Eventually, a Colorado district judge ruled that external uniformity was all that the homeowners association could impose on its members. He wrote, "Restrictions on external modifications are designed to protect the overall identity of the neighborhood. However, the residents are not actually identical people, with identical tastes, identical interests and identical interior decorating styles. The association cannot dictate the choices its members make in their most private spaces." The judge dismissed the assessments against Howard, ordered the association to pay his legal fees and court costs, and established that the board could not regulate the color, texture or style of drapes or any other interior feature of a home except the color of light bulbs visible from outside.

News of Howard's victory spread quickly, and he achieved a legendary status in Highlands Ranch. Residents, emboldened by this ruling, started remodeling the interiors of their homes, expressing their individuality in dramatic and unexpected ways. Howard knew one family that had converted the interior of its home into an enormous butterfly pavilion, with hundreds of tropical plants, humidifiers running twenty-four hours a day and nearly ten thousand butterflies fluttering around. To enter or exit the home, you had to walk through an air chamber that maintained the tropical environment and kept the insects safely indoors. Another family had created a maze modeled after the story of the Minotaur in Greek mythology, while another had built an indoor amusement park, replete with slides, trampolines, and water rides. All over the neighborhood, residents frustrated by the inability to modify the exteriors of their homes, radically transformed the interiors—Highlands Ranch became even more of a false façade than it had been.

# twelve

The rain continued to pound on the roof of Howard's BMW as he entered his section of Highlands Ranch, which had been built in the early-1990s by James R. Pendleton Construction. Howard turned left on Pendleton Boulevard, a wide, well-lit road that took him past Pendleton Place, Pendleton Court, and Pendleton Way. He turned left on Pendleton Avenue, passed Pendleton Street, turned right on Pendleton Lane, then left on Pendleton Drive. His was the nineteenth taupe house on the left, where Davis Delaney's van was still parked in the driveway.

As the garage door opened, the interior light illuminated the shimmering street. Howard turned into the driveway and came to a full stop, sitting back, wearily. Once again, Sophia had parked too close to the middle of the garage. For years Howard had explained to her that she needed to park as far to the left as she could so that he would have adequate room to pull in. The wheels of her Audi A8 were just touching the thin groove in the concrete demarcating the center of the main portion of the garage. The third bay was set back six feet from the rest of the garage, and it was cluttered with lawn equipment, bicycles, skis, potting soil, and boxes full of supplies for her gallery. They had so many storage items in that third bay that they had to cram their cars unnaturally far to the left in order to park.

Howard sighed and decided against going inside to get Sophia's keys and repositioning her car. He'd done that on many occasions in the past, but tonight he just wanted to get in the house and go to sleep. He thought about leaving the BMW in the driveway, but at exactly that moment, hard beads of hail started pelting the roof.

"Dammit!" he said, easing the SUV into the shelter of the garage. He inched forward until he was completely inside. The Beemer fit in the narrow space—just barely. He turned off the ignition and gently cracked the door. It swung open a little more than a foot before bumping against the Audi. There was not enough room for Howard to squeeze out. He leaned across to the passenger side and tried the door there, but it too was blocked. He sat still for a long moment, thinking that he'd have to pull out and start over.

"Screw it!" he said, leaning back over the center console. Howard pulled the switches that released the rear seats and laid them flat. Then he clamored awkwardly into the cargo area and crawled to the rear lift gate. He popped it open and started out of the SUV, accidentally stepping on the dangling end of his tie. He whooped in alarm as he tumbled gracelessly onto the slick driveway. He put his arms out to break his fall, but he still smacked his cheek and temple on the pavement. A bolt of pain shot through his skull, and Howard lay immobilized for several long seconds, while hard pellets of hail pummeled him. Finally, he lifted his head and crawled into the garage, fighting the urge to vomit.

He sat up and cradled his head in both hands for several minutes. His cheek bone throbbed with pain, and it felt as though someone had jabbed him hard in the eye. It was one-thirty in the morning, and the entire neighborhood was deserted. Howard wondered what would have happened if he had fractured his skull. He opened and closed his mouth several times, testing his jaw. Even though he was in pain, he couldn't help chuckling at the realization that if he had bled to death, the HOA probably would have fined Sophia for leaving a corpse in plain sight, and for staining the driveway blood red—a forbidden color.

He noticed the trash cans in the corner of the garage and remembered that the garbage trucks would rumble through the neighborhood in a few hours. According to the Residential Improvement Guidelines and Site Restrictions (which everyone referred to as the RIGs), residents could put their trash cans on the curb no earlier than 5 a.m. on Saturdays, and the receptacles had to be removed no later than 8 a.m. the same day. Trash trucks used to come on Mondays and Thursdays, and residents could put their cans out the night before, but the HOA board had changed this rule the previous year, just as it had changed most other reasonable procedures.

Howard checked up and down the block and saw no one, so he dragged his containers down to the curb and sprinted back up the driveway, ducking to shield his face from the hail. In his peripheral vision, he saw a light snap on across the street. He turned and saw Mrs. Stephenson, a 68-year-old retiree, standing in her bedroom window in a pink robe. Her drapes were wide open, and she was staring at him with a pair of high-powered binoculars—oddly, spying, even in one's bathrobe and even with magnification, was not a violation of the RIGs. In fact, overt and covert surveillance was encouraged by the board because it helped identify and punish covenant breakers. Howard waved at Mrs. Stephenson, but as usual, she did not wave back. He realized that if he *had* been dying in the driveway, Mrs. Stephenson would have watched his final breath, but she would not have called for help. Of course, he had no doubt that she would report him for putting his trash cans out at 1:30 a.m., but he didn't care. If the HOA came after him, it would be his word against hers.

When he entered the house, Sophia's two black suitcases were waiting in the kitchen. He stared at them for several minutes, recalling that she was leaving for New York in the morning. He wondered if this was really a business trip or if she was taking a vacation with Davis. Examining the contents of her bags might tell him a lot. He could see whether she had packed work clothes or party dresses, and if she had lingerie and condoms tucked into the pockets. Howard contemplated opening the bags, but decided that, despite feeling that he was suffocating in wet cement, he couldn't spy on his wife. He would talk to her in the morning. For now, he wheeled the suitcases into the garage and put them into the back of his SUV.

When Howard finally got upstairs, Sophia was lying with her almond-shaped face turned beatifically toward the ceiling. Her eyes were closed and her blonde hair was fanned out perfectly on the pillow. He might have suspected that she was feigning sleep if not for her intermittent snoring. Sophia snored through her nose, producing a high-pitched whine like a dentist's drill. More than once, this sound had intruded into Howard's subconscious, giving him nightmares about root canals.

He noticed that she didn't look angry or anxious in her sleep. Whatever had been bothering her at The Palm wasn't tormenting her dreams.

Howard climbed into bed and kissed her cheek. The light scent of her jasmine body lotion smelled familiar and soothing. He lay his head on the pillow—injured side up—and within seconds, he was asleep.

# *thirteen*

If Howard hadn't been so tired, he might have taken a moment to appreciate the fact that he'd noticed Sophia's jasmine scent. He rarely noticed odors unless someone prompted him, and based on this minor idiosyncrasy, Sophia had concluded that Howard suffered a major character flaw. Almost from the moment they'd started dating, Sophia had believed that Howard's inability to detect scents was proof that he had an immature emotional system.

"Sights and sounds are easy," Sophia often said, shoving an unlit candle, a bar of soap, or an opened bottle of shampoo under his nose. "Scents are all around you and they affect you in many subtle ways. Smell this. Doesn't it remind you of spring?"

Howard would give it a sniff and shrug indifferently. He could certainly *smell* the wonderful bouquet—lilac, vanilla, tangerine—but it never *reminded* him of anything.

"I'm just not very sensitive to odors," he'd said. He could detect strong smells, like vomit, over-full dumpsters, cheap perfume, and Sophia's bunnies. But most subtle scents slipped past him unnoticed.

"Mounds," she said, "you have to open your mind. If you don't notice scents or don't have memories attached to them, it means that you're not willing to be emotionally vulnerable."

Howard had rolled his eyes. "What emotional disability do blind people suffer?" If he was stunted for having an inadequate olfactory sense, then surely someone who lacked a more important sensory organ must have worse problems.

Sophia shook her head. "This isn't a simple logic problem, Howard." This was one of her favorite debating tactics. She'd say something outlandish, and when Howard countered with reason, she'd say that logic didn't count in this instance.

"Logic has its place, Mounds, but not when you're talking about emotions. How can logic explain love? Or happiness? Or sadness? Sometimes a person can feel happy despite a tragedy, or sad despite amazing good fortune. Emotions simply aren't logical."

The sweet aroma of popcorn reminded Sophia of movie theaters. She scrunched her nose against the repellant odor of mothballs and recalled her grandmother's musty attic full of old clothes. She caught a whiff of freshly baked chocolate chip cookies and thought of her mother baking on Sunday afternoons. Howard generally didn't notice these odors, and on the rare occasions that he did, they didn't provoke any memories. According to Sophia, that meant that he wasn't in touch with his deepest emotions.

# fourteen

Saturday morning, Howard woke up squinting at the sunlight slipping through the blinds. He groaned and grabbed a pillow to cover his face. Suddenly and inexplicably, in the fabric of that pillow he smelled Sophia's hair and remembered the way it had looked on the airplane when they'd first met. He smelled fabric softener and thought of the night a year ago when they had risked a major fine from the association by taking a blanket outside and having sex in the backyard.

Howard pulled the pillow away from his face, grinning, amazed, excited, and proud of himself. "I can *smell* you!" he exclaimed.

Sophia was sitting at her vanity, applying make-up. She dipped her nose toward an armpit. "Really?"

"Not over there, Bassiff." He pointed at the pillow. "I can smell you *here*."

"You can?"

"Yes! I woke up to the smell of you!"

"Mounds, that's wonderful!" She smiled at him in the mirror, then turned toward him with a scowl. "What happened to you?"

"What?"

"Did you get in a fight?" She stared at his black eye and bulging cheek.

"Oh," he said, gingerly touching his cheek. It was definitely sore. "I fell."

"You were drunk?" Her tone was disapproving.

"No, I—"

"I can't believe you drove home drunk, Mounds," she lectured.

"I wasn't drunk, Bassiff. Just tired and clumsy." He was tempted to mention her poor parking, but he didn't want to start a fight about the garage.

"Does it hurt?" Sophia asked.

"It's not too bad," Howard said. "The scents on the pillow reminded me of everything that I love about you."

She grinned and raised her eyebrows twice. Her pretty green eyes held his. "Thank ya, dawlin." She leaned toward the mirror, applying mascara. The waistband of her pajama bottoms was low on her hips, revealing a small tattoo of a Japanese symbol near the base of her spine.

"You smell yummy."

She said, "Sounds like someone is trying to get lucky." Bottles of earth-friendly Aveda hair and skin care products were clustered on the vanity top. Her family and friends stared out from pictures edging the mirror; an Eryka Badu concert ticket held top billing in the upper right corner. Her face was inches from the mirror as she worked carefully around her eyes.

"Actually, I—" Howard started, but he was interrupted by the sudden wail of a siren. He and Sophia looked at each other, then turned toward the window.

A voice boomed over a bullhorn. "ATTENTION HIGHLANDS RANCH RESIDENTS!" They both recognized the voice. It was J-Lo, chairperson of the HOA's architectural committee. "ACCORDING TO ARTICLE 5.28 OF THE CEE-DEE YOU MUST REMOVE YOUR TRASH CANS FROM THE STREET BY EIGHT A.M.! IT IS NOW EIGHT-FIFTEEN! YOU HAVE FIVE MINUTES TO COMPLY! FAILURE TO COMPLY, WILL RESULT IN AN ASSESSMENT!"

Every sentence out of J-Lo's mouth seemed to include one

of two acronyms: CD, for Community Declaration, or RIGs, for Residential Improvement Guidelines. She carried bound copies of each document with her and quoted from them as if she were a Baptist preacher at a revival.

"God, that woman is aggravating!" Sophia said, shaking her head.

Howard peeked out the window just as J-Lo passed their house. The siren squealed again, and she made another announcement.

"I don't know what you ever saw in her," Sophia said, watching Howard in the mirror.

He shrugged and thought, but didn't say, *mostly boobs.* He and Jennifer had dated years ago. "She wasn't like this back then," he said carefully. He didn't want to sound as though he was defending her. But it was true—she hadn't always been the petty tyrant that she'd become since joining the HOA board.

Howard had dated J-Lo briefly nearly five years ago, a few months *after* he first met Sophia. He and Sophia had been passionately in love, but in the early months, they had concluded that they had an irreconcilable difference—she wanted children, but he didn't—so they'd broken up. A few weeks later, Howard ran into J-Lo at a Denver Nuggets game, and they'd recognized each other from Highlands Ranch. They'd chatted near the concession stand for most of the second period. Howard was feeling morose about his breakup with Sophia, and J-Lo was depressed over a recent separation from her husband. Their sorrows had intensified the already strong sexual attraction they'd felt for each other. After the game, they'd retreated to the Blue Sky Grill for drinks, where Howard had stared obsessively at J-Lo's mouth.

She had a big, easy smile, pretty teeth, and a great voice,

with clear, precise enunciation and an expansive vocabulary. When she was listening, her eyes would blink languidly, as if she found his words physically pleasurable. The tip of her tongue occasionally flashed in the corner of her lips, like a fisherman's lure. She had a deep, throaty laugh that sent a gentle ripple of arousal through Howard's body every time she found something funny. Hours after the game, they finally left the bar, and in the parking lot, Jennifer leaned back against her car, grabbed the front of Howard's shirt and pulled him to her. Her plump lips pressed against his urgently, and he finally caught the lure. They kissed passionately for several minutes. Then she winked at him, got into her car and drove away.

Two days later, they had dinner at the Ruth Chris Steakhouse in Denver's LoDo district, and Jennifer slipped off her shoe and slid her bare foot up Howard's leg. She slowly unhooked two buttons of her blouse, revealing tanned D-cup breasts that bulged out of a push-up bra. When the waiter returned, he stammered over the dessert specials while trying to not stare at her cleavage. Howard and Jennifer fed each other chocolate cake and flirted obscenely. After dinner, they raced back to Howard's townhouse, ripped off their clothes and fell into bed, where Jennifer screamed and moaned as if she were having a continuous orgasm from start to finish. Initially, Howard had been turned off by her obviously faked performance. He wanted her to relax and enjoy the experience. He believed that he was a patient and competent lover, who would eventually help her achieve a real orgasm. But about fifteen minutes into the event, she had her legs wrapped around his waist, bucking her hips, and clutching him tightly as she screamed his name over and over—*Howard! Howard! Oh my God! Hoooooooowaaaaaard!!* He became convinced that she wasn't faking—he really was *that* good.

Lust and loneliness had held them together for nearly six months, despite having little else in common. Howard's fascination with her mouth faded, but his instant reaction to her enormous bosom remained. Most of their dates had been unapologetic booty calls, beginning and ending at one of their homes—usually after Jay Leno's monologue. At the time, Jennifer had a two-year-old son named Ethan, but Howard had never met the boy. She had rightly shielded her son from her social life, but she spent so many nights at Howard's house that he sometimes wondered if she really had a child.

"He's with his father," she would say, dismissively. Or "He's with his grandparents." Or "He's with a babysitter."

Eventually, Howard grew weary of empty sex and longed to have a meaningful relationship. He broke up with Jennifer—a decision she resented, even though he knew she was equally frustrated by their lack of emotional connection. A few months later, he stopped by Sophia's gallery and asked if he could take her to lunch. That day, they realized that, children or no children, they loved each other too much to be apart, so they'd resumed their relationship.

A year later, they were engaged.

# fifteen

Peeking out the bedroom window, Howard saw dozens of trash cans still on the curb, and scores of homeowners standing on the sidewalk in their pajamas and winter coats. The hail from the previous night had melted away, but despite the bright sunshine, the neighbors had their arms crossed tightly across their chests, and smoke emanated from their mouths when they talked. Some of them were looking closely at their cars, and Howard could see that a few windshields had spider-webbed impact circles from the hail. He was glad that he'd managed to get his SUV into the garage.

"I think we've got a mutiny out there," Howard said, pleased. He'd long advocated that the residents of Highlands Ranch band together and violate rules en mass. But who had initiated this trash rebellion? And why hadn't Howard been informed? "I'll go check it out."

He dressed quickly in jeans, a T-shirt, and a parka and walked down the street, greeting neighbors along the way.

"Good luck Tuesday night," said Tony Parker, a balding office supply manager who lived two houses down.

"Thanks," Howard said. Everyone knew about his upcoming confrontation with the HOA over Davis Delaney's van, and they all seemed to be rooting for him.

"Don't let them push you around!" yelled Elizabeth Duval, who lived across the street and four houses down. She was standing with one of her three children, a girl about twelve years old.

"I won't," Howard promised. He knew most of the parents by name, but not the kids—though he probably could have guessed. He had observed that the christening of children reflected roughly the same limited variety as the architecture in Highlands Ranch. Girls came in three versions—Madison, Emma and Bailey—and every boy was named Aiden, Ethan or Caleb.

Seven houses down, Adam and Miriam Hogan were huddled together, wearing heavy, fur-lined sailors' coats. Their two kids, Caleb and Emma, waved at Howard from the living room window. He showed them a clownish grin, and waved manically, his open palm darting back and forth so ridiculously fast that they giggled.

"They look like they're dying to come outside," he said, laughing.

"It's too cold," Miriam said, blowing a kiss to her children.

"Waste Management hasn't even come yet," Adam complained. They could hear J-Lo on the bullhorn a couple of streets over. She'd hit the siren for about five seconds, then make her announcement.

"What happened to your face?" Miriam asked.

Howard's right eye was swollen shut, but he smiled as best he could. "Either I was in a bar fight, or I fell out of the back of my SUV, your pick."

"Neither," Adam said. "I bet that psycho ex-girlfriend of yours belted you with her copy of the RIGs. Can you believe she expects us to take in our trash cans when the goddamned trash company hasn't come yet?"

Howard thought the Lord must be testing him. At work he had Bob Carson, who focused on the big picture and ignored any detail that conflicted with his perspective; at home he had J-Lo, who was obsessive about enforcing rules without ever seeming to consider context. A year ago, J-Lo had cited the Swansons on Pendleton Court for leaving their back gate open. The Swansons had called the fire department because their twelve-year-old son, Aiden, had broken his leg on the trampoline, and he was stuck in the coils. The EMS crew had worked diligently for nearly an hour to extricate the boy—his worried parents hovering as close as the techs would allow. During the ordeal, J-Lo, alerted by an overzealous neighbor, had written up a violation against the Swansons for leaving their back gate ajar for more than the ten minutes permitted under Article 2.28 of the RIGs.

"There was an *ambulance* in our driveway with its lights flashing!" the Swanson's had argued at a board meeting. "And our son was in the backyard in agonizing pain!"

The board had upheld the one hundred dollar assessment by a vote of five to two. The Swansons, screaming and vowing to file a lawsuit against the "Goddamned egomaniac micromanaging Nazis!" had been escorted out of the room by a pair of security guards. After they were gone, J-Lo said, "We don't *want* to fine them, but if we grant an exception in this case, then we'll be setting a dangerous precedent that will lead to problems down the road."

On another occasion, J-Lo had enraged hundreds of residents when she cited them for having brown spots in their yards *in the middle of a state-wide drought*. That night, the meeting room had erupted in screams, taunts, and violent threats. After several futile attempts to regain control by reminding the audience about the importance of precedents, the board members had escaped through a back door.

As they departed, someone yelled, "How about setting the precedent of having some Goddamned common sense!"

**\*\*\*\*\*\*\*\*\*\***

"A<small>TTENTION</small> H<small>IGHLANDS</small> R<small>ANCH</small> R<small>ESIDENTS</small>!" J-Lo's voice carried from two or three blocks away.

"You know why they changed our trash pickup to Saturday mornings?" Adam groused. Howard already knew the answer, but he didn't interrupt. "It's because they didn't want our trash cans sitting on the curb during the day while we were at work."

"Last year a Realtor complained that she was showing a house and the trash cans were *unsightly*," Miriam said.

"I'm sure she used the magic phrase, *lowered property values*," Howard suggested. The HOA feared lowered property values the way most Americans feared terrorists.

"To protect our property values," Adam said mockingly, "we have to buy twice as many garbage cans, make space to store them out of sight, and got up at dawn like fucking commandos to take out our trash."

J-Lo rolled back onto the street in her Lincoln Navigator. "Y<small>OU</small> <small>ARE ALL IN VIOLATION</small>!" she said through the bullhorn. "I <small>AM ASSESSING A FINE ON HOUSE NUMBER TWELVE-ONE-TWENTY-THREE</small>! I <small>AM ASSESSING A FINE ON HOUSE NUMBER TWELVE-ONE-TWENTY-FOUR</small>! I <small>AM ASSESSING A FINE ON HOUSE NUMBER TWELVE-ONE-TWENTY-FIVE</small>! I <small>AM ASSESSING A FINE ON HOUSE NUMBER</small> … ." All the way down the block.

J-Lo didn't actually have the direct power to issue citations, but she photographed infractions and turned them in to the board for consideration. The fact that she was president of the board just meant that she started with one vote in favor of each of her citations. She had her own website—chairperson.com—where she listed every complaint she'd ever filed along with the results of each investigation. Her home page was emblazoned with the message *Keeping Highlands Ranch*

*Beautiful. Jennifer Meagert-Logan's violation notices have been upheld 97.8 percent of the time.*

"I ran my campaign on that percentage," J-Lo often bragged. "I was elected onto this board because people want me to help keep our neighborhood beautiful."

# sixteen

Howard walked out into the street and stood in the path of J-Lo's SUV.

"Howard Marshall, it is a violation of the RIGs to block a roadway! Move out of the road or you will be fined!" J-Lo aimed her digital camera at him and snapped a photo.

Howard stood his ground, forcing her to a complete stop. Then he walked to the driver's window. "You didn't quote chapter and verse," he said.

J-Lo glared at him. Although it was early in the morning, she was, as always, perfectly groomed. Her pretty face was made up, her curly chestnut hair was flat-ironed straight, and every article of clothing was a carefully chosen designer piece—Rena Lange cardigan, Gara Danielle earrings, Kara Ross ring, St. John shoes, Miss Sixty Jeans and Liz Claiborne belt. She was classically pretty, sexy in a very adult way, yet adorable like a child—until she opened her mouth. Her corrosive tone quickly scrubbed the word *adorable* out of the mind; *pretty* didn't last long either, though *sexy* had some staying power. Her breasts, plump and prominently displayed, made a lasting impression.

"Chapter and verse?" she asked. "What do you mean?" If not for Botox, Howard knew that question would have been accompanied by an ugly furrow between her eyes, like an exclamation mark over her button nose. Instead her forehead was as emotionless as the architecture of the neighborhood.

Howard said, "When you said it was a violation to stand

in the road, you didn't mention where in the RIGs it says that. That suggests to me that you might be making it up."

"Your eye is disgusting," J-Lo said.

"Are you aware," he asked, "that the trash company hasn't come?" The enormous Lincoln Navigator seemed to overwhelm J-Lo's petite frame, but Howard knew her mouth needed the space.

"What I'm aware of," she said, her tone dripping with an acid that was completely at odds with the placid appearance of her face, "is that dozens of residents are in violation of the RIGs. What I'm aware of is that you've got a black eye because someone probably got tired of your bad attitude and taught you a lesson. What I'm aware of," she said, consulting a notebook in the passenger seat, "is that you put your trash cans out at one-thirty this morning, which is a violation of Article 2.83 of the RIGs."

"Who told you that?" Howard asked, knowing it was Mrs. Stephenson.

"I can't say," J-Lo said.

"Don't I have the right to confront my accuser?"

She shook her head. "We guarantee anonymity through our Whistle-Blowers Program."

That stopped Howard. "We have a *Whistle-Blowers* Program?"

"Let go of my door," she said. "I have work to do."

"Are you going to cite the trash company for violating the RIGs?" Howard asked.

"Don't be ridiculous."

"They're late. They're supposed to be here before 8 a.m., so they're in violation, right?"

"The trash company is not a signatory to the RIGs. *You* are, and so is everyone else in the neighborhood. The trash company has nothing to do with our residents' abiding by the covenant."

"What did you do with your trash cans this morning?" Howard asked.

J-Lo said, "I removed them from the curb at seven-fifty-nine."

"Still full?"

"Yes, still full," she said proudly.

"So you're going to keep your trash for another week?" Howard knew that J-Lo generated as much refuse as a medium-sized Indonesian village. She couldn't possibly survive with full trash cans for seven days.

"I'm waiting for the trash company to arrive, *then* I'll put my cans out."

"You'll be in violation," Howard said.

"No," she said. "I'll wait until the moment the truck reaches my house."

Howard gave her his most lawyerly look, which was difficult with a swollen cheek and bruised eye. "If I recall correctly, the wording of the RIGs allows trash cans to be *visible* to the public only during the designated three-hour period on Saturday mornings. It's not a question of whether you wait until the trash truck arrives. Once you're outside the three-hour window, merely bringing your trash cans down to the curb is a violation."

J-Lo leaned away from him. "I'm surprised whoever it was didn't dot both your eyes."

"Here are your choices," Howard said. "You can use your little bullhorn to tell everyone that you're making an exception to the rule because the trash company is late. Or you can continue with these fines, and I'll go sit in front of your house with my video camera and wait for you to bring your trash cans out to meet the garbage truck. I'll catch you in the act of violating the RIGs and put it on the Internet."

Howard knew he was hitting J-Lo where it hurt. As proud as she was of her 97.8 percent conviction rate, she was even prouder that no one had ever successfully filed a claim against her—though many had sought such revenge. She looked around wildly, as if searching for a counter proposal, but before she could respond, Howard patted the side of her SUV and said, "It's always good to see you, J-Lo." He strolled back to the curb.

"Do you think she'll cut us a break?" Adam asked.

"She said, 'Don't worry about it.'"

Miriam looked doubtful. She couldn't imagine J-Lo ever saying *Don't worry about it.*

As J-Lo continued down the street, she hit the siren and said, "Attention Highlands Ranch Residents! Due to unforeseen delays in the performance of track pick-up, today we will make a one-time exception …."

J-Lo didn't have the authority to make exceptions either, but her declaration meant that she wasn't going to report them to the board. Everyone on the block cheered and chanted Howard's name.

"I'm going back to bed," he said.

"Put some ice on that eye," Miriam suggested.

Howard walked back to his house, accepting congratulations along the way. He went up the stairs, stripped off his clothes, and slid under the covers with a groan of delight.

"Did I actually hear J-Lo make a retraction?" Sophia asked from her seat at the vanity.

"Give your husband some props for being a damned good negotiator," Howard said, doubling over a pillow and tucking it under his head.

"I hope you kick her ass Tuesday night. She's so damned annoying."

Howard shrugged. "What time are we picking up Kara?" Kara Williams was Sophia's best friend and assistant manager at the gallery.

"Ten." Sophia leaned forward and applied eyeliner. Howard looked at the clock. It was eight forty-five. Lenny Kravitz was playing softly on the stereo. The scent of vanilla floated on the air from a candle in the corner. He wanted to talk to Sophia, but she seemed to be in such a good mood, he wondered if he should wait until she returned from New York.

Sophia asked, "What are you planning to do during your week alone?"

"Oh, I'm going to live the life of a bachelor. I'll let the house get filthy, eat pizza every night, throw a couple of wild parties, and, if I get bored, I'll try on some of your panties."

"Sounds like fun."

"You don't know the half of it."

Sophia looked at Howard in the mirror. "I'm horny."

He shook his head in mock fatigue. "So what else is new?" After two years of marriage, they were still running a sexual marathon. They'd made love in every room of the house, in the car in the Denver Pavillions' parking garage, on the grass near the City Park boat house, and even in the laundry room at her mother's house. They'd played with each other in movie theaters, and on airplanes, and months ago, while on vacation in Costa Rica, Sophia had performed oral sex in the back of a van while a guide drove them to a volcano.

She dragged her eyes down the sheet, carefully examining the contours of his concealed body.

"Is it hard?"

"No," he said with a lewd smile, that looked slightly

grotesque under his bruised and closed eye, "but it *could* be." In fact, it was already swelling.

Sophia bit her bottom lip. "You've got thirty seconds." She glided out of the room, swinging her hips lasciviously.

Howard laughed. *Thirty seconds!* His wife loved to put him on the clock. They'd be in the middle of sex, going at it for fifteen or twenty minutes and she'd ask, "Are you close?" Howard would nod, and she'd look at the clock and give him a time. "I want you to finish in one minute and fifteen seconds. Can you do that, baby?" He'd nod again, and she'd whisper in his ear, counting him down. "One minute, baby … forty-five seconds … thirty … fifteen … ten … five … now! Give it to me, baby. Give it to me!"

She'd learned this technique in a book about Tantric sex. "Orgasms are mental, not physical," she'd explained. "I'm mentally stroking you, increasing our connection to each other, and allowing us to time our orgasms together."

Initially, Howard had thought this sounded a little kooky, but he'd quickly become a believer. Their sex life was remarkably mental and amazingly good. Now he had thirty seconds to get ready for her, and as usual, he was rising to the challenge. Yet despite the growing evidence under the sheet, Howard was not in the mood to make love to his wife. He needed to talk to her about his suspicions before she left; he simply couldn't let these feelings fester while she was gone.

Sophia walked back into the bedroom, kicking off her shoes and stripping away her clothes in one fluid motion. Naked, she pulled back the covers and nodded with an impish smirk.

"Well done!" She climbed into bed and kissed him hard. "Very well done." She rubbed her feet against Howard's legs, and he felt the fuzzy caress of her socks.

"Naked except for socks, huh?" Howard said. "Baby, you've got style."

Sophia said. "I fuck better with my socks on."

Howard ran a light hand down the length of her back and bottom, marveling, as always, at the silky warmth of her skin. As he traced his fingers back up her spine and into her hair, his smile slowly faded. "Do you have extensions?" he asked.

Sophia scowled at him good naturedly. "Have you been reading *Cosmo*?"

Howard waited, but she didn't respond. "Well?"

"Yes," she said, staring at him curiously. "Why?"

Howard had been disconcerted that Keiko had immediately noticed his wife's hair extensions. He didn't care how Sophia groomed herself, but this small secret, however meaningless, had reminded him that he probably didn't know his wife as well as he thought he did.

"What's Davis going to do while you're in New York?" Howard asked carefully. Davis might not survive a full week alone with Howard.

"He stayed up in Evergreen last night and left for Santa Fe this morning," Sophia said, nuzzling Howard's neck.

"Really? Why?" As far as Howard knew, Davis planned to live with them forever.

"He's scouting out some work down there."

"But his van is still out front."

"He rode his motorcycle."

"So he went looking for work, but he didn't take his *van*?" That didn't sound right to Howard. "All his equipment is in the van."

"Let's not talk about Davis right now," Sophia said, kissing Howard's cheek—the undamaged one. "You know, your black eye makes you look kind of tough. Like a hockey player who took a major defending his mates."

Howard wasn't willing to change the subject. "So he's gone for a week?"

"Yes," she said, impatiently.

"He was supposed to go to the board meeting with me Tuesday night to fight the assessment."

"Well ... baby, that's not important at the moment." She reached down and rubbed his crotch. "*This* is important."

Howard said, "Hold on, Bassiff. I need to ask you something serious."

She brought her lips back to his and gave him a long, wet, sensual kiss.

"Of course, Mounds," she purred.

Howard cleared his throat; it was clogged with suspicion.

"Are you"—he paused—"having an affair with Davis?"

She was about to kiss him again, but stopped inches from his lips. She didn't speak for a couple of beats. She just stared at him with a look that said more in an instant than she could have said in a week. Howard saw a flicker of ... of what? He watched her carefully, but he couldn't quite make out what she was thinking. He thought he saw a trace of guilt—something had happened, but she had prayed that she would get away with it. But now she'd been caught and she felt guilty. Or maybe it was shame he detected. Or could it be regret? Howard thought he saw a lot in Sophia's face.

When she finally spoke, she said, "Yes," with a calmness that startled Howard. He realized then that he had completely misread her expression. It wasn't guilt, shame, or regret that had flushed her cheeks during that long hesitation—it was *relief*. She'd been waiting for the right moment to tell him, and now, she was glad to have released her secret.

Howard stared at the ceiling, trying to decipher her reaction.

"Honey," Sophia said, hugging him. "I'm *sorry*." Now, she actually sounded sorry.

Their naked bodies were pressed together. After a moment, she tilted her hips back against him, and he slid inside of her. The last thing Howard wanted to do was make love to his wife, but he simply couldn't stop. Sophia rocked back and forth slowly. "I'm sorry, baby," she said into his ear over and over. She didn't count him down, but Howard finished quickly, exploding with a truly anguished groan.

They lay still for several minutes. "You'd better get going," he said, his voice distant and cold.

"Howard—" Sophia pleaded.

"You'll miss your flight."

She slowly rose from the bed, watching his face, but he didn't look at her. He stared at the ceiling in a daze as she gathered up her clothes and crept into the bathroom. He heard the shower, and when she returned fully dressed, he was still lying in the same position. She sat down at the vanity to re-apply her makeup.

Howard turned his head and watched her in a fog. She was six feet away and drifting steadily farther from him. Although he'd been suspicious for more than a week, he had somehow fought off any firm conclusions about his wife or his marriage. But now all of his assumptions about her honesty had been toppled by this *one* admission. Sophia was a fundamentally different person than she'd been ten minutes ago. She had a secret sex life that Howard knew little about. She wasn't just his wife any more; she was also someone's mistress. She had divided loyalties, and Howard had no idea whether he could trust her.

After a while, he asked, "Are you going to sleep with him again?"

Sophia looked down at her hands and didn't answer for a moment. Finally, she said, "I don't know."

Howard was batting zero. He'd known this woman for five years, yet he had no clue what was going on inside her head. He'd asked a simple yes-or-no question. Her options were, "*Yes, honey, I'm going to fuck Davis again the first chance I get,*" or "*No, honey, it was the biggest mistake of my life and I'll never do it again.*" Instead, she had responded, "*I don't know.*" For some reason Sophia had maintained a secret affair, yet had confessed instantly when asked about it. But now she wasn't sure if she was going to keep sleeping with the guy. What the hell was going on? And if she *didn't know,* then what was she sorry about?

"He's meeting you in New York, isn't he?" Howard said

"No," she said, shaking her head slowly. "I told you. He's on his way to Santa Fe."

# seventeen

They stood in the driveway for a full minute, staring at the back of Howard's BMW without saying a word. The SUV was sandwiched so tightly between Sophia's Audi and the edge of the garage that Howard could hardly believe that he'd managed to drive it in.

"Why didn't you just move my car?" Sophia asked.

Nothing was ever *her* fault. "Why didn't *you* park like someone who *isn't* trying to squeeze her husband out of the marriage?"

Sophia looked at her watch. "I don't have time for this."

*So take a cab*, Howard wanted to say. Instead, he said, "We'll take your car."

"I'm out of gas," Sophia said.

"Again?"

Sophia ran out of gas about once a month. The low-fuel light would come on and she'd ignore it. Eventually, she'd call Howard from the road and ask him to come rescue her with a gallon of super-unleaded.

"Next time, you should call Triple-A," Howard had said after the third time. That was back when they were dating.

"Howard, why would I call Triple-A when I've got you?"

"I'm just saying that the reason you pay for the service is so you can—"

"Triple-A is a last resort," Sophia had said. "I have a *boyfriend*, so I don't have to sit on the side of the road in danger of getting kidnapped, waiting for some grungy tow truck driver to come rescue me."

Howard had given up the argument, but he thought that if Sophia were really worried about being kidnapped or attacked, she'd fill up every now and then.

**********

Standing in the driveway, she said, "I have enough to get to the gas station."

Howard shook his head. He'd heard that before. The nearest gas station was two miles away. More than once they'd stalled on the way to refuel. He didn't have time to run out of gas today. He needed to get her out of the state so that he could think.

"I'll just pull your car out to make some room," he said, holding out his hand for her car keys.

Sophia looked at his outstretched hand, annoyed, as if he were a homeless panhandler on a street corner. She crossed her arms to make it clear that she wasn't going to give him anything. "They're upstairs," she said.

Howard stared at her, exasperated.

"I never take my car keys when I travel, Mounds. I don't need them, and I don't want to risk losing them in New York."

Howard looked up at the clear blue sky and took a calming breath. "Will you climb through the back of the SUV and pull it out?" he asked, dangling his keys at her.

She scowled at him as if he had asked her to do something difficult—like be faithful to her husband, park her car properly, or fill her tank with gas.

When she didn't respond or move to take the keys, Howard said, "I'm too big to climb through. This"—he pointed at his eye—"is what happened last time."

"Mounds, I'm wearing a skirt." It was a Herringbone

tweed skirt trimmed with black lace and satin ribbon, and it extended well past her knees.

"So? Who's watching except me and Mrs. Stephenson?" Howard turned to look across the street, and sure enough, the old lady was in the window with her binoculars. "Trust me, she's seen everything you've got."

Sophia glared at him with bored, half-lidded eyes.

"Fine!" Howard said, getting an idea. He asked Sophia to squeeze between the two vehicles and put the key into the door lock.

"I won't be able to get in this way, Mounds."

He grinned at her. "You don't need to. This is a special feature on BMW's. Put the key in the door, turn it to the right and hold it … *voila!*" All four windows descended, and the sunroof slid open."

"Neato," Sophia said sarcastically.

"It's a convenience feature," he explained. "On hot days, I can let the car cool off before I get in."

"So now what?"

Howard smiled brilliantly. "Just reach inside and put the key in the ignition, shift the SUV into neutral, and step out of the way." After she'd done as he'd instructed, he said, "I'm going to push the Beemer back about five feet so that the driver's door will clear the trunk of your car. Then I'm going to open the door, get in like a normal human being and drive you to the airport."

Sophia stood just inside the threshold of the garage with her arms crossed and her hip cocked.

Moving the BMW was harder than Howard had expected. He was pushing on the nose of the SUV with full force, and though it rocked an inch or two, it didn't roll. Finally, Howard imagined Davis Delaney's head wedged behind the back wheel, and he felt a Hulk-like surge of strength. The Beemer started to move.

"See?" he said triumphantly. The SUV rolled easily now that it had some momentum. "I'll just take it back a few feet."

The one factor Howard hadn't considered in his plan was that the floor of the garage was flat—the concrete driveway was not.

When the rear wheels hit the two-percent grade, the SUV sped up.

"Whoa!" Howard said. The BMW rocketed away from his outstretched hands as if it were falling off a steep precipice. The SUV barreled down the driveway, turning slightly, scraping the rear quarter panel of Davis' van. It backed over the full trash bins, knocking them over and dragging them under the bumper. It plowed through the mailbox, snapping the wood at the base. It continued across the road, slamming into the curb, crumpling the trash cans with a thunderous *boom!* Garbage exploded in every direction. The BMW climbed over the curb, showing surprising agility considering the engine was off and the transmission was merely in neutral. It ran through Mrs. Stephenson's flower bed and finally stopped just three feet from her front window.

Red-faced and stunned, Howard stood in the driveway, staring helplessly at the mess.

"You're a fucking maniac!" Sophia said. She ran into the house.

# eighteen

Howard crossed the street slowly, wondering how he would explain this to his neighbor, but when he looked up, he saw that Mrs. Stephenson was in her familiar place, staring at him with the binoculars. He waved tentatively, and pointed at her door, silently asking her to come down. But she didn't move. He rang her doorbell several times, but she didn't answer. He backed away from the door and looked up at her again. He wondered, not for the first time, if Mrs. Stephenson was a cardboard cut-out rather than a real woman. He wouldn't put it past the homeowners association to erect a fake sentinel—like a scarecrow—to intimidate potential covenant offenders. But he could tell by the subtle movements as she tracked him with the binoculars that she was a live person rather than a cardboard figure. He crawled around on her lawn, gathering up soiled papers, soggy fruit peels, and the slimy remains from dinner plates that had been scraped into the trash can.

Most of Howard's neighbors had come out to survey the scene, but they all kept a careful distance, and no one offered to help. Howard looked down the street, hoping to see Adam, but, apparently, he was gone.

Howard moved as quickly as he could, pushing Sophia's bags forward in the SUV, and scooping up the trash. The rubber cans were completely destroyed, and he didn't have time to run back to his house for new trash bags, so he heaped a week's worth of rotting garbage into the back of his BMW, cleaning up Mrs. Stephenson's yard as well as he could, checking his watch repeatedly.

Finally, he turned back to her window and yelled, "I have to take my wife to the airport! But I'll come back to take care of your yard!"

He pulled a stained envelope from the trash, wrote a note to Mrs. Stephenson explaining the situation and wedged it in her front door.

Then he ran up his driveway, opened the kitchen door, and said, "Sophia, come on." She was standing at the counter talking on her cell phone. They were fifteen minutes behind schedule.

"Ewww!" Sophia said when she climbed into the BMW and saw the trash.

Howard said, "I had to do something."

"But, Mounds—"

"You weren't exactly running out with trash bags to help me."

"I'm not the idiot who launched the SUV!"

Sometimes things acquire a momentum of their own, Howard thought. Maybe things with Davis had started innocently, and before Sophia could stop it, the situation had rocketed out of control. They drove in silence for several minutes. Finally, Howard said, "Later, I want to talk to you about Davis."

Sophia stared out the window for a while, and then said, "I'm glad it happened."

Howard gripped the steering wheel hard. What could she possibly be glad about? And what did she mean by *it* happened? Nothing had *happened* to her. She wasn't an innocent bystander. She had decided to cheat on her husband. "Why would you be glad?" he asked finally.

"Because we never talk," she said. "*Now* you want to talk to me."

That shocked Howard. "When have I *not* wanted to talk to you?"

"*Now* you want to hear what I have to say."

He looked over at her and said coldly, "If you had something to say, you should have opened your mouth not your legs."

Sophia wasn't looking at him. "I feel like what happened with Davis was what needed to happen in my life at this moment. The energy of it was good."

The *energy* of it? What the fuck? Howard let out a slow breath but didn't say another word.

Kara Williams ran out to the BMW with a smile that turned sour when she first smelled and then saw the mess in the back. "What the hell?"

"It's a long story," Howard said. He raised one of the rear seats and pushed the garbage over to the other side."

"I'm not riding in trash," Kara said.

"You're not riding *in* it," Howard said.

She backed away from the SUV.

Howard blew out a hard breath. He was barely holding it together. "Sophia," he said, "you drive. Kara, get in the front seat. I'll ride in the back."

"What about my bag?" Kara asked.

"What about it?"

"I don't want it sitting on the trash."

"I'll hold it in my lap," Howard promised.

She tentatively handed him her suitcase.

She scowled. "What happened to your face?"

Howard said, "Girl, get your ass in the car!"

\*\*\*\*\*\*\*\*\*\*

Kara and Sophia chatted amiably during the forty-minute

drive to the airport. If Kara noticed the tension between Sophia and Howard, she didn't mention it. At the airport, Kara jumped out and snatched her bag from Howard, checking it for stains. He pulled Sophia's bags out and brushed the garbage off of them. Sophia grabbed the back of Howard's head and kissed him hard.

"I'm sorry, Mounds," she said. Her standoffishness was gone. "I love you."

Howard just nodded and walked around to the driver's seat. Sophia backed toward the terminal, holding his gaze, dragging her suitcases. He found it ironic that *now* she didn't want to turn her back on him. *Now* she felt some sense of loyalty. She mouthed, "I'm sorry," and "I love you." Howard pointed, trying to warn her that she was about to bump into a family. The parents and their two adolescent children nearly fell over each other trying to avoid her, but Sophia continued to backpedal, oblivious to everyone else. The *energy* of backpedaling must have felt good to her, like the *energy* of parking in the middle of the garage, the *energy* of making people come rescue her when she ran out of gas, and the *energy* of fucking her lover.

When she mouthed, "I love you," again, Howard put the Beemer in gear and sped away.

# nineteen

Howard had held back his emotions for nearly an hour, focusing instead on getting out of the house, pushing the SUV out of the garage, cleaning up the trash, picking up Kara, and driving the women to the airport. He had resisted the impulse to argue with Sophia because he wasn't sure what he would say. He needed time to think.

Howard started shaking. He noticed it in his hands first, but then he felt his entire body trembling in the grip of a betrayal so profound that it left him lightheaded. It wasn't the sex. Although the thought of Sophia and Davis in bed together made him nauseous, he knew he would get over that part. It was the deception that gnawed at him. He thought about all the secrets Sophia must have kept. He recalled her cavalier tone on the nights that she'd called to say that she'd be late getting home from work. He remembered the calmness in her face when he'd found her in the kitchen two nights earlier, pretending to read *The Amazing Adventures of Kavalier and Clay*. Sophia was a talented liar—Howard had never known that about her.

He backtracked in their relationship, trying to discern what had been true, and what had been a lie, but he had no clue just how deep the deception ran. Was this her first affair? How long had she been sleeping with Davis? She'd claimed to have met him at an art show in Seattle three months ago. Was that true?

He latched onto the steering wheel with both hands, trying to stop the shaking. He gnashed his teeth and mashed the gas pedal. The sweet scent of Sophia's perfume lingered in the car and mixed with the acrid odor of the trash. Howard lowered the windows, trying to flush out the smell, and the cool October wind tousled his hair and stung his eyes. His cell phone rang, and the name *Sophia* flashed on the caller ID.

He turned off the phone and tossed it into the passenger seat. A few tears leaked down his cheeks and dried quickly in the harsh wind. Loose trash flew out of the open windows, littering the highway, but Howard barely noticed.

A siren blared behind him—his second of the day—but this time it wasn't J-Lo scolding the neighbors about the garbage cans. In the rearview mirror he saw a Denver motorcycle cop motioning toward the shoulder. Howard checked the speedometer and saw that he was up over ninety mph, *Jesus!* He looked back at the cop, and saw the officer reach forward to remove a scrap of paper flapping against his windshield.

Howard turned on his blinker and eased onto the shoulder of I-225. He wiped his eyes, dug his wallet out of his back pocket, and got the registration from the glove box. The cop stopped the motorcycle and leaned it on its kickstand. He said a few words into his radio, and then slowly pulled his gloves tight. He swung his leg over the bike and marched forward stiffly, stopping behind the doorpost; Howard had to crane his neck to see him.

"Is that *trash* you're spreading all over the highway?" the cop asked, eyeing Howard suspiciously. His last name—SCHLEIDEN—was printed on his badge, which was speckled with red marinara splotches. Howard noted with alarm a band of marinara running from the officer's left shoulder to his right.

Howard wiped his good eye. "I had an accident."

Officer Schleiden scrunched his nose against the smell and took inventory of the mess. Soiled napkins, paper towels, cherry pits, apple cores, banana peels, stained sheets of paper, baked beans, a little spaghetti, lettuce, envelopes, Q-tips, balled up toilet paper, torn white plastic trash bags and more.

"What kind of accident?" the cop asked.

"It's actually a funny story," Howard said, smiling awkwardly, hoping the cop would see the humor in it. "I ran over the garbage cans in our driveway and trash sprayed everywhere." He tried to block out the image of Sophia backpedaling into the terminal.

Officer Schleiden studied him closely, noticing that one eye was swollen and the other was red and teary. Howard's hair was uncombed, and his stomach rumbled loudly with hunger pangs. "You been drinking?"

Howard looked shocked. It wasn't even eleven in the morning. "No, sir!"

"Taking anything?"

"Absolutely not!" Howard tried to look as sober as he could, but he was haunted by the thought of Sophia and Davis moaning and panting in bed.

"License and registration."

Howard handed over the documents.

Officer Schleiden looked at them for a moment, and said, "So your story is that you ran over a garbage can and all this trash was catapulted *into* your vehicle?"

"No, no, no," Howard said, laughing a little too loudly. "After I hit the garbage can, I scooped everything up off the street and threw it in the SUV."

Officer Schleiden nodded. "Step out of the vehicle, please."

Howard opened the door. Cars and trucks zipped past, buffeting them with cool wind that tore at their clothes. The tires screaming against the cold asphalt sounded like jet planes rocketing into the air. As Howard's body swung out of the SUV, his right foot eased off the brake. The BMW, still in gear, shot forward.

"Whoa! Whoa!" the cop screamed, grabbing Howard and pulling him away from the moving SUV.

The momentum pulled the driver's door shut with a crisp German thunk.

Howard and Officer Schleiden stared at the rolling BMW for a moment of shared disbelief, then the cop whirled toward the approaching traffic and waved frantically, urging the cars barreling past him to slow down and shift into the left lane. He ran to his motorcycle, turned on his siren, and threw up a long-rooster tail of dirt as he fish-tailed after the wayward SUV.

Howard, suddenly alone on the side of I-225, shivered in the cool wind. *Sometimes things acquire a momentum of their own.* Up ahead, he watched Officer Schleiden take up a position in the middle of the road, keeping traffic from passing the slow-moving BMW. Small bits of trash continued to billow out of the open windows. Two long lines of cars formed as the BMW X5 demonstrated the superiority of its German engineering. The wheels were perfectly aligned, the suspension perfectly tuned, and the SUV perfectly balanced. It clung to the contour of the road, rolling confidently along the shoulder with its right blinker on as if someone were still sitting in the driver's seat. Howard wiped moisture from his cheeks and started walking after his SUV.

Less than a minute later, a college-aged guy in a Nissan Maxima pulled up next to him.

"You need a ride?" he asked. He didn't seem the least bit uncomfortable about picking up a teary-eyed stranger with a badly blackened eye, who was strolling down the highway.

Howard pointed and said, "My SUV got away from me."
The guy said. "Hop in."

They drove in silence for about a minute. "So there's no one in there?" the driver asked, pointing at the BMW.

"Nope," Howard said.

"At first I thought this was another O.J. chase. You know, slow-moving vehicle and all."

"I forgot to put it in park."

"Like it had somewhere to go, huh?" the kid chuckled.

*Like my wife*, Howard thought morosely.

"They say BMWs practically drive themselves," the kid said. The highway curved gently to the left, and the BMW turned gently with it. "Now we know it's true."

Finally, after nearly a mile and a half, the BMW's passenger wheels drifted off the pavement. The SUV rolled into the dirt, and clamored through a gulley. It finally stopped on a slightly uphill slope. Officer Schleiden jumped off his motorcycle and ran to put the vehicle in park.

The cop turned and stared down the highway, looking for Howard, and he seemed to panic when he didn't see his suspect. He was just starting to head back that way when a Nissan pulled onto the shoulder, and Howard climbed out.

The cop was breathing hard. "I should have told you to put your vehicle in park." He sounded apologetic, as if he'd neglected part of his training.

Howard shrugged blankly.

"Don't feel bad about it," the cop said. "This isn't the first time that's happened."

Howard knew Officer Schleiden was talking about the BMW, but his comment could easily have applied to Sophia.

"It doesn't look like anything got damaged," the cop said. "You think we can drive it back to the shoulder, or should I call a tow truck?" He sounded worried that Howard would request a tow, and then the officer would have to write up a formal report.

"I think we can drive it out," Howard said as cheerfully as he could.

"Want me to hop in and give it a shot?"

Howard nodded.

Officer Schleiden climbed aboard and put the SUV into reverse. He backed toward the shoulder, following the same path it had taken to enter the gully. He ended up about twenty feet behind his motorcycle. He eased forward, put the BMW in park, raised all the windows, and turned off the ignition.

"I figured it was safer to back over the known terrain than risk running over something sharp in the ground in front of me," he explained.

"Good thinking," Howard said. Could he backtrack with Sophia and get their marriage back on solid ground? Did he even *want* to?

The officer took a moment to regain his composure. He said, "Come around to the back with me, please."

Howard followed him to the rear of the BMW. Officer Schleiden pointed at a black scrape mark on the bumper. "*That's* from a rubber garbage can?" The bumper was slightly dented and the abrasion had clear, sharp lines. A rubber trash can couldn't have made that mark.

Howard was confused for a moment, but then he recalled the SUV's trajectory down the driveway. "I hit a mailbox, too."

Officer Schleiden nodded slowly. "You hit anything else? Any people, pets, bicycles, cars, or other objects?"

Howard had imagined that Davis Delaney's head was behind the back wheel of the SUV, but he hadn't actually done any harm to the artist. He shook his head.

"Okay," the cop said. "I pulled you over because I clocked you at ninety-three."

"That's pretty fast," Howard confessed. Bile bit at the back of his throat.

"And you had trash blowing all over the road."

"Yes, sir." Howard nodded, looking back at the litter still floating across the highway.

"This whole garbage thing,"—Officer Schleiden gestured with his hand—"just isn't making sense."

"I'm gonna throw up." Howard hunched over, waiting for vomit that, fortunately, didn't come.

"What did you take?" Officer Schleiden asked.

Howard stood up. "Nothing," he said, swallowing heavily.

Officer Schleiden hooked a thumb in his belt and drummed his fingers against the hard leather. "What happened to your eye?"

"I fell."

"When?"

"Last night."

"Where?"

"In my driveway."

The officer considered this for a long moment. "Your driveway sounds like a dangerous place."

Howard said. "I was climbing out of my SUV, stepped on my tie and lost my balance."

Officer Schleiden looked perplexed. "Okay," he said, putting his notebook into his pocket and removing his sunglasses, "you've got to tell me something, because I'm getting a strange read on you. So far, nothing you've said makes any sense. Last night, you somehow stepped on your tie, fell in your driveway, and got a black eye. This morning you ran over your mailbox and your garbage can and piled trash into the back of your SUV. Then I clock you at ninety-three in a sixty-five, while you've got paper and napkins flying out of your back windows, and you get out of the SUV while it's still in gear, and it goes rolling down the highway. Now you're weepy and about to puke. You see how this looks to me? I can tell by looking at you that that you're not drunk or high, but something is seriously wrong with this picture."

Howard nodded and stood up straight. "Let me explain." Over the next several minutes, he told Officer Schleiden about getting home late last night and having to wedge his BMW into the garage because of his wife's lousy parking. He described how he'd climbed out of the back, stepping on his tie and tumbling into the hail-splattered driveway. He told him about pushing the SUV out of the garage, losing control of it, and watching it barrel through the trash cans and mailbox as it crossed the street.

Officer Schleiden was laughing by the time Howard got to the end. "So then I tell you to get out and your Beemer drives away from you *again*!"

"I couldn't believe it," Howard said.

"It's almost like the SUV is trying to escape!"

"I guess so," Howard said.

Officer Schleiden thought for a few moments, and then asked, "So why are you crying and nauseous?"

"I'm just upset," Howard said.

"You *couldn't* be this upset about running over your garbage can."

Howard's vision was watery, and his stomach was still gurgling. He carefully rubbed his face; the whole right side was sore. "I'd rather not say." He imagined Sophia, writhing in bed under Davis, crying out in pleasure. "It's personal."

Officer Schleiden waited a moment. "You sound like you've had a rough go. But technically, when I pull over a guy doing ninety-three in a sixty-five, and he's bleary eyed and vomity, has an SUV full of trash, and gets out without putting it in park, I gotta do a field sobriety test and maybe take him down to the station for a Breathalyzer. But I believe you're just upset, so maybe if you tell me what's bothering you, it'll confirm my suspicions, and I can send you on your way."

He seemed like a nice guy, trying to help Howard out. Howard stared at the mountains in the distance and figured if he was going to tell anyone about the affair, he might as well start with a complete stranger. He took a deep breath, exhaled and said, "I just found out my wife is cheating on me." That was a lie—he'd known for weeks.

"Aww, Christ!" Officer Schleiden looked down the road and clenched his fists. "*Jesus Christ*!" He put a hand on Howard's shoulder and bowed his head. "I'm sorry to hear that."

Howard looked at the cop's hand for a moment. This oddly friendly gesture made him feel uncomfortable. "Me too," he said.

"What's her name?" Officer Schleiden looked at Howard under his hooded brow.

Howard wondered why the officer wanted to know. "Sophia."

"Sophia *Marshall*?"

That stopped Howard. For a moment it sounded as if the cop actually knew his wife, but then he remembered that Officer Schleiden was still holding his driver's license. He was simply repeating Howard's last name.

"Yes," Howard said. "Sophia Marshall."

Officer Schleiden pulled his hand back and slipped his glasses on. "That's tough." He pulled out his notebook, but didn't open it. "Been through that myself."

"Yeah?"

"Caught my wife in bed with my best friend," he said contemptuously. "They were lucky I'd just come back from jogging and didn't have my gun on my hip. I might have shot 'em both." He glared at Howard. "You get that feeling?"

Howard shook his head, defensively. "I don't own a gun."

"But you wanna kill 'em, right?"

"No!" Howard insisted, scowling in disapproval. A police officer shouldn't make homicidal suggestions to a man in Howard's emotional state! "I would *never* hurt my wife!" And then with an honesty that surprised even himself Howard said, "Actually, I just wish I didn't know." If he didn't know, he wouldn't have to act. If he didn't know, he wouldn't be thinking about divorce. If he didn't know—

"Wish you *didn't know*?" Officer Schleiden looked at him carefully, as if he were reassessing Howard's sobriety. He put his hand on the butt of his gun, resting it there as if the thought of *any* wife stepping out on *any* husband gave him a homicidal urge. "Not me," he said, unconsciously baring his teeth. "I wanted to know every detail. *Had* to know. Couldn't sleep until she told me everything. And after that, I divorced her sorry cheatin' ass."

"Yeah?"

"I wasn't gonna be a cuckhold!"

"Yeah."

"'Cause that's what you are right now." He jabbed Howard in the chest. "A cuckhold!"

Howard refused to be provoked. The more Officer Schleiden

pushed him, the more resolute he felt. It was okay for *Howard* to criticize his wife, but he didn't think the cop should pile on.

The officer thought for a moment. "Was it someone you know?"

"Who?"

"The guy sleeping with your wife."

"Oh," Howard said. A pained look flashed across his face. "One of her clients … an artist who has been staying with us for a while."

Officer Schleiden jerked backward. "That motherfucker! Took advantage of your hospitality and turned you into a cuckhold!"

Howard was tempted to point out that Sophia didn't have any children; therefore, Davis Delaney wasn't a *mother*fucker, just a wife-fucker. It seemed like a lesser offense.

"Let me run your license." Officer Schleiden walked over to his motorcycle, leaving Howard shivering in the cool October air, thinking about Sophia on a week-long vacation with her lover.

When the cop returned, he said, "You've got a be-on-the-lookout-for."

"A what?" Howard asked.

"It's not quite a warrant, the Douglas County Sheriff's Office put out a be-on-the-lookout-for you, because of your little accident this morning. You got cited for a hit and run."

Howard said, "I didn't hit anything other than my own trash can and my mailbox!" Then, "Oh, I guess I also clipped the van of the guy who's been sleeping with my wife. It was parked in the driveway."

"Damn! There's a lot of action in your driveway!"

"But I didn't *run*. I rang Mrs. Stephenson's doorbell half

a dozen times, but she wouldn't answer. She just watched me from the window."

The cop looked at his notes. The complainant was Edith Stephenson, whose address appeared to be right across the street from Howard's. Surprisingly, the official report corroborated Howard's outlandish story.

"If I let you go, you'll go straight home?" Officer Schleiden asked.

"Absolutely," Howard promised.

Officer Schleiden returned Howard's license and registration. "You gonna divorce her?"

*Was he?* Howard wondered if he'd end up miserable and bitter like the cop.

"You should," the officer said. "Once they go astray you can never trust 'em again."

# twenty

Howard did not get a ticket for speeding or littering—just orders to keep his windows up, slow down, and take a hard line with his wife when he got home.

"If you decide to keep her—which would be a big mistake!" Officer Schleiden said. White spittle sprayed off his lips and landed on Howard's shirt, which seemed fair considering the cop had Howard's salsa on his uniform. "Make her beg!" The cop glared until Howard promised, as solemnly as he could, that he would be tough on Sophia. The officer gave Howard his business card and said, "Call me if you ever need anything." When Howard pulled away from the shoulder, Officer Schleiden stood at attention and saluted.

Howard stayed under the speed limit down I-225, and then merged onto I-25, heading south toward Lincoln Avenue. His stomach groaned again, and he remembered that they didn't have much food in the refrigerator at home. He impulsively jerked the wheel and sped across two lanes—drawing several angry honks—to take the Dry Creek Road exit. He stopped at Tokyo Joe's and numbly ate a bowl of salmon, brown rice, teriyaki sauce, vegetables, and avocado.

Back on the road, Howard returned to The Bubble without further incident. On Pendleton Boulevard, young children were playing in their front yards. On Pendleton Court a teenager was washing a Chevy F-350 dually in his driveway— an act that would earn him a fine if J-Lo spotted him, because Article 2.48 of the RIGs outlawed trucks with more than four wheels, even if they were just parked in the driveway temporarily for cleaning or loading. A group of middle school kids in baggy clothes turned down Pendleton Way. Pendleton Drive was crowded with families in minivans and SUVs undoubtedly rushing off to afternoon soccer games.

Howard turned onto his street and saw yellow crime-scene tape stretched around Mrs. Stephenson's yard. There were deep brown gouges in the turf, and the flower bed was destroyed. Howard's broken mailbox had been removed from the street, but someone had etched a chalk outline of it onto the pavement.

As Howard pulled into his driveway, he was startled by another vehicle pulling in next to him. It was J-Lo. She shot out of her SUV as if propelled by an ejection seat and scurried around to meet him just as he climbed out of the BMW. She had changed clothes since his confrontation with her about the garbage cans. Now she was wearing *bebe* jeans with studded rhinestones on the rear pockets, a tight-fitting, cream-colored, button-up cardigan with a neckline that plunged to her solar plexus, and a shimmering translucent cream scarf that covered her substantial cleavage, without totally obscuring it. A Coach purse hung from her bent elbow.

"I've got something you want," she sang suggestively. Her breasts were still jiggling from the sprint around the SUV, and Howard had to work hard to keep his eyes on her face.

"Did you make the chalk outline?" he asked, pointing toward the street. It looked like her work.

J-Lo said, "I sure did, and that's just the start of it." She shifted her weight onto one leg, which launched her breasts into another massive repositioning. "You're in a lot of trouble, mister." Oddly, she sounded playful rather than angry—and unexpectedly flirtatious. Howard had to judge her emotions by her tone of voice, because her Botoxed face didn't offer any clues.

"Did you call the police and try to get a warrant put out on me?" he asked.

"I had no choice," she said. "It was a hit-and-run." She pointed across the street. "That's the crime scene."

"It was *not* a hit and run!"

"You hit something, and then you ran," she stated, as if the evidence were incontrovertible.

"It was *my* mailbox and *my* trash can."

"That's the thing," J-Lo said. "They don't belong to you alone. They belong to the whole community, and when you destroy them, you're hurting all of us."

"The whole community didn't pay for them, and the whole community sure as hell didn't help me clean up the mess!"

"The whole community didn't drive into a neighbor's yard like a maniac."

"I didn't *drive* into her yard," Howard said, though he wasn't eager to explain the SUV's solo journey down the driveway.

"You should go see a doctor about that eye." J-Lo handed him three envelopes. "These are notices for the damage to Mrs. Stephenson's yard, your trash cans, and your mail box. You've got forty-eight hours to make the repairs, and these letters give you authorization to proceed without getting specific approval from the board. However, after the repairs are completed, the board will review the work, and if anything violates the RIGs, you'll have to start over again."

Howard snatched the envelopes and started walking away.

J-Lo pointed at Davis' van. "And *that* has got to go."

Howard followed her gaze and thought *yeah, and the guy who owns it.* "We'll find out Tuesday night."

"I have a 97.8 percent conviction rate," J-Lo reminded him.

"Yeah," Howard countered, "but you're 0-2 against me."

"You're going to lose this time," J-Lo promised.

"We'll see."

"Don't you want to know what I have for you?" She shifted her weight again; her pendulous breasts shuddered for several seconds.

"I'm not interested," Howard said.

"Oh, you'll be interested all right," she said with a wink. "You'll be begging for—hey, what stinks?" She stood on her tiptoes and saw the garbage spread out in the back of Howard's BMW. "Oh my God!" She pulled a camera out of her purse—*snap, snap.*

"Why are you taking pictures?"

"You're not allowed to haul trash in your SUV. Only the garbage company can do that, and they already came this morning."

"I'm not *hauling* it," Howard said. "I just picked it up."

"And took it *out* of the neighborhood."

"*And* brought it back in with me," he said.

She took another picture.

Howard sighed. "Shouldn't you be spending time with your kids?" J-Lo had two boys, ages seven and three.

"They're in daycare," she said.

"On a Saturday?"

"They're too much on the weekends," J-Lo said, blowing air from her cheeks. She and her husband were separated—again. They'd been married eight years, but they'd been separated at various times for a total of thirty-seven months. J-Lo's husband took the boys every other weekend, so Howard was surprised to learn that the kids went to daycare on their weekends with her.

"It's a great program," J-Lo said. "They teach the kids foreign languages, let them watch animated movies, take them on field trips, play with them, and just let them explore and discover the world for themselves."

"It sounds like a *parenting* service," Howard said cruelly.

All the good humor instantly drained out of J-Lo's face. "You wouldn't know anything about parenting, would you?" she snapped. "Clean up your goddamned mess!" She stormed around to the driver's side of her SUV.

Howard sighed regretfully. "Hold on a second," he said, chasing after her. "I'm sorry. I'm having a really shitty day, but I shouldn't take it out on you."

She crossed her arms below her breasts and glared at him.

"Really," he said. "I'm sorry. What is it that you were going to give me?"

"You said you weren't interested."

Howard said, "Okay, I'm interested."

J-Lo studied him for a moment. "It's information."

"About what?"

"About your wife."

"Yeah?" Howard asked. His pulse thudded in his temples. "What about her?"

"She's having an affair."

Despite the Botox, Howard noticed a subtle victorious shift in J-Lo's face. He saw calculation in her eyes, the flush of opportunity in her cheeks, the quick flicker of a smile.

"Did you hear me?" J-Lo said. "She's cheating on you."

"What makes you say that?" He wondered if J-Lo was talking about Davis or if his wife was sleeping with someone else, too.

J-Lo said, "I have lots of spies in the neighborhood."

"Who's she supposed to be having the affair with?"

"Don't be a dumbass, Howard. She's been fucking Davis for months."

*Months? How could J-Lo know that?* "I already knew about the affair," Howard said.

"You don't know everything I know," J-Lo sang.

"What else is there?"

"Invite me inside, and we'll talk about it." She laid her palm flat against his chest and dragged it down to his abdomen.

Howard, groaned, silently cursing his penis' instant response. It really did have a mind of its own. He flushed red and stepped back

J-Lo looked down at his crotch, and grinned lasciviously, reached out to touch his chest again, but Howard avoided her hand.

Then he wondered why he was being such a Boy Scout when Sophia certainly hadn't restrained herself. Having sex with J-Lo would be the perfect revenge, Howard thought, because Sophia hated her.

J-Lo shifted her mammoth bosom again, and Howard took his time looking at it. "You've been thinking about me," she said.

"What do you know about my wife?"

"I'll tell you inside," she said coyly. "But I only have a few minutes."

As they entered the garage, J-Lo gently tucked her hair behind her ears and stopped in front of him. "I see you still don't have Ferrari Testarossa," she said suggestively. She was standing very close. Howard noticed the gentle scent of her perfume, and remembered the intimate details of their torrid affair. It was interesting to discover that despite the gulf of nearly five years, his marriage, and her transformation into an HOA Nazi, he was drawn to her physically today as much as he had been then.

Howard knew he should send J-Lo away before he did something he would regret, but his mind kept replaying the events of the past few days—Sophia's calm deception, her confession, their passionless love making, and Officer Schleiden's parting words—*Once they go astray you can never trust 'em again.* His sense of loyalty was fading in and out like an overloaded circuit.

Suddenly, he said, "I see you still don't have a Range Rover."

J-Lo smiled at him, pleased by his response. *Ferrari Testarossa* and *Range Rover* were sexy code words from their previous relationship.

# *twenty-one*

After an amazing session in bed, Howard and Jennifer (this was long before he started calling her J-Lo) were sprawled on the crumpled sheets in his bed.

Jennifer purred, "You're my Range Rover." Her plump chest rose sensuously with every breath, and Howard reached over to gently lay a hand on the breast nearest him.

He was fading fast, but he managed to give her a weak smile. He'd heard all about her fascination with Range Rovers. Her best friend in college had owned one, and *Range Rover* had become the compliment that J-Lo bestowed upon the best of everything. Where other people might say, "That's the Cadillac of computers" or "That's the Cadillac of golf carts," J-Lo would substitute Range Rover. Even in Howard's dazed, post-organsmic state, he knew the significance of the compliment.

"Thank you, honey," he said quietly, realizing too late that he should have said her name. Years earlier, Howard had accidentally said "Michelle" during an intimate moment with his girlfriend Nicole, and she'd never forgiven him. As a defense against further mistakes, he'd started using terms of endearment—honey, sweetie, darling—instead of names, but after Jennifer called him her Range Rover, he knew he should have said her name. But *honey* was already out of his mouth and there was nothing he could do about it. His breathing became regular. Soon he started to snore.

She poked him in the side. "Am I your Testarossa?"

Howard didn't answer for a moment.

"Are you my what?" he asked, groggily.

"Your Ferrari Testarossa?"

That was Howard's if-money-were-no-object dream car. Years ago, he'd used his business card and a lot of confidence to trick a Ferrari salesman into giving him a test drive, and, ever since, he'd raved about the car's smooth acceleration and tight cornering.

"Well," he said sighing, "no … you're more like my Honda Accord." This was the car Howard had purchased after extricating himself from the exasperated Ferrari salesman.

Jennifer popped up against the headboard like bread jumping out of a toaster—her mood instantly darkened to an angry crisp.

"Your *Honda Accord*?" she asked in disbelief.

"Don't take that the wrong way," Howard said quickly. He thought about sitting up with her, but then thought better of it. He liked being on his back looking up toward heaven for guidance. "That's a compliment."

"I tell you that you're my Range Rover, and you tell me that I'm your Honda Accord, and I should take that as a compliment?"

"Yes, honey," Howard said, regretting again that he hadn't used her name. "I would never buy a Testarossa. It's a fun fantasy car, but it's too impractical. A Ferrari costs too much; it's too small; it's no good in the snow, and it doesn't get good gas mileage. But a Honda Accord is the car I actually bought, because it meets all of my needs." He paused to consider its positive attributes. "It's sporty, but it has four doors, a good-sized trunk, and front-wheel drive. It's good in the snow, inexpensive to insure, and cheap to repair. It's the best value on the road. That's why I say that you're my Honda Accord, Jennifer." He felt proud of himself for using her name at the end.

Jennifer stared at Howard, her head cocked at an angle, her arms tightly crossed. "Did you just say," she asked, glowering at him, "that I'm like your Honda Accord because it has a good-sized *trunk*?"

She knew damned well he didn't mean it like that.

"I said sporty, too," he offered.

"And cheap!" she pointed out.

"Jennifer" (he managed to squeeze in her name again), "what I'm saying is that I chose my car because it was a perfect fit for my life."

"First of all," she said, loosening one hand from her crossed arms and extending her index finger as if it were a rusty nail she wanted to jab into Howard's eye, "you bought a Honda Accord because it was all your cheap ass could afford. Second," another finger shot out of her fist, "there are a million Honda Accords on the road. They're plain. They're boring. No one ever does a double take and says, 'Ooh, look at that Honda Accord.' And third" (another finger), "I retract my Range Rover compliment, because you are not a smooth ride!"

"Jennifer," Howard said, trying without success to hold her liberated hand. "I'm sorry. I was drowsy. I didn't know what I was saying." Sometimes, as she decompressed, Jennifer would slide down the headboard incrementally like the temperature gauge on an overheated engine slowly drifting back to normal. This wasn't one of those times. "Can I take another crack at it?" Howard asked.

"Go ahead!" she barked. She had re-crossed her arms and clenched her jaw—the engine had seized up.

Howard let out a breath. "You *are* my Ferrari Testarossa."

The hard look melted away instantly. This was long before her Botox treatments, so when she smiled, her eyes crinkled and her cheeks bunched adorably. "Really?" she cooed. She unfolded her arms and leaned over to give him a kiss. "You're so sweet, my big Range Rover."

That was the formula that had allowed their lustful, but otherwise vapid, relationship to survive for as long as it did. Howard would tell Jennifer the truth, and she'd get upset. Then he'd make up a lie, and she'd say, "Really?" as if his first statement had never existed.

# twenty-two

Howard led J-Lo through the garage and into the home he shared with his wife (and now Davis). He knew that he was making a mistake, but all he could think about were J-Lo's super-sized breasts and her sensual lips. He was mentally replaying one of their intense sexual sessions from years ago. But as they crossed the threshold into the kitchen, J-Lo stopped.

"What *is* that?" she demanded.

"What is *what*?" Howard asked, looking around the kitchen. He didn't see anything strange. Before he could say another word, she shoved him out of the way and sprinted back out through the garage. Howard looked inside again, but didn't see anything that would have provoked such a fearful reaction. He trotted out of the garage. J-Lo had left her SUV in the driveway and was running down the sidewalk. Howard started chasing her, calling out to her, but she never glanced back. He started sprinting in earnest, running on the balls of his feet the way he had when he was a college football player. But he'd been young and fit back then. Now he was heavier, older, and out of shape; J-Lo was pulling away—in heels.

She paused briefly at a house with its backyard gate open. A few dozen people were milling around in the backyard eating barbecue. "Close that gate!" J-Lo screamed.

"What?" a man in a red Kansas City Chiefs hat asked.

"Section 2.28 of the RIGs!" J-Lo screamed as she ran away. "That gate must be closed! I'll issue an assessment!"

"Jennifer!" Howard pleaded, stumbling after her.

"Hey Art," the guy in the Chiefs hat said, "some hot chick is out here screaming, and some dude is chasing her."

Finally, Jennifer ducked behind a parked car, and Howard came to a stop a few feet away, gasping for breath, hands on his knees.

"What's … wrong?" he managed.

"What's going on here?" a man's voice demanded.

Howard turned to face three men staring at him suspiciously. A fifty-something man in the middle had cobalt blue eyes and a salt-and-pepper mustache that drooped over his mouth. An apron cinched around his thick waist read KISS THE CHEF. The younger men, who had the same blue eyes, similar mustaches and the same thick build, started to flank Howard. A stream of people in jeans and sweaters made their way down the sidewalk, some with kids in their arms, most eating barbecue. The men stared unabashedly at J-Lo, who was crouched down, breathing hard. The translucent scarf had unraveled during her sprint, and was no longer draped over her cleavage. So her breasts were even more exposed. The buttons of her sweater were under tremendous strain, and all the men seemed to be praying that something would pop loose. Although the neighbors resented J-Lo for micromanaging their lives, most of the men simply couldn't take their eyes off of her.

The chef pointed a spatula at Howard. "Just what the hell are you doing, son?"

"It's not … what … you … think." Howard said, panting. Before he could say another word, the two younger men hit him from both sides, forcing the last bit of air from his lungs. They shoved him to the ground.

"Young lady," the chef asked J-Lo, cautiously, "are you okay?"

"There's a gas leak!" J-Lo shrieked.

The chef was nonplussed.

Howard said, "She's—" But the men holding him shoved his face into the grass.

A female voice said, "Art, you *asshole!*"

Howard was able to turn his head just enough to see an enormous woman with a yapping cocker spaniel clutched to her massive bosom. "I told you that damned propane tank was leaking!" Apparently, she was the woman most likely to *kiss* the chef, although at the moment, she didn't seem to be in a loving mood. The crowd ate their ribs and beans and watched the scene with what seemed like amusement.

The chef set his jaw. "Jackie, the grill is *not* leaking."

"You're gonna blow us all up, you damned *maniac!*" Jackie turned and stormed back toward their house.

"Don't you touch my grill!" Art yelled. His wife was picking up speed; the dog had climbed up to her shoulder, barking ferociously. The chef started after her. "Don't you touch my grill, you *bitch!*"

Jackie broke into a jumbled trot, her wide hips rolling from side to side. Art stumbled after her, clutching the spatula as if it were a baton in a relay race. Trying to cut a corner, he tripped in bark landscaping and thudded heavily on the driveway.

"Don't you touch—" was all Howard heard as Art rolled over slowly.

"I think," Howard said drawing the crowd's attention back to him, "J-Lo was talking about a leak at *my* house."

"Don't call me that," J-Lo said.

Howard wondered how Sophia's theory about scents would explain J-Lo's odd olfactory abilities. She had a tiny— surgically reduced—nose that somehow detected odors that no one else knew existed. J-Lo would walk into a room and proclaim that it smelled *sad*. She'd cure the sadness by lighting a candle, but not with a match. According to J-Lo's sensitive nose, an extinguished match made the room smell *hostile*.

Howard had once asked her what *hostile* smelled like, and she said "prison."

He had paused and asked cautiously, "How do you know what prison smells like?"

"I've smelled it on TV," J-Lo said matter-of-factly.

She lit candles with a flame gun that had a green handle and a long metal barrel; she said the smell it produced was *cool*. J-Lo thought the stereo smelled *dusty*, yellow paint smelled *clumsy*, and leather furniture smelled like the *suffering of innocent animals*.

This last observation surprised Howard, because J-Lo was the type of woman who wouldn't go grocery shopping unless the store had valet parking. He couldn't imagine her lying awake at night worrying about cows being slaughtered to make furniture.

"What about your shoes?" he asked. "They're leather."

"Leather shoes smell comfortable," she said dismissively.

"They don't smell like suffering, just like furniture?" he pressed.

She stared at him. "Howard, you *sit* on furniture. That's different."

**********

About the alleged gas leak, J-Lo said, "It smelled like a runaway train in there!"

The brothers, suddenly recalling that J-Lo was the wacko neighborhood Gestapo, loosened their grip on Howard and looked down at him with real sympathy.

"You were running from him," one of the men asked,

"because you thought there was a gas leak?"

"There *is* a leak!" she hissed as if she had a leak of her own.

The brothers helped Howard to his feet. The crowd continued to eat their barbecue and waited to see what would happen next—as if watching a scene on a sitcom.

"I'll go check," Howard said, dusting himself off and smiling at the crowd. Most of them must have been guests, because he didn't recognize them as residents of Highlands Ranch.

A boy who looked about seven years old, tugged at Howard's shirt. "What happened to your eye?" He wore jeans, a Broncos sweatshirt, and a wool cap. He had a rose-colored bruise on his cheek.

"I fell down," Howard said. "What happened to you?"

The kid raised his hand and delicately probed the wound. He shrugged and said, "My little sister hit me with a Bratz doll."

"Ouch! That must have hurt," Howard said sympathetically.

The boy shrugged again. "She's only three years old."

"Oh, so it was an accident," Howard said.

"She was aiming for my eye," the boy said, shaking his head wearily. "She's always aiming for my eyes."

"Aiden, get back over here!" A woman in her early-thirties rushed down the sidewalk to rescue her son.

Aiden backed away and took his mother's hand. Howard started toward the house, and J-Lo kept pace with him, ducking behind parked cars as if she were a soldier in a war zone. The barbecue crowd followed closely, murmuring to one another.

"You could have said something to me," Howard said with just a hint of anger. "You left me there to get blown up." He looked over at J-Lo and realized he was talking to himself. She was twenty feet back, hiding behind a maroon Lexus.

"Don't turn on any lights!" she advised. "Don't slam any

doors! Don't do anything that might make a spark!" By now, more neighbors—somehow aware that something of historical importance was brewing—had come out of their houses. They watched with their arms draped protectively over their children's shoulders.

Howard gave the crowd a thumb's up; only Aiden returned it. Cautiously, Howard walked into the house, lifted his nose in the air, and turned back from the door.

"I don't smell anything," he called to J-Lo.

"You *never* smell anything!" she screamed, as if it were a felony charge.

*Has she been talking to Sophia?* Howard wondered. He walked through the living room, sniffing. He checked the kitchen, the den, and the garage. He detected no odors. The hot water heater and furnace were in the basement. He walked slowly across the kitchen to the basement door, his feet growing heavier with each step. He didn't want to confront what he might see downstairs. He assumed that Davis' bed would be unmade, and he knew the twisted and tangled sheets would provoke unbearable images of Sophia and Davis naked. Howard's sweaty palm slipped on the doorknob several times before finally getting a grip. The door opened slowly, as if warning him against proceeding. He stood on the top step for several minutes, staring down into the gloom. Eventually, he stepped back, closed the door, and left the house.

By the time he reached J-Lo's sheltered bivouac, his breathing had returned to normal. He said, "I don't think there's a—"

"*Yes,* there is!" she insisted.

"You should call the utility company," one of the neighbors suggested.

"I already did," J-Lo said. She raised her cell phone. "They'll have someone here in half an hour."

The neighbors, perhaps fearing that J-Lo would penalize them for loitering, returned to their homes. The barbecue attendees drifted back to their party, and Howard sat down on the curb next to J-Lo to wait for the Xcel truck.

"You don't have to wait," Howard told her.

"I'm not starting my SUV while there's a gas leak," she said.

"I'll go get it for you."

"You think the deadly gas swirling in the air cares *who* starts the SUV? You think it'll blow up if *I* turn the key, but not if *you* do it?"

Howard knew better than to argue with J-Lo when she was in the grip of sarcasm.

"Why are you crying?" she asked

"I'm not," Howard said, but when he raised his hand to his face, his cheeks were moist.

"And your face is all red."

"I don't know," Howard said. "I guess it was hot in there."

"Maybe the gas affected you," she concluded.

"What do you know about Sophia and Davis?"

"I know that she's humiliating you."

"You said you knew about other things that were happening."

"I do."

"So tell me."

"Information is never free."

"What will it cost?"

"What do you have to offer?" She traced a finger down his leg.

"Not that."

"Why not?"

"Because I'm married ... because you're married ... and because I'm not interested."

"Your wife has already trashed your marriage; my jerk husband has probably left for good this time, and I know you're still interested. I can see the way that you look at me."

"Men look at you because you have big boobs, J-Lo. Don't confuse that with real interest."

Her mouth fell open, but before she could respond, an Xcel truck turned onto Pendleton Drive. "There he is!" Howard said. He jogged down to meet the driver.

"Damn, this place is confusing!" the Xcel man exclaimed, hitching up his utility belt. He wore dark gray pants and a light gray shirt with the name Ed stitched over his heart. "I had to call my dispatcher three times to guide me in."

"Sorry about that," Howard said, as if it were his fault that all the streets had the same bland appearance.

"So what's the problem here?" Ed asked.

"There's a gas leak!" J-Lo screamed from down the street.

Ed looked at Howard with raised eyebrows.

"She's overreacting," Howard said confidentially.

"I heard that, you *dick*!" J-Lo had great hearing, too.

Ed went inside. He came back out after five minutes and signaled to J-Lo. "There ain't no leak!" He smiled, waving a black meter.

She came back cautiously, shaking her head. "I could smell it!"

"That ain't possible ma'am." He pointed to his meter, but he was transfixed by J-Lo's cleavage. "This thing, uh," he stuttered, "picks up, uh, levels as low as five ... as low as five parts per hundred million. I put it right up against ... against the uh ..."

154

"Valve?" Howard suggested.

"Against the value, and it, uh, didn't bulge … I mean budge. There ain't no leak in there."

"I smelled it as soon as I walked in the door, didn't I?" she said to Howard, putting her hands on her hips, pulling her sweater even tighter. Ed gasped as her breasts appeared poised to leap out at him. J-Lo glared at Howard, daring him to contradict her. "It smelled messy," she said, dusting off her hands, which caused her breasts to quiver.

Ed's eyes seemed to be quivering, too. "Well, there's no leak," he repeated.

J-Lo grunted, and turned to Howard, "Call me when you're ready to talk … or whatever." She jumped into her SUV and peeled rubber as she backed out of the driveway.

Ed exhaled heavily and shook his head. "You're a lucky man," he said, grinning at Howard.

"Yeah?" Howard asked absently.

"That's, uh, quite a lady." Ed watched her SUV as it continued down the street. "When she said you could call her or whatever, she sure packed a lot into that *or whatever.*"

Howard said, "Ed, how did the basement look to you?"

# twenty-three

Howard trudged inside to get a box of lawn and leaf bags and a pair of yellow cleaning gloves. He returned to the driveway and started scooping the garbage out of his BMW. He gagged several times over the rotten smell and wondered if the SUV would be forever ruined. Although the Beemer had leather seats, dash and door panels, the cargo area and the headliner were covered in cloth, and he worried that the smell—and the memory of this horrible day—would stay embedded in the fibers. Two hours later, when he finally picked up the last clump of spaghetti, he left the windows, sunroof and rear gate open to air out the interior, and then walked across the street to knock on Mrs. Stephenson's door. Again, she didn't respond, but he waved at her as she watched him remove the police tape around her yard and pluck the dead flowers out of her garden. He walked back into his kitchen, grabbed the phone book, picked a landscaping company at random, and had an oddly alliterative conversation with a man who promised to "stop by Sunday to survey the site of the sullied soil."

Howard drove to the Car Wash Express on University Blvd. and got the interior of his SUV shampooed. He bought a gallon of gas for Sophia's Audi, and picked up a new mailbox post from Ranch Mart—he had no difficulty choosing one that would match the neighborhood because the store adjacent to the Park Meadows Mall sold only mailbox posts that had been pre-approved by the homeowners association. Howard simply went to the lumber section and typed his address into a computer. It told him the exact model to purchase.

Back at the house, he emptied the gas into Sophia's Audi and then drove it to a gas station to fill the tank. When he returned, he positioned her car perfectly in the garage, pulled his SUV in next to it, spent an hour installing the new mailbox post, and finally walked into the house just after 7 p.m., exhausted.

The first thing Howard noticed was that the house seemed musty with the scent of illicit sex. He wondered if *that* had been the smell J-Lo had detected. Suddenly, he had no trouble sorting through the odors around him. He smelled the delicate fragrance of potpourri in the bathroom next to the kitchen, a banana peel from Sophia's breakfast turning rotten in the garbage can, the lingering wisps of her perfume— and he smelled Davis, too. The artist's scent burrowed into everything like a virulent intruder. Howard wanted to get a bottle of Lysol and scrub until he destroyed every molecule of Davis Delaney.

He started for the cabinet under the sink. His footsteps echoed hollowly off the kitchen tiles, and seemed to reflect his increasingly hollow marriage. If he walked all the way across the kitchen, he could rip the basement door off its hinges and march downstairs, pack up all of Davis' belongings, throw them into the back of his van, and set the whole mess on fire in the driveway. Howard had seen Angela Bassett do that in the movie, *Waiting to Exhale*, and at the time, he'd thought that burning her husband's property had been immature and expensive. But now, Howard thought, *God, that would be fun!* He could siphon the fuel out of the van so that there wouldn't be a big explosion, just a nice steady burn of everything Davis had brought into their home.

Of course, Howard would never do it. A felony arson conviction would keep him from becoming a lawyer. To douse the rage burning in the pit of his stomach, he grabbed a six pack of Coors from the refrigerator and gulped most of the first can before the door swung shut. He plodded into the living room with the other five and collapsed in his recliner, where he stared up at the eight pieces of Cynthia Mason's work decorating the walls. From the moment Sophia had first hung the paintings, Howard had thought it was ridiculous to have eight identical green squiggly squares hanging in the same room, but Sophia had insisted that each painting was different, and visitors always seemed to enjoy trying to find the hidden images they contained. The newest picture, hanging over the fireplace, was called *Hidden Treasure*. It was the only original painting in the entire house.

"Why are you keeping *this* original?" Howard had asked when she brought it home.

"It's a gift from Cynthia. Can you believe she painted it in just two days?" Sophia had shaken her head in amazement, but Howard had shrugged indifferently. This painting was identical to the rest; he wouldn't have been surprised if Cynthia Mason churned out one an hour.

"So what's the hidden image in this one?"

"It's a sunken treasure chest, overflowing with jewelry," Sophia said.

Howard stared at the painting for a long time—he couldn't see anything.

# twenty-four

Howard guzzled the last of his sixth beer and belched loudly. He said, "What would Jesus do?" Then he started laughing—deep, drunken, belly laughter that bent him over at the waist and nearly spilled him out of the chair. He stood up and walked slowly into the kitchen, where he pulled a second six-pack out of the fridge. What would Jesus have done? was a perfect question, because when Jesus died, he was a thirty-three-year-old *bachelor*.

"He had enough sense to not get married!" Howard exclaimed marching back into the living room and falling back into his recliner, chuckling.

After a while, thoughts of his wife in bed with Davis Delaney pushed aside the humor, and he shook his head, trying to get serious. For some reason, Howard was suddenly certain that his *mother* would *not* be surprised to learn about Sophia's affair. He almost felt that Sophia's taking a lover would affirm some secret suspicion his mother had held for years.

"Then why am I surprised?" he asked aloud. He sucked down half a beer, and wondered if he had missed warning signs. If her affair was predictable, then *why* was it predictable? What did it say about her character, her values, and her commitment? Was she likely to cheat on Howard because she was likely to cheat on *anyone*? Or had she cheated *because* of Howard?

"Her affair has nothing to do with me. Nothing to do with me. Nothing-to-do-with-me. Nothingtodowithme," Howard chanted. He took another long swallow, trying to drown the bubble of anger rising from his gut; the can trembled in his hand.

Suddenly, the front door opened and two boys burst into the house, talking loudly and laughing. Their voices stopped abruptly after three or four strides, but by then they were in the middle of the living room. They were both dark-haired, about nine years old, wearing worn jeans, sweatshirts, wool caps, and gloves. One had a football in his hands. By the time they stopped, they'd tracked muddy footprints across the tile entryway and onto the carpet.

"Hey," Howard said calmly. It wasn't the first time that children had accidentally come into the house.

"Ah, jeez," one of the boys said. "Sorry, Mister."

"No pro'lem," Howard slurred, rising clumsily from the recliner. "Who ya lookin' fer?"

The boy wearing a University of Colorado sweatshirt raised his hand. "My house, sir."

"Las' name?"

"Jensen," the kid said.

Howard flicked his hand at the boys, waving them back to the tiles near the door. "Off tha carpet."

The boys stepped back gingerly, carefully retracing their muddy steps.

Howard went into the kitchen and fumbled through several drawers before finding his copy of the *Highlands Ranch Homefinder Directory,* which contained maps of every street in the neighborhood and a three-dimensional depiction of each house. Typed inside the frame of each home was a phone number, address, the name of every person who lived there, including pets, and the vehicles registered to the residence. A detailed index allowed residents to cross reference any known fact about a family or residence to find the home they were seeking. The HOA had created the directory more than a decade ago, because the absence of distinctive landmarks in the neighborhood had proved too disorienting for children, senior citizens, and visitors. After a spate of lost children in the 1990s, the association had been forced to create a system that would quickly reunite kids with their parents.

Howard's vision was swimming. He held the book at arm's length. "How ya spell Jensen? S-O-N or S-E-N?"

"S-E-N," the boy said.

"Jensen, Jensen, Jensen," Howard said, tracing his finger down the index. He opened and closed his eyes several times, trying to improve his vision. "I can't read it." He lurched across the room to the foyer and handed the directory to the Jensen boy.

"I don't know how to use this," the kid said, holding up the book helplessly.

"Just look fer yer las' name."

The boy turned the pages of the big book until he found the J's.

"Whoa! There's a lot of them," he said.

"Was yer daddy's firs' name?"

"William," the boy said.

"You see a Wil'um Jensen?"

"There's four of them."

"Yer mother's name shoul' be there, too."

"There's two William and Jennifers."

"For Chris' sake," Howard said. "You see yer name?"

"Both of them have sons named Caleb, but hey!" he exclaimed, "Our dog, Elway, is in here!"

"Good, you found you."

"The other family has a dog named Plummer and a cat named Shanahan."

"Wha' page it say yer on?

"One seventy-two." Caleb flipped through the pages until he got to a map that showed his home.

"That's a cool picture," Caleb's friend said, pointing at the framed green squiggles over the fireplace.

"Sweet," Caleb said. "It's like three-D!"

"Yeah, tha's our hidden treasure," Howard said, gazing at the picture as if he could actually see the image it contained. He lowered his head to study the map in the directory. Though the image was blurry, he could just make out the location of Caleb's home. He said, "Yer jes two streets off."

He walked them down to the sidewalk, while Mrs. Stephenson monitored the action with her binoculars. He pointed down the street. "Go enda tha block, lef', two blocks, lef' and then fin' yer house."

"Thanks, Mister!" they said in unison. They ran down the sidewalk, tossing the ball back and forth.

Howard waved at Mrs. Stephenson, and she bobbed as if she were about to lower the binoculars and wave back, but in the end, she just tracked him, as usual. He burped, and the taste was rancid in his mouth. He threw a resentful glance at Davis Delaney's van and stumbled back into the house.

# twenty-five

The first time Howard ever saw Sophia, she was sitting at gate thirty-seven on the B Concourse at Denver International Airport. As Howard walked toward the boarding area a little before 8 a.m., her golden hair had glowed at him like a beacon. Even with her face turned down to her book, it was obvious that she was a beautiful woman. Her blonde hair was tied back loosely, and she wore black tights and a long black, brocade sweater. Her left leg was tucked underneath her; the right was crossed over her left knee, dangling sensuously.

The waiting area was almost full, but there was an empty seat next to her, so Howard walked straight over and sat down. He didn't have an opening line, but he trusted that something would come to him if he just got close to her. She shifted slightly away from him as he slid into the seat. He glanced at her with a smile ready, but she didn't look up from her book. After a few moments, Howard opened his McDonald's bag and started eating a breakfast sandwich.

A few minutes later, she asked, "Where are you off to?"

They still argued about who had picked up whom. Sophia would claim that she had made the first move by starting a conversation; Howard would counter that he had made the first move by sitting next to her.

He turned toward her with a mouth full of sausage, biscuit, and egg, and put a hand over his lips as he chewed hurriedly. Sophia waited for him, watching with child-like directness. He saw no guise in her face; no guile, no discomfort, and

165

no fear of rejection. She had flawless alabaster skin, delicate freckles, light green eyes and soft lips. She watched him with a pleasant, peaceful expression, and waited for an answer.

"I'm going to Dallas," he managed finally. "And you?"

"Baton Rouge," she said. "For my grandfather's funeral."

"Oh," Howard said awkwardly. "I'm sorry."

"It's okay," she shrugged. "He was 88, and he got to experience a lot of wonderful things in his life. Now his energy has moved on."

Howard nodded slowly. He liked the way she balanced her grief against the certainty that her grandfather was now in a better place.

"I'm Howard Marshall."

"Sophia Andreasson." She offered her hand.

They shook, and somehow Howard knew he'd be holding her hand for years. He noted with quiet delight that she wasn't wearing a wedding ring.

"Oh, look at that cute baby!" Sophia exclaimed.

Howard followed her gaze and saw a seven- or eight-month-old infant in a stroller with his twenty-something mother at the helm. The boy was awake, but barely. He gently sucked a pacifier while his head lolled to one side and his eyes fluttered at half mast.

Sophia said, "He's adorable!"

"He sure is," Howard agreed, though he barely noticed the boy's face. Howard's eyes were drawn instead to his Osh Kosh B'Gosh outfit, his Nike tennis shoes, the blue and white stroller with its oversized wheels and sun canopy, the diaper bag hanging from the handles, the bottles and baggies of food protruding from various pockets, and the extra clothing visible in the top. Another heavy bag weighted the mother's left shoulder. Everything must have cost nearly a thousand dollars.

When Howard was a teenager, his father had urged him to think beyond the perceived benefits of parenthood to notice the costs.

"I sometimes hear young people talking about becoming parents, and they sound like people talking about fancy cars," John Marshall had said.

"Huh?" Howard had asked. His father was fond of analogies, but this one seemed a little off the mark.

"They see a Mercedes rolling down the street, and they dream about owning one. But they're only seeing the benefits. They think about how they'll look behind the wheel. They're not thinking about the payments, the price of the rims, the insurance premiums, the gas, the taxes, or the cost of routine maintenance."

"People think of kids like that?" Howard asked.

"They see a cute kid and say, 'I want one of those,' as if it's all fun and games, and there are no financial, emotional or behavioral costs."

Howard looked at the young mother in the airport and saw the costs. He said, "She looks like she could use another set of hands."

Sophia said, "I'll hold that little cutie the whole flight if she needs help."

Howard thought holding the baby was the least of it. He stood up as the woman approached. "Can I help you with your bag?"

The mother hesitated and looked down the concourse. "I still have a ways to go," she said dejectedly.

Howard glanced at his watch. "I've got time." He reached for the bag on her shoulder, and she let him take it.

She sighed gratefully, groaning as she rolled her shoulders. "Thank you *so* much."

"Your son is adorable," Sophia said as the boy rolled past.

"Thank you," the woman said, smiling at Sophia.

Howard and the mother continued down the terminal. She told him that her name was Rebecca Olson. She and her son, Isaiah, had started in Des Moines, Iowa, and had a connection in Denver on their way to Sacramento.

"It's my first time traveling with him," she said wearily. She had a pleasant, round face and shoulder-length brown hair. She was wearing a simple pale yellow T-shirt, a cream button-up sweater, and a wide-pleated skirt.

"It's hard to believe this little guy requires so much stuff," Howard said. The bag he was carrying must have weighed thirty pounds, and the stroller was loaded down with provisions like a Humvee heading into battle.

Rebecca laughed. "My husband calls me Isaiah's sherpa."

Howard left her at her gate and wished her luck with the rest of her trip. She thanked him and slumped, exhausted, into a chair.

Howard hustled back to his gate and was happy to see that the flight had not yet started boarding. He walked up to the ticket counter.

"Excuse me," he said to the attendant. "I just discovered that my friend Sophia Andreasson is on this flight, and I was hoping to sit next to her."

"It's a pretty full flight, but let me take a look," the woman said. She typed a few letters into the computer and studied the screen. "Well, she's in 17A, so that's the window, and there's a Mr. Garvey on the aisle. I can put you in 17B if you don't mind the middle."

Howard pulled out his boarding pass and smiled. "I wonder if Mr. Garvey might like to have my seat in the exit row?"

When he sat back down in the boarding area, Sophia said, "It was sweet of you to help that lady." Her eyes seemed to be soaking in every detail of him, and Howard felt his own gaze swimming. He had never believed in love at first sight, but he was warming to the idea.

He said goodbye to Sophia when she rose to board the plane. She hesitated as if waiting for him to ask for her phone number, but Howard just smiled and watched her go. He read his book while all the other passengers boarded the plane. Finally, when the attendant announced that all passengers should be on board, he slid the novel into his backpack and marched over to the gate.

Sophia grinned at Howard when he sauntered down the aisle of the nearly full airplane, and she threw her head back and laughed when he plopped down in the aisle seat in her row.

"I wondered what you were doing up at the counter!" she exclaimed. Her laughter was rich and lovely and gave Howard a shiver all the way to the bottom of his feet.

He pointed three rows ahead at a gray-haired, fifty-something man in the emergency exit row. "Mr. Garvey had no idea what he was giving up."

They talked non-stop for the next two hours. Howard couldn't stop staring at her. She had an easy smile and a gentle personality. She slipped off her shoes, and propped her feet up on the seat in front of her. Her tights fueled his imagination; they chastely covered every inch of her skin while brazenly revealing every swell and curve. Fortunately, Howard had left the seat between them empty; he probably saved himself being too forward, putting his hand on her knee.

She told him about her grandfather's poor health, and how her grandmother had had to give him sponge baths for the last two months of his life. "But she wouldn't wash his privates. She said, 'He can he can wash his own winky. I'm not touching it!'"

They looked at each other with wide-eyed intoxication and talked about religion, heaven and hell, sexual experimentation among adolescents, nakedness at any age, and the dieting and dating practices of sumo wrestlers. She told him that she was the thirty-year-old owner of an art gallery and confessed that she dyed her brown hair blonde. Howard told her that he was a thirty-three-year-old executive for a technology company, and confessed that his hair was starting to thin.

She had plenty of opinions, but she was not an opinionated conversationalist. She had a mind like a surgical knife and a voice like butter.

"I have a small voice," she said. "Everyone has always told me that."

It *was* soft like a little girl's voice. It wasn't so young that it would confuse a telemarketer on the phone, but it was the kind of voice that could get overrun in an argument.

Before they left the plane, they exchanged business cards, and Howard promised to call. A week later, he picked her up at her house, she "shot a bunny" in his car, and they fell in love.

**\*\*\*\*\*\*\*\*\***

Ancient history, Howard thought, as he belched and clumsily placed a half-full bottle of vodka on the end table. His vision was blurry and every nerve ending in his body seemed to be tingling, but he felt sober. He remembered having a pretty good buzz earlier, but since then, he must have slowed down. *Have I had dinner?* His brain felt perfectly normal. He could think clearly and speak without slurring, and he was sure he could walk effortlessly, though he didn't feel like trying at the moment.

Howard looked at his watch, bringing his wrist close to his eyes and then pushing it far away, but he couldn't read the numbers. It didn't matter. It was Saturday and he had nothing else on his schedule. Bob was in Beaver Creek, and Sophia was in New York. Howard's dance card was empty. Another belch sneaked up on him. He stuck out his tongue and made a face.

The phone rang. Howard looked at it, but didn't move. It had been ringing on and off for the past few hours. He figured Sophia must have reached New York, and now she was trying to reach him.

"Ha!" he said, raising his drink to the ceiling. "She wasn't trying to reach me when she was down in the basement with that little fucker!" Was he slurring? Howard didn't think so. He sounded normal, sober, rational. That was good. He fully intended to get drunk, but he wasn't in a hurry. He had all night. "Now she's in New York with *Davis*," he said, "and she can't stop thinking about *me*. Good! I hope she's having a shitty—"

He stopped, staring across the room at Davis Delaney, who was watching him from outside the window. The artist was smiling, almost gloating, but his expression was frozen and unnatural. Howard rubbed his eyes, trying to clear his vision. Davis looked eight feet tall, and all Howard could see was his head and long hair.

The doorbell rang and Howard jumped, instantly calculating that Davis' arm would have to be twenty feet long to reach the doorbell from where he was standing. Howard looked toward the door in amazement, and then back at Davis, but the artist was gone.

The doorbell rang again, and Howard stared at it, wondering who it could be. He couldn't recall much from the past few hours, but he was hungry. He hoped that he'd ordered a pizza. He got to his feet on the third try. The room kept jumping to the left as if dodging him. Beer cans were strewn everywhere, and the carpet was soggy under his socks. A bag of Lay's potato chips and the bottle of vodka were on the end table near the chair. *When the hell did I pull that out?* He stared at the bottle for a long time. Maybe he *was* a little drunk.

The doorbell rang again. *Oh yeah. That's what I was doing.* Howard stumbled across the room. He stopped to stare at the two sets of muddy footprints on the floor. They went halfway into the living room and then stopped as if the two people had suddenly leaped into the air and never come down. Howard looked up toward the ceiling to see where they might have disappeared to. The doorbell rang again, and he jumped. He took three quick steps forward and yanked the door open.

"Meer-ee-um!" he sang. "Meer-ee-um tha da-leer-ee-um!"

"Oh Lord," Miriam said, rushing into the house to catch him before he fell. "How much have you had to drink?"

"Jus' a cup-la beers."

"You poor baby," she said, helping him back into his chair. She brushed potato chip crumbs off his shirt and pants. "Sophia asked me to check on you."

That was the last thing Howard heard.

He woke up the next morning in the master bathtub, with a crick in his neck, a killer headache, and a puddle of vomit very near the toilet.

# twenty-six

Andrew Metcalf's eighty-seven painted eyes stared down at Howard from the cream-colored walls of the bathroom, and they seemed angry, as if they blamed him for giving them a hangover. Howard groaned and threw an arm over his face. He vowed—and this time he meant it!—that he would never take another drink. As soon as his headache went away, he was going to march downstairs and pour out every drop of alcohol in the house. Then he remembered that there was no more beer in the fridge—that's why he'd graduated to vodka. He pressed his bare feet against the cold porcelain at the other end of the tub. He briefly considered turning on the taps and taking a bath, but the thought of being immersed in hot water made him want to puke again.

*Gotta get cleaned up*, Howard thought. He could go to church. It *was* Sunday after all. He could forgo his usual lineup of NFL games, sit on a pew, say a few prayers, and do confession. How long had it been since his last confession? Twelve, fifteen years? Yesterday, Officer Schleiden had practically suggested that Howard shoot his wife. Today, it might be good to get advice from someone who wasn't armed.

He sat up slowly and looked around the bathroom. His vision wasn't jumping and jerking the way it had been last night, but it was still blurry. He went to the linen closet, grabbed an old towel and mopped up the congealed mess on the floor. *That* was a smell that sparked many bad memories. He would never ever *ever* let another drop of alcohol touch his lips.

The doorbell rang. That was probably the sound that had awakened him. He slipped a bathrobe over his shoulders and took a moment to use Colgate and Listerine to scrub the pungent taste of vomit out of his mouth. When he finally opened the front door, he was greeted by a couple in their mid-sixties, grinning at him as if he'd just won a contest.

"Mr. Marshall, we're Gene and Jean Johnson from Juniper Jungle Landscaping," the man said. He had a brochure in his hands and a pair of thick gardening gloves tucked under one arm.

Howard stared at him blankly. He and Sophia didn't need any landscaping, and even if they did, there was a six-month application process to get approval from the HOA.

"You rang regarding repairs required on the residence across the street," Gene continued, pointing at Mrs. Stephenson's house.

"Oh … Yes! Right!" Howard said.

"We've already taken a peek at it, and it doesn't look like much," Jean said. She had a kind face with laugh lines around her mouth and eyes. They both wore blue jeans and checkered red shirts with their company logo on the breast pocket. "The grass is pretty torn up," she said, "but lawns are easy to fix."

"Grass is glorious, don't you agree?" Gene asked.

Howard nodded indifferently.

"We love grass," his wife said. "We met at a turf management convention and fell in love immediately." She gazed lovingly at her husband. "He proposed to me three months later next to the Scott's fertilizer display at the hardware store."

"Green, glorious, grass!" Gene said. "We eat, sleep, and drink it."

"Do you smoke it, too?" Howard asked, chuckling.

"Certainly not!" Gene said, scowling and raising a protective arm in front of his wife. "Smoke spoils the spring in the stalk, causing it to shrink away from the sun and suffocate."

"It was a jo—" Howard started.

"Backyard barbecues and billowing blazes are the bane of budding blades!"

"Okay," Howard said. "I was kidding." His head was pounding. He would never *ever* drink again.

Gene eyed Howard suspiciously, and carefully extended a brochure toward him. An invoice was tucked inside. "I've itemized the costs," Gene said. "It'll be two hundred dollars to trade out the turf and tuck some new tulips into the garden."

"That sounds reasonable," Howard said.

"Are you okay?" Jean asked.

"Sure," Howard said.

"Your eye just looks so … Was it a bad accident?"

"Oh, no," Howard said. "I wasn't in the SUV at the time."

"Was your wife at the wheel?" Gene asked.

"No one was driving," Howard said. "I was trying to push it out of the garage and lost control."

Gene and Jean stared at him for a long awkward moment. Then Jean turned to her husband and said, "Remember that old Ford you used to have to push start?"

"Oh yes," Gene said with a chortle. "Perpetually parked on a hill, so I could push her away, pop the clutch and pound the gas pedal."

Howard's hangover couldn't take much more of this. "So about the lawn …?"

"Do you have an assessment notice?" Jean asked.

Howard shuffled through the mail stacked on the hall table and handed them one of the letters J-Lo had given him the day before.

After they left, Howard retreated to the kitchen and poured

himself a cup of coffee. He ate two bowls of Cheerios and was contemplating a third when the phone rang. He knew it was Sophia before he saw her cell phone number on the caller ID. He looked at the clock. It was nearly noon. She'd probably been calling all night and morning, but he'd been too drunk to respond.

He picked up the phone.

"Hi, Mounds," Sophia said. He could tell that she was surprised to hear his voice.

"Hey." His throat was still raw from vomiting.

"Did you get my messages?"

"No." He sat in his recliner and leaned all the way back, but that was a mistake. The room started spinning. He sat up and leaned forward, resting his forehead on the heel of one hand.

"You should check the messages and delete some," she said. "The mailbox is full."

That sounded like more work than Howard needed. "Why don't *you* delete them? You filled it up."

She didn't answer right away. "You don't want to hear what I have to say?"

"I don't have the *energy* for that," he said, throwing her word back at her.

"We need to talk."

"Do we?"

"I want to apologize. I know what I did was wrong."

"Is he there with you?"

"Who?"

Who did she think she was kidding? "Davis Delaney," Howard said. "The guy you've been fucking. About five-ten, one-eighty, long brown hair, talks like a gansta rapper. Remember him?"

"You don't have to be like that," she said. "He's not here."

"You sure?"

"I told you he wasn't coming to New York."

"So he's really in Santa Fe?"

"Yes."

"You said he'd be there for a few days. How long is a few days?"

Sophia thought for a moment. "I don't know. Maybe a week."

"That's convenient."

"Mounds, it's the truth."

"It's complicated, too. You have a week-long trip to New York and he's got a week-long trip to Santa Fe. A simpler story would be that he went to New York with you."

"He's not in New York."

"Yeah, that's what you said."

Silence again. Howard wondered if he was going to heave up the Cheerios.

"I don't blame you for not trusting me," Sophia said quietly.

"I want to know about the affair," Howard said.

"What do you want to know?" she asked carefully.

"Why?" Howard said. "I want to know *why* you did this?"

Sophia didn't answer for a moment. "It just … happened, Mounds. I don't know why."

"You're lying," Howard said. He could tell by the hitch in her voice that she was hiding something.

"I'm not lying," she said. "I just don't have a good answer for *why.*"

Howard snorted. "How long have you been involved with him?"

"A few weeks."

"That's not what I heard."

"Who have you been talking to?"

"I heard you've been sleeping with him for months."

"That's not true, Mounds."

"Where did you meet him?"

"I told you, Seattle."

"I know that's what you *told* me, Bassiff. I'm asking you if it's true."

"Yes, it's true."

"How soon after meeting him did you fuck him?"

"Mounds, we don't have to get into that."

"Why not?"

"Because those details don't matter."

"They matter to me."

"No, they don't. You think that you want to know everything, but telling you every little detail would just hurt you more."

"You almost sound like a woman who loves her husband and thinks about his feelings before she acts, but I guess if that were true, we wouldn't be having this conversation, would we?"

"I do love you, Mounds."

"Hmm."

"And I *don't* love him."

Howard hung up—the first time he had ever done that to Sophia.

The phone rang right way, but he didn't answer. Although he was desperate to understand why she had betrayed him, he just wasn't in the mood to listen to Sophia talk about love. Clearly, she wasn't an expert on the subject.

*What has happened to her?* Sophia had always seemed so honest and direct. As far as Howard knew, she had never kept any significant secrets from him, and until recently, she'd never been mean-spirited. So why had she made her affair with Davis so obvious that even J-Lo knew about it? Why had she been so flagrant during the past few weeks that she had aroused Howard's suspicion? Why had she so readily said, "Yes," when he'd asked her about the affair? It was almost felt as if she had *wanted* him to know. But why?

Howard knew where he could find some answers. He put on a jacket and walked out into the sunlight.

"Damn!" he exclaimed, turning back inside. He spent five minutes searching for his sunglasses, which he finally found in the center console of his BMW, and then he went back out the front door, still squinting as the bright sun penetrated the tint of his Nike lenses. He kept his head bowed as he shuffled down the sidewalk, trying not to jostle his pounding head. When he did look up, he saw dozens of tiny Denver Broncos flags rippling on the antennas of cars parked along the street. Broncos banners also hung from flag poles on a third of the houses on the block. During football season, the neighborhood turned orange and blue in accordance with Article 2.71 of the RIGs. Only four types of signs were permitted in the neighborhood—for-sale signs, the work-in-progress signs that tradesmen put up, political signs (one per yard up to three weeks before each election and five days after), and Broncos banners and flags from 5 a.m. to midnight every day that the Broncos played. There was no limit on the size, shape or number of Broncos emblems a resident could display, but no other professional or college team logos were permitted. Today the Broncos were in Oakland to face the Raiders.

Miriam and Adam had the Walker floor plan, which was identical to Sophia and Howard's Oxford model except for a subtle difference in the pattern of the trim. However, all similarities ended at the threshold of the house. Miriam and

Adam were avid sailors, so after Howard's landmark court victory, which had secured the right of every resident to control the interior of their homes, Miriam and Adam had transformed their house into an opulent yacht.

Howard stepped onto the front porch, which Miriam and Adam called the *prow,* and rang the bell, which sounded nautical whistles inside the house. He leaned forward and looked through the *portal* to see if anyone was coming. The glass was pleasantly cool against his forehead, but when he exhaled, the stale odor of vodka bounced back and made him shudder with regret.

"Never again," he vowed, closing his eyes.

"Hey, there," Miriam said, when she opened the door. She gave him a sad, sympathetic smile as if he were a dog that had been hit by a car. Howard averted his eyes. He hated everything her expression said about him. *Do I look that pathetic?*

"Come aboard. It's chilly out there." She was dressed like a cruise director, in white Bermuda shorts, white and blue deck shoes, and a blue golf shirt. She had a clipboard crooked in one elbow.

"How are you?" she asked.

"I've been better," Howard said.

She made a note.

The foyer had been painted to resemble a dock and gangplank leading up to the portal of a ship. In the original floor plan the front door had opened into a broad and open living room with a staircase on the left leading up to a hallway loft that overlooked the foyer. Miriam and Adam had blocked the view of the interior with an enormous, slightly curved wall just ten feet inside the front door. It was painted to look like the starboard flank of a white, ultramodern yacht that spent more days on the open sea than in harbor. The paint near the bottom was slightly discolored by lapping waves, and a few smudges indicated the spots at which the hull had rubbed up against docks. There was even guano painted high up on the bow from seagulls that had perched on the *gunwale*. Below the guano was the name of the ship—Suburban Schooner. A swirling blue and white pattern on the floor of the foyer looked like a choppy sea, and a humidifier in the corner pumped the smell of saltwater into the room. Miriam led Howard over a slightly raised loading ramp that swayed under his feet. She marched ahead gracefully, but Howard had to hold on to a waist-level rope to keep his balance. A pair of weathered and frayed *bow lines* arced down from the side of the ship and tied off to cleats on the *dock*.

"Whew!" Miriam said. "You smell like booze—a lot of it."

"I'll try not to give the *galley hands* a contact high."

She led him through the door in the *hull* into the main stateroom. All the furniture was bolted in place, and the *bulkheads* were high-gloss, varnished, curved teak that divided the *ship* into segments that could be sealed off in the event of a leak. Howard thought it was a pity that Miriam and Adam didn't live in a flood zone. Their house probably would have floated in rising water.

"Can I get you some coffee?" Miriam asked.

"That would be great," Howard said.

She wrote something on the clipboard. "Cream and Splenda, right?"

"That's right," Howard said. She made another note. "And thanks for cleaning up my living room." He barely remembered what he'd done the night before, but he recalled that the room had been trashed. This morning, everything was neat and ordered. The beer cans had been discarded, the liquor bottles stored, the ghostly muddy footprints shampooed away, and the carpets vacuumed.

"You're welcome," Miriam said. "Adam's in the den."

Their two *galley hands*—Caleb, 8, and Emma, 6—ran into the room.

"Hey, Uncle Howard!" they screamed, jumping into his outstretched arms. He smothered them with kisses as they giggled and tried to slither away. They were both wearing blue-and-white sailor outfits.

"You smell funny," Caleb said.

"That's what your mother said," Howard said.

Emma scrunched her nose. "Maybe you should take a bath."

"Sounds like a good idea," Howard agreed.

"You *should*," Miriam said. "Why don't you go upstairs and freshen up?"

"I'll show you where the bathtub is," Emma said.

"There's a *bathtub* on the ship?" Howard asked, amazed.

The girl giggled and nodded dramatically. "It's upstairs next to my cabin."

"Do you think I'll fit in the tub?" Howard asked. "I'm awfully tall."

Emma laughed and said, "Aunt Sophia and Uncle Davis fit."

In an instant, all the color drained out of Howard's face.

"Kids!" Miriam yelled quickly. "Leave Uncle Howard alone! *Batten down* your toys and go upstairs!" Howard lowered the children, and they immediately picked up their toys and started running upstairs with them.

"They took a bath *here*?" Howard asked numbly.

Miriam ignored the question. "There are extra towels in the hall cabinet, and Adam's in the den!" She raced off to the kitchen.

Howard trudged up the stairs. *Why would Sophia and Davis bathe together in Miriam and Adam's house? Why would Miriam and Adam let them? Why hadn't his friends told him what was going on?*

Emma and Caleb shrieked as he crested the top step, and they ran to his side. "It's this way!" Emma cried, grabbing him by the hand and dragging him down the hall. Emma's enthusiasm, normally so contagious, couldn't penetrate Howard's gloomy confusion.

He stepped into the bathroom and quickly closed the door, leaning against it heavily as if he were trying to stop someone from breaking it down. The olive-colored walls seemed to creep in on him, and his breath grew shallow and quick in the disorienting realization that cancerous secrets lurked beneath the surface of his marriage. At any moment, a child's innocent remark—*Aunt Sophia and Uncle Davis fit*—could cause a misstep that would send him crashing through a rotten plank into the murky bilge water of his life. Howard looked around the room suspiciously, everything seemed normal, but he could no longer trust his own perceptions. Even the sunlight streaming through the window seemed to mock him with the shimmer of fool's gold.

He stumbled to the sink and turned on the water, scooping it onto his face and hair. The cool water stung his skin and refreshed his senses. He stared at his reflection in the mirror and willed himself to calm down. He had to pay attention. The truth was within his reach, but he had to keep his emotions in check and pay attention. He dried his hands and face, and gargled with Listerine. He stepped out of the bathroom into the hall, where the giggling kids grabbed his hands and dragged him back down the stairs.

"You smell better now!" Emma exclaimed.

Howard found Adam watching the Patriots-Dolphins game on a seventy-inch flat screen TV. New England was leading 17-7.

"Heard you went on a bender last night," Adam said, sipping a Coors Light. He was wearing a red, white, and blue captain's uniform with a hat and deck shoes, and he was sitting in a captain's chair in front of a full-fledged helm with gauges, knobs, and a big naval steering wheel that had handles that looked liked beer taps protruding every twelve inches. Howard had heard Adam explain to the kids that if he were actually on the water, he would never drink a beer while sitting at the helm. "I can only do this on the *Suburban Schooner* while we're docked here in the neighborhood," he told them.

Howard settled into an arm chair and said, "How does Emma know that Sophia and Davis took a bath together?"

Miriam came into the room and set a cup of coffee on the table next to Howard.

"They took a bath *here*?" Adam asked, scowling.

Miriam wrung her hands. "A shower."

"Why?" Adam demanded.

"Howard, I'm so sorry," Miriam said. "I just didn't know what to do. I didn't feel that it was my place to tell you, but I didn't want to help her hide it either."

"Why did they take a shower here?" Howard asked.

"They'd been out at a farm somewhere, and when they came back, they had straw all over them. They didn't want to walk into your house like that, so they asked me if they could use the shower. I didn't expect them to jump in together."

"Emma *saw* them?" Adam demanded.

"No, no, no," Miriam said quickly. "She *heard* them talking, and then she saw them when they came out of the bathroom."

Adam stared at the plasma screen while Miriam said, "I

just didn't know what to do."

Howard asked, "How long has this been going on?"

Adam's eyes darted to Howard. "The showering together?"

"The affair."

Adam spun the steering wheel hard to the left, and the volume on the TV dropped to a whisper. "You didn't know Sophia was having an affair?"

Howard shook his head. "Not until yesterday."

Adam pushed himself out of the chair. "Come with me."

"Where are you going?" Miriam asked.

"To talk," he said.

"About what?" She sounded panicked.

"Man stuff."

Howard followed Adam through a series of staterooms, each protected by a water-tight door. Adam would wait until Howard closed the door behind them, before opening the next one, always making sure that any leak on the ship would be contained. Eventually, they reached the three-car garage, which Adam referred to as a dry dock. His behemoth Hummer 2 was wedged in next to Miriam's mammoth Ford Excursion. Howard always marveled at how perfectly the SUVs were parked—leaving adequate room for *each* driver to get in and out. In the slot for a third vehicle were two Arctic Cat snowmobiles, a pair of jet skis, a riding lawn mower, and a gas-powered snow-blower. Their speedboat was in a storage unit near Chatfield Reservoir because the RIGs prohibited parking it in the driveway.

Adam threw his empty beer can into a purple recycling bin in the corner.

"*You* recycle?" Howard asked.

Adam shrugged. "We've only got one Earth, right?"

They climbed into the Hummer, which was where they

convened whenever Adam wanted to have a man-to-man talk.

"Look," Adam said, "Sophia and Davis have been groping each other in front of everybody. I wanted to tell you, but Miriam said I should keep my nose out of it."

Howard took a slow sip of his coffee. "In front of whom?" He didn't like the way Adam had said *everybody.*

Adam turned to study Howard carefully. "How could you *not* have known?"

Howard stared out the windshield. Of course, he *had* known. His subconscious had sniffed out the ugly scent of her affair long before his conscious mind caught the first tendrils. He scowled, recalling the subtle changes in her demeanor—the coldness that had crept into her eyes when she looked at him, the slightly impatient tone that had lately turned aggressive. He saw Davis and Sophia at the breakfast table planning their day at the gallery, pulling out of the driveway in her car, or walking into the house at night laughing, telling stories over dinner. Sophia had always spent a lot of time with her artists, so initially, Howard hadn't been suspicious. However, in retrospect, he could see them for what they were—lovers. He felt the wet concrete start to engulf him again.

Adam said, "She calls him 'The Big O.' Did you know that?"

Howard shook his head. He didn't trust his voice.

"Apparently, the first time they had sex, she had some mind-blowing orgasm, and she's been chasing it ever since."

*The Big O?* Howard kneaded his forehead with one hand. He set his coffee mug down and tried to figure this out. Nothing made sense. He and Sophia had a great sex life. They made love three or four times a week, though Howard now recalled that the frequency of their love-making had recently declined. He had figured that the decrease was due

186

to stress—they'd both been so busy at work and he'd been consumed with studying for the bar exam. *Has she been faking with me?* That was a sobering and intimidating thought. He'd never suspected her of faking orgasms, and now … no …. He shook his head … she couldn't have been faking. She put a lot of energy into the positions, natural stimulants, and mental provocations she learned from the Kama Sutra, Tantric guides, and other instructional manuals. As a result, their lovemaking was fantastically rewarding for both of them. At least he had thought so, until now.

*The Big O?*

*How many people had she told?* Howard wondered. He couldn't believe that Adam knew such detail.

Then, as if he'd read Howard's mind, Adam said, "Everyone in our immediate circle knows."

Howard felt the wet concrete creep up to his chin.

"Every day she and Davis go to lunch—alone—and she comes back to the gallery looking disheveled, her face glowing. The other girls in the gallery start joking, '*Oh*, Sophia,' '*Oh*, my,' 'Did you go *oh*-verboard?' You know, anything with an 'O' in it."

Howard was struck again by the realization that he simply did not know his wife. It was enough of a shock to discover that she was having an affair. He would never have expected her to be so indiscreet.

Adam said, "She fucking rubbed your nose in it."

# twenty-seven

Howard stumbled down the sidewalk, as if the *Suburban Schooner* had been a real ship that had taken him on a long journey and now he had to regain his land legs. He walked blindly, disoriented by the houses around him.

"Mr. Marshall!" a man called as Howard neared the house. "Mr. Marshall!"

Howard looked across the street and saw a white van emblazoned with the logo, *Juniper Jungles Landscaping*, parked in front of Mrs. Stephenson's house. Gene and Jean strode toward him with soiled red knee pads over their blue jeans, and muddy spades in their hands.

"How are the repairs coming?" Howard asked, numbly.

"Dandy!" Gene reported.

Jean said, "We put down fresh Merion Kentucky Bluegrass sod to cover the tire tracks, and we're nearly finished planting bulbs in the garden. This isn't the best time of year to put in sod, but this stuff is pretty hardy. A week from now, the new strips will be integrated. They'll just be a little greener than the rest of the yard. By spring, everything will look perfect."

"I'm glad to hear that," Howard said, scowling at what appeared to be grass stuck in Gene's teeth.

"There is another area of attention," Gene said. "As you might expect, we routinely repair fouled foliage after deranged drivers deviate from their path and plow through the impatiens and petunias, so—"

"No, I wouldn't have expected that," Howard said. A car

barreling across someone's front lawn didn't sound like an everyday occurrence to him.

"Oh, it's quite common!" Gene said, smiling broadly. Howard saw flecks of green color throughout his mouth. It looked as if Gene had just finished eating a salad, and hadn't had a drink to wash it down. "The strip of sod shouldering the driveway is typically the target of unintended tread—"

"Gene, quit talking the man's head off," Jean said. "The Broncos game is about to start." Howard noted that she too had grass stuck in her teeth. He shuddered recalling Gene's proclamation earlier—*Green, glorious, grass! We eat, sleep, and drink it.*

"We found this in the bushes." Jean held up a small, handled bag from a Hyde Park jewelry store. "There were a few other trash items that we threw away, but when I saw the receipt, I thought you might need it."

Howard didn't recognize the bag. He accepted it from Jean and studied the credit slip. It was a charge for a twenty-one-hundred-dollar TAG Heuer watch engraved with the message, "To my favorite artist—S." It was dated three weeks ago.

"Is that important?" Jean asked.

Howard nodded slowly.

"See, Gene!"

Gene shrugged indifferently and grinned at Howard with grass-spackled teeth. "Wish I'd witnessed the wreck. BMW barreling backward, blowing through trash bins and bumping over the curb. Must have been quite a sight …."

# twenty-eight

Howard sat in his living room, staring at the Hyde Park receipt. The hangover headache had dissipated, but it had been replaced by a throbbing confusion. Years ago, he and Sophia had vowed that their marriage would be different from most. They would love each other *unconditionally*. Not unconditionally the way most newlyweds professed it—"I-love-you-honey-bunny-as-long-as-you-treat-me-nice-listen-to-me-every-day-stay-interested-in-the-same-things-I'm-interested-in-stay-physically-fit-style-your-hair-the-way-that-I-like-dress-the-way-I-like-do-the-chores-I-want-you-to-do-never-contradict-me-remember-my-birthday-remember-the-day-we-first-met-always-remember-our-wedding-anniversary-and-Valentine's-Day-think-I'm-sexy-and-be-faithful-to-me-in-thought-word-and-deed." No, they weren't talking about *that* kind of unconditional love. Sophia and Howard had vowed to love each other without selfishness, without judgment, without viciousness, and without the clingy insecurity that battered so many marriages and dragged them into the salvage yard of divorce.

But now Howard understood what *unconditional* really meant, and he knew that he and Sophia had never loved each other unconditionally.

There were many conditions they had to meet if they wanted to be loved, and *fidelity* was one of them. If Howard truly loved Sophia *unconditionally*, then he wouldn't judge her or reject her for anything that she did. Loving her unconditionally would mean that he would continue to love her even if she had a dozen affairs, spent all their savings, went on a murderous rampage, or—heaven forbid—chopped off his penis. *Unconditional* love had sounded powerful and sacred when they'd pledged it to each other on their wedding day. They had written their vows themselves, promising to love, honor and protect each other in sickness and in health, in good times and bad, for richer and for poorer, unconditionally until death did them part. Now Howard realized just how meaningless their vows had been.

He had no idea how the phone got into his hand. He didn't remember picking it up or dialing. One moment he was sitting in his recliner, the next Sophia was saying hello in his ear.

"I see you bought your boyfriend a watch," Howard said with no script, just letting the words slip out of his mouth unedited.

"What?"

"You spent two grand on a watch. You don't remember it?"

"Of course, I remember. You just caught me off guard."

"That's a mighty big present."

"He's an important client," Sophia said. "I've sold more than twenty-five-thousand dollars worth of his paintings."

"That's why you gave him a watch?"

"Of course."

"Not because he's *The Big O*?"

Sophia didn't respond. It sounded to Howard as if she'd stopped breathing.

He said, "Yesterday, when I dropped you at the airport, you said you were sorry."

"Yes." She sounded guarded.

"Why?"

He could tell the question confused her. "Because I *am* sorry."

"Sorry for what?"

More confusion. "Sorry for hurting your feelings, I guess."

"Where are you?" Howard said, looking at his watch. He'd expected her to be at her booth at the art show with thousands of people milling around. It sounded quiet on her end.

"I'm in my hotel room."

Howard said, "Sorry for hurting my feelings is an interesting way to put it."

"What's so interesting about it?" she asked, defensively.

"You're not sorry for *cheating* on me, you're only sorry for *hurting my feelings*."

She paused. "What's the difference?"

"You're not sorry for fucking Davis. You're only sorry because you got caught."

"I didn't get *caught*," she said indignantly.

"Oh, you got caught all right."

"I *confessed*. You asked me if I was sleeping with anyone, and I said yes. You didn't *catch* me."

Now *she* sounded like a lawyer. "Bassiff, you got caught by everyone we know."

"That's ridiculous."

"Is it?"

"Of course it is."

"Name someone who *didn't* know that you were sleeping with Davis." The silence stretched out for five full beats. "Maybe there's someone in the Big Apple who didn't know."

"Fuck you!"

"Yeah, you could have done that, but you chose to fuck Davis instead!" Howard stabbed the off button and just barely resisted the urge to throw the phone across the room. He'd never been the type to hang up in the middle of a conversation, but he was in the grip of a trembling rage unlike anything he'd ever experienced. Strangely, hanging up discharged his anger

193

like a lightning bolt releasing energy in a storm. The moment the phone went dead, calmness surged through him.

Sophia called right back.

Howard answered.

She was breathing hard, as if she had just run up a flight of stairs. Hanging up might have discharged his anger, but it had energized hers.

"Isn't that one of the things we promised never to do," she said through clenched teeth. "We promised to talk things out rather than hanging up the goddamned phone!"

"We promised to be faithful too," Howard calmly reminded her.

Sophia continued to pant. "I told you I was sorry." Howard could tell by her tone that she was in her angry pose—feet shoulder-width apart, left hand clenched so tightly that it was bone white from the wrist down, eyebrows pinched toward her nose and the muscles at the back of her jaw pulsing slowly.

"Sorry doesn't quite cut it," he said.

"What do you want, Mounds?" she spat. "You want me to go back in time and change the past?"

"How about just changing the present. I asked if you were going to sleep with Davis again, and you said you weren't sure."

"Well, now I'm sure."

Howard waited for her to clarify. When she didn't elaborate, he asked, "So which is it? Are you sure you're *going* to sleep with him or sure that you're *not*?"

"It's over."

"When did this happen?"

"Yesterday."

"Why?" Howard asked. "The only difference between now and last week is that now I know about the affair. Is that the reason you're ending it? Because I know?"

"No," she said, quietly. She was ramping down. "I just realized that I'd made a mistake."

"Helloooo—understatement," Howard said derisively.

Sophia didn't speak for several moments. Finally, she said, "I didn't mean for this to happen."

Howard said, "Isn't there an Eminem song about a woman who slips, falls, and lands on a man's dick?"

"Don't be a jerk!" Sophia snapped. "People make mistakes."

"People make vows, too!"

"Okay Mounds! I'm sorry! What do you want me to say?"

Howard said, "It would be one thing if you'd slept with Davis one time while you were falling-down drunk. That would sound like a regrettable, but brief, lapse in judgment. But sleeping with the guy day-after-day for weeks and parading him around in front of our friends? That's just deliberately spitting on our vows!"

"Spitting on our vows? Come on, Mounds! Don't blow things out of proportion!"

Howard pulled the phone away from his ear and stared at it for a moment. He laughed humorlessly, and said, "I'm not the one *blowing* anyone!"

For the third time in two days, he hung up on his wife.

# twenty-nine

Howard ate a whole bag of chocolate chip cookies and guzzled sodas while he watched the Broncos game. Denver was up ten points over Oakland late in the fourth quarter, and CBS's lead broadcast team—Jim Nantz and Phil Simms—praised the Broncos for dominating in Oakland, where the Raiders usually enjoyed a home-field advantage. Howard slammed his fist into the arm of the recliner, outraged that *his* home-field advantage had been undermined by Sophia's repeated personal fouls.

Simms, with his Southern drawl, said, "In this league you have to be able to go into somebody else's house, take away what they do best and silence the crowd. Look at these guys"—he circled several Raiders defenders—"they've got their hands on their hips, they're breathing hard, and they're not looking at each other. Over on the other side of the ball"—he circled several Denver players—"these guys still have a little pep in their step. You don't have to check the scoreboard. You can look at the field and tell who's winning this game."

Howard stared at the bright yellow lines Simms had drawn on the screen and saw too much of himself in the posture of the Raiders defenders. He was standing around looking defeated while the game spiraled away from him. *I should do something,* he thought. *But what?* He looked around the living room He didn't have a scoreboard to show him exactly how often Davis had scored or how much time was left on the clock of his marriage. He stared at the receipt on the table next to him and wondered if there might be other clues in the house.

There could be letters, pictures, a journal, a dayplanner, special lingerie or something that would help him better understand what had happened. Howard got out of his recliner and walked slowly into the kitchen. He stared at the basement door for several minutes. It was the natural place to start, but every time he got close to the door, the sinking feeling returned.

Howard turned away from the kitchen and went up the stairs, past the prints of enraged spirits stuck in their star prisons, down the hall and into the master bedroom, where ghastly pictures of bloody umbilical cords were mounted every few feet.

He'd never known Sophia to keep a journal, but he looked for one any way. He opened the drawer in her bedside table and found two novels, several bobby pins, about three dollars in change, a dirty tan rubber band—a keepsake from their third date—a vibrator, sex lube, and a stack of fashion and art magazines. Under the bed he found an abdominal machine they'd ordered but never used, two pairs of shoes—one his, one hers—several magazines and a lot of dust. He checked all of her dresser drawers, and though he found plenty of lacy lingerie, he didn't see anything that he didn't recognize— nothing that appeared to have been purchased especially for a lover. He pawed through the clothes in her walk-in closet; he opened all the drawers and cabinets in the bathroom and shuffled through her toiletries. It took more than an hour to scour every potential hiding place in the master bedroom, but he found no secrets. He checked the two guest rooms upstairs, but each looked as though no one had entered in months. Then he started on Sophia's neat, sparse home office. She did the bulk of her bookkeeping at the gallery, so the home office was mostly ceremonial, but there were a few stacks of papers arranged on top of the desk.

A folder sitting under a lamp contained her credit card statements from American Express, Master Card, and Visa. He and Sophia had never consolidated their finances, so they still had separate credit cards, bank accounts and loans. Each of their cars was titled in one name only, and the house and the gallery were still owned solely by Sophia. Howard traced his finger down the list of charges, not sure exactly what he was looking for. The bills were recent—two of them had payments due in the next ten days. On her American Express statement, he saw restaurants, clothing stores, gas stations, the charge at Hyde Park for the expensive watch, grocery stores, the monthly fee for her membership at Bally's, a flower shop … and the Hotel Monaco Denver.

*The Hotel Monaco?* He stared at that entry for a long time.

# *thirty*

Three years ago, on Howard's birthday, he and Sophia had dined at Panzano, an Italian restaurant on the ground floor of the Hotel Monaco. They'd fed each other fried calamari, baked salmon, mashed potatoes and little bites of chocolate cake. He remembered exactly how she'd looked that night, her face shining with excitement, blonde hair hanging in long, dangling curls, light green eye shadow perfectly accentuating the color of her irises. She'd worn a cropped, brown shrug sweater, over a peach blouse and Tommy Hilfiger, extra-low hip-hugger jeans.

"I wonder what the rooms in the hotel look like?" She wrapped her lips sensuously around a small wedge of cake that Howard held out to her on the end of his fork. She moaned softly as the rich flavor exploded in her mouth.

They'd admired the ornate lobby of the Hotel Monaco on their way into the restaurant. "I've heard the rooms are pretty amazing," Howard said.

"And super contemporary."

"Maybe they'll let us see a room," Howard suggested.

"Tonight?" Sophia asked doubtfully. She wiped a tiny crumb from the corner of her mouth. "You think they'd just give us a key and let us take a look?"

"Well, no, not by ourselves," Howard said, staring at her lips, thinking of how soft they would feel against his. "They wouldn't trust us to leave the room unscathed." He kissed her gently, once, twice.

"Scathe me, baby," Sophia whispered, gently holding his face and kissing him more earnestly. "Scathe me."

"But maybe someone could escort us," Howard suggested.

The waiter brought their check, and Sophia said, "Don't forget to be generous."

"I won't," Howard promised. It was a tradition of theirs to leave a big tip—regardless of the actual service—whenever they were celebrating a special occasion.

"It's our way of showing gratitude to the universe," Sophia had explained when she'd first suggested the practice. "We've got a good life, and we've just enjoyed a good meal, so we should leave a big tribute."

Howard knew the waiter would be pleasantly surprised when he discovered the fifty percent tip.

At the front desk, the manager told them that he'd be delighted to let them preview a suite.

"That's the term you use, *preview*?" Howard asked.

"Yes, sir," the manager said. "Let me see what we have vacant at the moment." He tapped on the computer.

Howard said to Sophia. "If they have a special word for it, then this must be a fairly common request."

"Ah, here's a nice suite on the tenth floor," the manager said. He programmed a key and led them to the elevator. He discreetly kept his eyes forward while they whispered behind him.

"This is a very special suite," the manager said when they reached the door marked 1034. He slid the card key into the lock and pushed the door open. Howard stepped into the room with his arm draped around Sophia and stopped, shocked, his mind slow to process what should have been obvious at a glance. The room had been decorated with flowers, balloons, a cake, and a sign that read, "HAPPY BIRTHDAY, MOUNDS!"

"Surprise!" Sophia said, jumping up and down. She clapped her hands, and laughed, loving the baffled look on her husband's face.

Howard couldn't believe that she had gotten him all the way up to the room without his suspecting, even for a moment, that she might have organized a birthday surprise.

The manager placed the key on a small table near the door and slipped out of the room.

"Come here," Howard said. She walked slowly into his arms. "I love you, Bassiff."

"I love you, too, Mounds," she said softly. She pushed him back against the door and kissed him passionately as she unbuttoned his shirt. Howard, undid her jeans, and slid them and her panties down over her hips. She stepped out of them quickly, and he turned her around and pressed her against the door. She wrapped her legs around his waist, and they made love standing against the door.

The next morning, they snuggled in the big hotel bed with a thick down comforter pulled around them.

"That was the best birthday present I've ever received," Howard said. The balloons swayed from side to side as the air conditioner kicked on. The flowers had filled the room with so much fragrance that even Howard noticed the aroma.

"You should have seen the look on your face!" Sophia said. In the morning light her face was flushed with a delicate blush.

"I never suspected a thing," Howard said.

"The manager was so perfect! I talked to him yesterday and told him what I wanted to do, and he just said, 'No problem. When you finish your meal, just ask me if you can preview a room, and I'll take you up.'"

"And then *I* suggested that we ask about a room."

"I know!" Sophia exclaimed. "I couldn't believe it! I almost started cracking up right then."

"Thank you," Howard said, kissing her softly.

Sophia groaned contentedly and burrowed deeper into the covers. "From now on this is our special hotel. This is where we'll come whenever we have something to celebrate."

"But only if we can stay in *this* room," Howard stipulated. "We'll call ahead and reserve our special suite. We'll have dinner at Panzano, and then come up here."

"And have sex against the door," Sophia said, nuzzling his neck.

They'd followed through on that promise three times since their wedding day, and each visit had been sweeter and more romantic than the previous one.

◦◦◦◦◦ ┃ ┃ ◦◦◦◦◦◦

Howard and Sophia hadn't been to the Hotel Monaco in more than six months, yet her American Express statement showed a charge there just two weeks ago. She'd paid $198.32 for a room. The night before, she'd spent $150 on dinner at Panzano. The American Express Gold Card statement broke down each restaurant charge into two categories—FOOD/BEV and TIP. The tab at Panzano had been $100.05, but Sophia had *celebrated* with an overly generous tip of $49.95.

Howard couldn't tear his eyes away from the statement. The Hotel Monaco was *their* hotel, Panzano was *their* restaurant, and leaving a big tip was the way *they* celebrated *their* good fortune. The suffocating feeling was coming back, but this time Howard wasn't sinking into a mushy, formless bog; instead it felt as if the wet concrete was hardening around him. His chest hurt, and he groaned as his face turned red and veins popped up in his face. Sophia seemed to be going down a checklist of everything she could do to show contempt for their marriage.

The pages fell out of his hands and he slumped over on the desk.

# *thirty-one*

Howard was sinking again. This time he was wearing a charcoal, four-button suit that Sophia had given him for Christmas a year ago, and he was in his BMW. A few minutes earlier he'd been inching forward in rush-hour traffic on his way to work, when suddenly a bog had opened up in front of him and the nose of the SUV had angled down. He looked at the man in the car next to him, but the guy had snorted and shaken his head, as if Howard were stupid for allowing himself to become mired in such a predicament. The woman on the other side never even glanced at Howard as he slipped deeper into the road. The hood was nearly completely covered, and the front doors wouldn't open. Howard reached back and lowered the rear seats, climbed into the cargo area and pushed open the trunk lid. All the other cars on the highway veered around him. A few drivers honked in outrage, but no one stopped to help. Howard thought that he might be able to jump to safety. He steadied himself on the rear bumper and tried to leap. But when he bent his knees and pushed against the Beemer, it simply sank deeper, taking him with it. Soon, the murky substance was gathering around his ankles and he was standing on the submerged SUV, sinking with nothing to grab on to and no one to call out to. He watched as his body sank into the thick, wet substance, and again he saw a warm glow below him, as if the BMW's headlights were illuminating a path. He tilted his head back as the bog sucked at his throat and pulled him under the surface.

Howard came awake with a sudden gasp. He breathed hard and fast, looking around the room, trying to get his bearings. He was still in Sophia's home office. His neck and back were sore from sleeping slumped over on her desk. He twisted his head from side to side and stretched his arms up high. It was nearly six in the morning; he decided to head into the office.

He walked down the hall to the master bathroom and turned on the shower. Andrew Metcalf's eighty-seven eyes watched him as he shuffled over to the toilet to empty his bladder and then stood at the sink brushing his teeth. By the time he finally stepped into the shower, steam had begun to fill the room. He stood motionless under the cascade. He felt numb—no fear, no anger, no disappointment. Not a single thought flashed through his mind. He was like a robot simply following a routine. He turned off the shower, dried himself with a thick cotton towel and walked back to the sink to shave. Steam from the shower had coated every glass surface in the room, and the eighty-seven eyes glistened with moisture, but they, like him, seemed otherwise emotionless.

Howard selected a tan, double-vented suit from the closet and put on a yellow shirt with a blue and tan striped tie. He threaded a brown belt through his loops, and slipped on a pair of brown dress shoes. He plodded down the stairs, past the nearly exploded stars and into the kitchen. He stared forlornly at the basement door while he poured coffee into his travel mug and took the first slow sips.

At the office, Howard spent most of the day as if in a stupor, not speaking to anyone, not answering his phone. He tried to ignore his boss, but Bob Carson was not the type of man who would allow anyone to ignore him.

In the late afternoon, Bob said for the tenth time, "So you're not going to tell me who punched you?" Howard's eye had mellowed to light purple with a yellow haze at the edges.

"I told you, I fell," Howard said. He assumed that Sophia had tried to call him during the day, but he'd turned off his cell phone and had changed the greeting on his outgoing message to say that he was out of the office and would return on Tuesday.

"Maybe you got in a fight with your wife's lover," Bob said. "Duked it out with the guy to see who was gonna win the girl."

"Chief, seriously," Howard said. "I had a rough weekend, and I'd rather not talk about it."

Bob was quiet for several minutes. "I had a wild weekend with the strippers."

"Yeah?" Howard said, without betraying that he knew that Bob had not had sex with the strippers. "What did you do?"

"The easier question is what *didn't* we do! Those girls kept me twisted in knots the whole weekend. It was incredible!"

"I'm glad to hear it."

Bob sighed heavily. "Come on Howard. A shiner like that's gotta have a better story than 'I fell.' Did you go somewhere after Platinum Heels on Friday? Did you go out with those two girls we picked up? What were their names?"

"Aziza and Keiko," Howard said.

"You hook up with them?"

"No," Howard said.

"You sure?"

"Of course, I'm sure."

"'Cause they called me today," Bob said.

"Good for you."

"They were looking for *you*. Said they're leaving town Wednesday afternoon, and wanted to see you again before they left."

"Yeah?"

"Said they'd called your line, but got some mumbo jumbo about you being out of the office."

Howard grunted.

"I naturally assumed that you had … you know … hooked up with them, and they wanted a little more."

"Sorry to disappoint you," Howard said.

Bob was quiet for several minutes, but then said, "You're not canceling on Hooters are you?"

Howard had been meeting Adam and Mark Hewerdine, a lawyer, at Hooters for Monday Night Football for the past three years. This season, Bob had horned in on their ritual.

"I have a lot of work to do," Howard said, pointing at the papers littering the table.

"You need the distraction," Bob said. "You can't sit home brooding about whatever it is that you don't want to talk about. And what better distraction than Shelly?" She was their favorite server at Hooters.

Howard shrugged indifferently.

Bob fidgeted for several moments. "Look," he started, and then hesitated. "I'm sorry we didn't tell you."

Howard looked up suddenly. "Tell me what?"

"About Sophia."

"*You* knew?"

"We *all* knew."

Howard shook his head in disbelief. "How in the hell did *you* know?"

"Adam told me."

# thirty-two

The traffic on I-25 moved briskly despite the coned-off lanes, closed exits, and unexpected bottle-necks of a seven-year construction project. Howard got off at Colorado Boulevard and pulled into the Hooters parking lot. As he walked past Bob's limo, Howard tapped on the glass and waved at Edward. The driver waved back, and then returned to his book. Inside the restaurant, Howard had to squeeze through the crowd near the door to get to their usual table in the back. Before Bob forced his way into their Monday Night tradition, one of the guys had always had to arrive before six p.m. to save a table. But Bob had promised Shelly a two-hundred-dollar tip each week if she reserved a spot for them, and they'd never again had to worry about where they would sit.

When Howard reached the table the Bills were leading 3-0, and they'd just kicked off to the Chiefs. Bob, Adam and Mark were hunched over their plates, eyes glued to the big screen, fingers sticky with barbecue sauce from the platter of hot wings on the center of the table.

"What's up?" Adam said without looking at Howard. At home, he always wore sailing gear, but during the week, he was an advertising salesman for Clear Channel, and he dressed the part. He had heavily moussed hair, designer dress shirts, and fifteen-hundred-dollar suits.

"Hey," Mark said, also not looking over. He was a partner at Hamilton Hewerdine and Harper, and he was Howard's mentor in the legal profession.

Howard slipped into his seat and stared at his friends

Shelly came to the table with a mug of beer in one hand. She had long blonde hair with dark roots and crowd-stopping electric blue eyes. She put the beer in front of Howard.

"Here ya go, sweet—Oh my goodness! What happened to you?" Like a concerned mother, she squared up on Howard and trained those amazing eyes on his bruised face.

Howard tried to muster a smile. "It's a long story."

"Poor baby." Shelly gave him a hug. Her enormous breasts pressed against the side of his head like warm pillows. "Don't you worry. In a week that shiner will be gone and you'll be as handsome as ever."

"Thank you," Howard said.

She backed away and scowled prettily. "To tell you the truth, the black eye adds to your whole rugged appeal, like you got in a fight."

"Pu-leeze!" Bob said. "Howard wouldn't know what to do in a fight. He's a pacifist." Bob had no idea that Howard was a former Golden Gloves champion.

Howard said, "Here's to *looking* like I got in a fight." He raised the glass to his lips, and without a second thought, broke his promise to never drink again.

Shelly gave him a warm smile. Her generous breasts overflowed her tight tank top, and her belly button ring sparkled above the low waistband of her shorts.

"Everybody having their usual tonight?" she asked. The men nodded. "I'll be back in a flash," she said with a wink and turned away. Though men were standing shoulder to shoulder at the bar, there was plenty of room in the dining area for the waitresses to move around. Howard, Bob, Mark and Adam watched Shelly's amazing, bouncing butt cheeks undulating beneath the orange fabric of her shorts.

"I admire her," Bob said.

"That's not admiration," Mark said. "That's ogling."

The Chiefs fumbled and Buffalo recovered at the thirty-two-yard line. Cheers erupted in the crowded restaurant, and Indian war chant music blared over the sound system. Everyone started doing the tomahawk chop, mocking the traditional celebration of the Chiefs' faithful. The Broncos win on Sunday had put Denver half a game behind the Chiefs in the AFC West. If Kansas City lost tonight, the two teams would have identical records, but Denver would own the tie-breaking edge with fewer conference losses.

When the noise died down, Howard said, "All of you knew about Sophia?"

Bob looked guilty. Adam glanced away. Mark said, "Howard, this hasn't been easy for any of us."

They all rose to their feet as the Bills' quarterback launched a pass to the corner of the end zone, and groaned as one when the receiver came down out of bounds.

"It's been a little hard on me, too," Howard said sarcastically.

"It was so obvious," Mark said, talking out of the side of his mouth so that he could keep his eyes on the television screen. "We all just thought that you must not care or didn't want to do anything about it."

Yesterday, Adam had said that everyone in their immediate circle knew about the affair, but Howard had assumed he was exaggerating. "Obvious in what way?" he asked. He couldn't imagine how Bob or Mark could have known what Sophia was doing.

They jumped to their feet again as a Bills' running back burst through the middle of the defense and carried the ball down to the fifteen-yard-line.

"That's what I'm talking about!" Mark exclaimed, pumping his fist at the screen.

"The Chiefs are gonna get their asses kicked tonight!" a man at the next table said.

Adam said, "Two weeks ago, you brought Davis to Hooters with you for the game." He took a long pull on his beer.

"Yeah, but that was before I knew he was sleeping with my wife."

Someone whooped as the Bills' quarterback threw another fade to the back corner of the end zone. This time the receiver came down in bounds and the Hooters crowd went crazy. The war chant came on again, and everyone started swinging his arm forward in a rhythmic tomahawk motion. Buffalo was up 10-0, putting the Broncos a little closer to first place in their division.

Buffalo kicked off again, and the Kansas City returner brought the ball out to the twenty-eight yard-line.

"Look at that!" Bob exclaimed, pointing, his fingers dripping with barbecue sauce.

Shelly was bending over a table near the big screen, gently swaying her ass from side to side. The thin fabric of her shorts crept up into the cleft, exposing the bottoms of her sumptuously rounded cheeks. The Chiefs' third-down pass fell incomplete, but none of the men in Shelly's section seemed to notice.

"Goddamn!" Bob said when she finally stood up and walked away.

Mark cleared his throat.

Howard said to Adam, "So you knew about this before I brought Davis here?"

"I'd known about it for a while," Adam nodded. "There were a couple of times I was gonna talk to you, but then when you brought him here, I figured you must be cool with everything.

I didn't know if you and Sophia had an open marriage, and I didn't *want* to know. So I just stayed out of it."

"But that's when we all found out," Mark said through a mouthful of chicken. "Adam told us about all the time that Sophia had been spending with Davis and all the rumors about them."

"These girls are fucking *hot!*" Bob said. His eyes were locked on a server named Amanda, a raven-haired, twenty-one-year-old with enormous breasts and a sweet smile. She'd just started working at Hooters a few weeks ago.

Suddenly, as if sensing that her special place in Bob's heart—and wallet—might be at risk, Shelly showed up with their food. "Here ya go, boys!" She set four burgers and two baskets of fries on the table. She plopped into Bob's lap, threw her arm around his shoulders and gave him a stern glare. "Bob, are you looking at other girls?"

"Of course not," he stammered.

"I could have sworn I saw you staring at Amanda."

"Who's Amanda?" Bob asked innocently.

"Good answer," Shelly said. She rubbed his head, and then stood up and put her hands on her hips. "I'll get another round of drinks. Ya'll want anything else?" She gestured at her body as if it were a menu. The men smiled guiltily and shook their heads.

Buffalo's quarterback scrambled to his right, looking downfield for an open receiver. Before he could make the pass, a Chiefs' defensive end caught up with him and swatted the ball out of his hands. Everyone in the restaurant groaned. Another Chiefs' player recovered the loose football.

Everyone booed when the Chiefs scored on a weak-side toss. The Bills were still up 10-7, but the momentum had shifted.

A few minutes later, the Bills completed a 40-yard pass and drew another cheer from the crowd. The war song played again, and everyone chopped their tomahawks. Shortly before halftime, the Bills scored again to take a 17-7 lead, as the teams trotted into their locker rooms.

Shelly returned. "You boys doing okay?"

Bob said, "I'm looking for wife number four. You interested?"

Shelly said, "You're so cute!" She patted Bob gently on the cheek. He returned the pat—on her butt cheek—drawing a reproachful glance.

"Careful Chief," she said.

She walked off, and Bob said, "I would marry that girl in a heartbeat. Sweet, sexy, sassy, and she's always flirting with me."

Mark said, "She's not flirting with *you*. She's flirting with the two-hundred-dollar tip."

"Why are you always on the prowl for a new wife?" Adam asked.

Bob said, "I'm pre-wired to spread my seed. I look at women the way a botanist looks at plants—variety is the most important thing."

The second half started, and the crowd roared again as the Bills scored on a long pass down the sideline on the very first play.

"Sophia must have a green thumb," Howard said.

Everyone at the table fell silent.

"Shake it off, buddy" Adam said, tapping Howard's arm with a closed fist.

"I just don't understand why she would do this."

"You never will," Bob said.

Howard scowled. "What do you mean *never*?"

"Has she told you the reason?" Mark asked.

216

"She's in New York," Howard said.

"Oh, I forgot," Bob said. "They don't have phones in New York."

Howard glared at him. "She won't tell me."

"Doesn't matter," Bob said. "You'll never understand. Women are just different from men."

"Ain't that the truth," Adam said.

"I hate to break it to you," Bob said, sipping his beer and giving Howard a serious look, "but wives are *allowed* to cheat."

"Get out of here," Mark said.

Kansas City completed three passes in a row, but eventually was forced to punt.

"Says who?" Howard demanded. He certainly hadn't given Sophia permission to step out on him.

"Society,"—Bob took another slow sip—"women can cheat *if they have a good reason.*"

Howard laughed incredulously. "What about vows and commitments and promises? What about through sickness and health, good times and bad, for richer or for poorer?"

Bob said, "You see the movie *The Bridges of Madison County?*"

"Yeah."

"One of my exes dragged me to it," Bob said. "It's a love story."

"I know that," Howard almost snapped at his boss. "So?"

"Meryl Streep is a Midwestern wife with a nice, devoted husband. But while hubby is out of town with the kids, she falls in love with Clint Eastwood. Why? Because she was bored and wanted something different. Women all over the country cried at the end when she had to decide whether to stay with her husband or go with Clint." Bob stopped talking and nodded as if he'd said something profound.

Howard asked, "How does that prove that women have permission to cheat?"

Bob said, "The movie was a *love story*. That means society believes that a story about a cheating wife can be romantic. If *The Bridges of Madison County* had been about a bored husband cheating on his devoted wife, it wouldn't have been a love story."

"Hell no!" Adam said. "Remember that movie, *Unfaithful*, where Diane Lang was married to Richard Gere, but she was sleeping with that French guy."

"Another love story," Bob said conclusively.

Mark said, "But in those movies, the wives didn't leave their husbands."

"So?" Bob asked.

"That makes a difference, doesn't it?" Mark argued. "If the wife leaves, then It's not a love story. She has a crisis of conscience, but in the end she stays with her husband. That's what makes them love stories."

"I hadn't thought about it that way," Adam said. "Staying does kinda make a difference."

"All I'm saying," Bob continued, "is that women have a free pass to cheat. These movies make it seem like the wife isn't a slut out sowing her wild oats—she's just a lonely woman looking for attention." Then in a high falsetto, Bob said, "*My husband doesn't pay enough attention to me.*"

"*He's a workaholic and he forgot my anniversary,*" Adam offered in an even more ridiculous falsetto. "*I'm sitting at the dining table in a sexy dress waiting for him, but now I have to blow out the candles, because he's not coming.*"

"Okay," Mark said. "In the movies, there's a formula, but that doesn't mean that they have permission."

"What else could it mean?" Adam asked.

They ate in silence for several minutes. The third quarter was nearly over, and the Bills were still up by ten points.

Eventually, Bob said. "If any wife gets caught cheating, I guarantee you she's got some reason why it was justified. That's the way women are."

"You're serious about this?" Howard asked.

"You want to know why Sophia cheated on you?" Adam asked.

"Of course I do."

"Figure out what motivated her. What would Sophia use as her excuse? Are you not paying enough attention to her? Did you forget to send her flowers on your anniversary? Have you become too predictable? Was she looking for more than just sex?"

Howard drained his beer. Suddenly he realized that Adam was trying to tell him something. "*You* know why she did it," he said.

"Yes," Adam confessed, holding Howard's gaze. "But you need to ask *her.*"

"Why don't *you* tell me," Howard said. "You're sitting right here."

Mark said, "For a lot of very good reasons, none of us is allowed to testify in this trial. If you want to know what Sophia thinks, put her on the stand and cross-examine her.

# thirty-three

The Bills beat the Chiefs 27-14, vaulting the Broncos into first place in the AFC West. On the drive home from Hooters, Howard was suddenly curious about the spate of messages he'd ignored for the past forty-eight hours. He snatched up his cell phone and checked the voicemail on all his lines. Every account—home, office, and cell—was full. He exhaled wearily as the various computerized voices told him that he had a total of fifty-three new messages. He started with his cell phone.

"*Mounds, I'm so sorry,*" Sophia said in the first message. "*I just watched you drive away from the airport, and I feel so bad. My heart hurts. I wish I was in your arms right now. Please call me, baby. My flight doesn't leave for another hour. Please call me. I'm so sorry. I hope you'll forgive me. I love you so much.*"

The next dozen messages had the same flavor. I'm sorry; I feel bad; I made it to New York; I miss you; I wish I were in your arms. Call me. Please forgive me. I love you.

Howard sped through them, looking for something different, looking for a clue. She filled up his cell phone mailbox on Saturday and then started on the home phone. There, her tone grew less conciliatory, more aggressive. She sounded frustrated by his refusal to take her calls, so she quit pandering, quit delivering the standard I-got-caught-and-now-I-feel-regret script.

"*Hey Mounds,*" she said in a not-quite drunken tone. She'd recorded this one late Saturday night. "*It's your wife ... Sophia ... in case you forgot. Or maybe I'm your ex-wife by now. Maybe you got one of your little attorney friends to draw up the divorce papers so you can serve them to me the minute I get back next Saturday. That would be just like you to not talk to me and start making plans of your own, wouldn't it? Yeah, I screwed up. I shouldn't have slept with Davis, but what the hell. It happened. It's over. I can't change it. What did you expect?"*

*What did you expect?* That threw Howard. He'd expected fidelity. Hadn't she?

He moved on, skipping through messages that all sounded the same, but eventually he heard something different. There was a lot of background noise—a murmuring crowd, light music. Howard could hear a woman talking, but he didn't recognize the voice.

"*...salmon with a teriyaki*"—the next few words were inaudible—"*spinach orzo pasta*"—inaudible—"*I can give you a few more minutes...*"

A waitress.

Howard heard Sophia ask, "*What do you think?*"

Another female voice said, "*I'm gonna have a salad.*"

"*I think I'll try the salmon,*" Sophia said.

This wasn't the first time that Sophia's phone had accidentally redialed the last number. She'd inadvertently called Howard's voicemail many times in the past, but he'd always deleted the messages without listening; he hadn't wanted to eavesdrop on his wife. He had tried to teach her how to lock her phone so that this wouldn't keep happening, but like parking her car correctly in the garage or filling up on gas, Sophia had never caught on.

"*Are you going to leave Howard?*" the other woman asked after the server departed. Howard recognized Kara's voice.

Sophia didn't respond audibly, and the silence sounded ominously like a shrug to Howard.

Sophia said, "*Davis drives me a little bit crazy sometimes. He's so damned flirty with everyone, and he lives totally in the moment. He doesn't think about his next meal, let alone the next step in his career, or the direction he'll take in life.*" Howard closed his eyes. Her friend had asked Sophia about her husband, and Sophia had quickly changed the subject to her lover. Was she gone already?

"*Uh huh,*" Kara said. "*But at least he's not boring like Howard.*"

Boring? Howard pulled the phone away from his ear and stared at it.

"*I guess—,*" Sophia said doubtfully, and the doubt in her voice sounded, to Howard, like a powerful argument in his defense.

"*I can see why you like Davis,*" Kara said. Howard wished she would shut the fuck up. "*He's definitely a hottie.*"

"*That's for sure,* "Sophia agreed. "*The crazy thing is that I wasn't trying to fall in love with him. You know how you hook up with someone and you immediately start imagining what it would be like to be in love with him? I didn't have that with Davis. The sex was great, and the sneaking around was exciting, but he's really not husband material. But, after a while, his perpetual good mood and his impulsiveness started to grow on me.*"

"*And grow and grow and grow,*" the other woman said.

"*Yeah,*" Sophia giggled. "*He's—*"

The message ended, and Howard was left sitting in the car with the phone cutting into his ear like a knife.

Until that moment, the torturous images running continuously on Howard's mental projector had been of Sophia writhing in orgasmic ecstasy, calling out Davis' name. She had dubbed him "*The Big O*" for Christ's sake. Howard had assumed that Davis Delaney was her equivalent of a Hooters girl—a nice fantasy, and fun to flirt with, but not someone she would risk her marriage for.

Howard replayed the message half a dozen times, scowling fearfully as his wife contemplated a future without him. He moved on to the next batch of messages, the ones on his office line. There were a handful of business calls, two messages from Aziza and Keiko saying that they wanted to see him again, and another dozen or so from Sophia.

She told him that things were going well in New York, that she was sorry for cheating on him, sorry for filling up his voice mail, and sorry for hurting him. He could still hear the anger in the clipped tone of her words, and the businesslike pace of her sentences. Finally, he got to a message that was different from the rest. He could hear background noise, music playing lightly and people's voices, but Sophia sounded echoed, as if she were in a tiled room.

*"Mounds, I know you don't want to talk to me, and frankly I don't want to talk to you either,"* she said. *"I'm only calling because I know you won't pick up the phone. You're too much of a coward to talk to me about* our *marriage!"* She paused and took several deep breaths. *"You're probably sitting in the house getting drunk, or maybe you're out getting some pussy. That would be like you, wouldn't it? Since I had sex with someone else, then you should have sex with someone else, right? Go ahead if you think it will make you feel better."*

Another long pause. Howard thought the message had ended.

*"What did you expect, Mounds? Huh? I'm your wife and you're my husband, but you don't want to have kids, so where does that leave me? I want a baby. There I said it. I want to know what it feels like to make love when you're trying to make a baby. I want to know what it feels like to be pregnant. I want to know*

*what it feels like to be a mother. I can't do that with you, can I? You don't want kids. No way. No how. No nothing. So what did you expect? Did you expect me to waste my whole life with you? Did you expect me to grow old without—"*

She ran out of time, which was probably fortunate for Howard, because he hadn't taken a breath since the beginning of the message. He gasped loudly as if he'd been trapped under water.

The next message pushed him back under the surface. *"No, I wasn't trying to fall in love with Davis,"* she said as if answering a question Howard had asked. *"But I do love him. I love his spirit; I love his energy. And he's handsome."* A long pause. *"He would make pretty babies."*

When Howard reached the house, he pulled into the garage and barely noticed Mrs. Stephenson watching him. He plodded up the stairs and fell onto the bed fully clothed. He felt like a spirit trapped in one of Geraldine Crawford's stars. No matter how hard he pushed, he simply could not break out.

Lying alone in their darkened bedroom, Howard wondered how he could have been so unaware of Sophia's feelings. Maybe she was right—maybe his inability to detect odors *was* indicative of his general failure with emotions. If he knew his wife—*really* knew her—wouldn't he have known just how desperately she wanted children? Wouldn't he have sensed that she'd been shopping for a new husband?

But why hadn't she talked to him about it? Why hadn't she divorced him before starting a relationship with Davis? Howard had never known that his wife was capable of such deceit.

# thirty-four

The issue of children had been the source of angst in each of Howard's three serious relationships before he met Sophia. It first cropped up at the University of Tennessee when his girlfriend, Katie, invited him to her dorm room after class on a Thursday afternoon. She was nineteen, auburn-haired, thin and brainy. Her face was always slightly flushed, but when she was nervous, dark splotchy patterns emerged on her cheeks, forehead, and neck—one of which roughly resembled the Australian continent.

Howard plopped down on her bed and shrugged off his backpack, completely unprepared for what was to follow.

"I love you," she said.

"I love you, too."

"Why don't you ever tell me that you love me?"

"I just did."

"You only say it after I say it."

"I can never beat you to the punch," Howard countered. For months he had complained that she peppered him with so many I-love-you's that the phrase was losing its meaning.

Katie shook her head. "If I didn't say 'I love you' first, you'd never say it."

"Well," Howard said, "we'll never find out, because you can't restrain yourself." He smiled at her to let her know that he was joking—sort of.

"I've *restrained* myself for the past three days," she said tersely. She pulled out a dayplanner and showed him a notation she'd made three days earlier, vowing a moratorium on "I love you's" until Howard said it to her first. After seventy-two hours, she'd concluded the experiment.

Howard sighed. She was always putting their relationship through some sort of trial—usually based on something she'd read in *Cosmo*. "Is that why you invited me over here, to tell me that I've failed another test?"

Katie jumped off the bed and ran into the bathroom. Howard closed his eyes and pinched the bridge of his nose. Why is she so upset? he wondered. This was not a new issue for them.

"Honey," he called through the door. "I'm sorry!"

He heard the toilet flush and then the door cracked open.

"I love you," he said preemptively when Katie peeked out.

She emerged from the bathroom with her hands behind her back.

"What are you hiding?" Howard asked with a smile, his hands unconsciously moving to his crotch. "I hope it's not a butcher knife. I don't want to get Bobbet-tized."

She pulled her hands out to reveal something much worse than a knife—it was a pregnancy stick bearing a royal blue line.

"Blue means pregnant," she said quietly.

Howard's mood instantly shifted from humor to anger. He realized that the I-love-you test had merely been an opening salvo. Round two was coming out of the bathroom pretending that she had just discovered her condition. *Does she think I'm a complete idiot?* he wondered.

"What do you mean, you're pregnant? I thought you were on the pill," Howard said, though even as he said it he recalled that Katie sometimes forgot to take her daily pill or she'd sometimes take it at different times of day, which Howard had read diminished its effectiveness.

"I was," Katie said. "I still am. I guess it didn't work."

She was chewing on the collar of her sweatshirt, and a pair of pimples had risen on her forehead. She walked back to the bed and sat next to him, smiling anxiously as tears gathered in the corners of her eyes. The pregnancy stick was in one hand, and a wad of tissue was in the other.

Howard stared absently at the frayed ends of his Levis and his scuffed, scarred boots. Every thought he'd ever had about parenthood ran through his mind; the joy and love that people professed to feel toward their own children; his father's instruction to consider the costs, not just the benefits, and his own nascent feelings that he might not want to become a father. All of this had been theoretical, but now his nineteen-year-old girlfriend was actually pregnant; Howard had to face reality.

"Well?" Katie asked, her nervous smile collapsing.

"Let me think for a minute," Howard said, lying back and staring up at the ceiling.

Furrows formed in her brow. "What's there to think about? Either you're excited or you're not."

"It's not that simple."

A key turned in the lock and the door swung open. Katie's roommate, Tara, entered wearing headphones plugged into her iPod. She stopped, apparently sensing the tension in the air.

"I'll come back," she said, and was gone.

Howard asked, "Does *she* know?"

Katie nodded. "This isn't how I expected you to react." She grabbed his hand and pulled it toward her face as if she were going to kiss it.

"Don't!" Howard snapped, ripping his hand away. He stood up and glared at her, massaging his hand as if she had hurt him. "I need to think."

"There's nothing to think about!" she screamed.

He paced the room in short agitated steps. "How long

have you known?" He asked in a tone that foreshadowed his future legal training.

Katie looked down at the pregnancy test in her hand, but she knew better than to claim that she had just found out.

"I took a test a couple of days ago," she said quietly.

"Why?"

She paused. "Because I was late."

"How late?"

She shrugged. "A week and a half."

"So you were a week and a half late, *then* you took a test, *then* you talked about it for two days with Tara and who knows who else…"

"Just Tara and Vickie." Katie crossed her arms.

"Well, if you needed all that time to think about it before you told me, can't you give me just a couple of minutes to let this sink in?"

Her mouth snapped shut, but she never took her eyes off him. Howard sat down and planted his head in his hands. He wondered if *she* was ready to become a mother, if *he* was ready to become a father, and if *they* were ready to raise a child together. He wondered what their parents would say and what it would be like to live the next nine months, knowing that their lives were about to change—forever.

Katie looked off into the distance and ran her tongue along her teeth. She shook her head slowly. "Why don't you just say what you're thinking?"

"Don't try to think for me."

"You want me to have an abortion and make your problem go away."

She wasn't completely wrong. For as long as Howard had been old enough to have an opinion on the issue, he'd been pro-choice. He believed it was a woman's right to choose, and he thought that most teenagers and even women in their early twenties were probably better off having abortions than children. But now that he was faced with the decision himself, he wasn't sure what he believed. Katie had been on the pill, and he'd thought that they were being responsible. But he knew that abstinence was the only foolproof birth control. Now what? Was it appropriate to get an abortion as backup birth control? Did the fact that Katie was pregnant mean that, despite Howard's reservations, he had to step up to the responsibility? It would certainly change their lives, but not necessarily for the worse. His parents had been nineteen and twenty when they'd had their first child, and they'd made it. So had Katie's parents and billions of other people in the long history of the planet.

Howard knelt down in front of Katie and took both her hands. "I'm sorry that I didn't immediately get excited, but I love you, and I'll support you no matter what you decide to do." They both took a couple of deep breaths.

"I didn't mean for this to happen," Katie said, sniffling.

"Of course you didn't," Howard said, brushing a strand of hair away from her eyes. "This is the way it happens. People get pregnant by accident, and then they adjust and make it work. We'll do the same."

For the next two weeks they planned their future as parents. Howard was surprised at how quickly his fears about fatherhood had faded away, replaced by a euphoric confidence that everything would be fine. They had no idea how much money they'd need to maintain a home and raise a baby, but they were confident that they'd figure it out. Their plan was for Katie to drop out of school temporarily. They would both move out of the dorms into an apartment. Howard would continue taking classes part time, but he'd get a full-time job.

Thus far in his college career he hadn't worked because he was a full-scholarship football player and the NCAA prohibited jobs for full-scholarship athletes. He would quit the football team and apply for a position in one of the stores at the mall. His friend Thomas was making twelve dollars an hour as a sales associate at Abercrombie and Fitch, and Howard figured he could get by on that type of salary. After staying home with the baby for a semester or two, Katie would resume her studies with a reduced class load. They stayed up late night after night, lying in bed, considering baby names, talking about child-rearing priorities and wondering just how cute their infant would be.

In this glow of excitement, they drove to Jacksonville to share their plans with Katie's parents. They'd agreed that Howard would do most of the talking because he felt it was important for him to break the news to Katie's father.

Her parents, Adrian and Ryan Cooper greeted them in the driveway, and ushered them into the house. Katie's parents helped them get settled into separate bedrooms and then escorted them into the dining room where dinner was waiting. They had rotisserie chicken, mashed potatoes, green beans, rolls, and pecan pie. Katie and Howard told the Coopers about everything that had transpired on campus since the start of the semester—except the pregnancy—and the Coopers caught the kids up on life in Jacksonville. During dinner, Howard thought there had been several perfect moments to mention the baby, but each time he'd raised a questioning eyebrow at Katie, her face had bloomed red, and she'd shaken her head minutely.

After dinner, they moved into the living room to watch a Cirque du Soleil tape. Howard and Katie sat on the couch, while the Coopers got into matching recliners positioned facing the TV. Howard took Katie's hand and gave it a gentle squeeze of encouragement. He raised his eyebrows again, but she squinted at him and crushed his fingers in her grip. Howard turned away angrily. *How much longer does she want to wait?*

"Mr. Cooper," Howard said, deciding that he had to take charge, "would you mind turning down the TV for a—"

Katie raised his hand toward her face and before he could pull away, she bit down hard on the meaty section.

Howard screamed, reaching an operatic pitch that he held for an impressively long breath as Katie sank her teeth deep into his flesh. He tried to yank his hand away, but she had a firm grip; he succeeded only in dragging her halfway off the couch, forcing her teeth even farther into his hand.

"Katie!" he begged, his eyes wide and his mouth contorted in agony. *"Kay-Teee!"*

Her parents ran to her side. Howard's arm was locked ramrod straight, and she was held at the end of it, slumped partly on the floor.

"Katie, honey," Mr. Cooper said in a calm voice, "you have to relax." Her father eased her back onto the couch, drawing tears from Howard as his trapped hand shifted position in her tight grip. Blood ran grotesquely down Katie's chin.

"Get a towel!" Mr. Cooper commanded.

Mrs. Cooper ran into the kitchen and came back with two dish towels. She spread one in Katie's lap and used the other to dab at the dripping blood.

None of them was surprised. Katie had been a biter ever since she'd grown her second tooth. She'd bitten kids at day care, grade school, junior high, and the Girl Scouts. She'd even sent her senior prom date to the hospital after biting through his tuxedo and taking a chunk out of his bicep on the dance floor—the tuxedo *and* his pitching arm had been ruined. She'd developed some control over her biting in adulthood, but she still loved to have something between her teeth. The collars of all of her shirts were worn through by her constant chewing. She chomped on her hair whenever it drifted toward her mouth, and when she hugged Howard, she'd sometimes nibble on his shoulder playfully. In bed, she'd bitten his nipples, earlobes, and lips. Fortunately, she'd never bitten his penis, but Howard never relaxed when she gave him a blowjob.

The biting was light and tolerable when Katie was relaxed, but when she was stressed, a playful nibble could turn into a fierce grip, and, once she clamped down, her jaw would lock in place. It could take as long as half an hour to get her to release. A year earlier, Mrs. Cooper had broken her hip in a car accident, and Katie, Howard, and Mr. Cooper had waited at the hospital for hours while she was in surgery. When the doctor came out to tell them the result of the operation, Katie had turned bright red and bit down on the webbing between the thumb and index finger on Howard's left hand. He'd jumped out of his chair with a yowl, dragging Katie with him. They'd squirmed on the floor—Howard writhing in pain, Katie actually growling like an angry terrier. After ten minutes of desperate, but futile, coaxing, a nurse had injected a muscle relaxant into Katie's jaw. Once Howard was free, they'd rushed him into an examination room where he received thirteen stitches and a tetanus shot. He thought he had gotten off easy.

After biting him at the hospital, Katie had been extremely apologetic. Although Howard knew that her assault was the result of an uncontrollable impulse, it had taken months to actually forgive her. He'd never before been assaulted by a girlfriend, and it was terrifying to spend time with her, worrying that next time she might nick an artery.

Yet despite the danger, Howard hadn't broken up with

her, because, between bites, she was sweet, intelligent and funny—stress just bought out the animal in her.

**********

"Take deep breaths," Mr. Cooper instructed, gently stroking Katie's hair. Her eyes darted back and forth frantically; Howard thought that she might bite all the way through his hand and swallow the ball of flesh.

"Let's go to the hospital," Mrs. Cooper suggested.

The Coopers helped Katie and Howard rise from the couch and walk gingerly to the garage. Every step was agonizing for Howard.

He slumped in the backseat of their Isuzu Rodeo, trying to get as comfortable as he could with his arm extended and his hand trapped in his girlfriend's mouth. Mrs. Cooper spread thick towels to soak up the blood that continued to trickle down Katie's chin. Katie sat up primly with her hands folded in her lap. She didn't look upset any more. Her face was clear, and her eyes had stopped dancing around. Occasionally she gave Howard a sympathetic look.

"Don't turn your head!" he urged. "Stay still!" He closed his eyes and tried to think of anything but the fear that Katie's top teeth were actually touching her bottom teeth and all the flesh in her mouth was completely severed from his hand except for the thin slivers trapped in the gaps like dental floss.

They drove in silence for several minutes, but when they stopped at a long traffic light Mr. Cooper asked, "Howard, what did you want to tell me?"

Howard had been resting his head against the window. Suddenly, his eyes popped open. "Sir?" he gulped.

"You were going to tell me something."

"Oh, it was nothing," Howard lied, sounding unexpectedly

cheerful given the condition of his hand. "I don't even remember what it was."

"My daughter only gets like this when she's really nervous. The boy she bit at the prom had just asked her to go to a hotel." Mr. Cooper watched Howard carefully in the rearview mirror. "Something you were about to say must have scared her."

Howard smiled awkwardly, then looked at Katie. She was staring at him, with her head forward and her eyes cut all the way to the side, but he couldn't tell what she was thinking. He took a deep breath and decided that, eventually, her parents had to know, so now was as good a time as any.

He said, "We're going to have—aaaaaahhhhh! Shit! Shit! Shit!"

Katie bit down and rocked her head from side to side as if she were trying to rip his flesh off. Howard panted in agony.

"Katie, stop that!" Mr. Cooper said, reaching back to swat her leg. She glared at her father for a moment, but stopped moving. Her face was covered in red patches again.

"We're going to have a baby!" Howard said quickly.

Mr. Cooper lowered the volume on the radio. "You're what?" he whispered.

Howard sneered at Katie. Despite her brutal attempt to silence him, he'd outfoxed her.

"We're—"

"You're *what?*" her father spat.

Vaguely Howard registered that Mr. Cooper was angry, but he was still focused on the victory over Katie. "We're going to—" Howard continued gamely.

"YOU'RE *WHAT?*" her father screamed. He had turned in his seat to stare directly at Howard.

Howard finally realized that the Coopers were upset. He

swallowed hard and fell silent. Katie's mother buried her face in her hands, sobbing.

"Sir ...," Howard started.

"*YOU'RE WHAT?*" Mr. Cooper bellowed, bursting the euphoric bubble that had enveloped the young lovers for two weeks. The traffic light had turned green and drivers behind them honked impatiently, but Mr. Cooper didn't budge. He glared at Howard, and the combined effects of Mr. Cooper's rage and Katie's firm grip made Howard feel faint.

"What about *marriage?*" Mrs. Cooper wailed. "I thought you were going to tell us that you wanted to get *married.*"

Howard and Katie looked at each other in surprise. During two weeks of discussions about their future, they had not once mentioned marriage. *How was that possible?* Howard wondered. They had discussed marriage earlier in their relationship, and they'd agreed that they would wait until after they'd both graduated from college. But now, as they prepared for parenthood, neither of them had raised the question again. Howard wondered if the fact that they hadn't talked about it meant that they weren't ready for a life-long commitment. And if they weren't ready for marriage, how could they possibly be ready for parenthood? Having a child would bind them together more permanently than a marriage ever could.

Howard thought realistically about their situation for the first time in weeks. Yes, he could quit the UT football team, but he'd lose his scholarship. Could he really earn enough working at the mall to pay the rent on an apartment, feed three people, *and* pay tuition? His parents had three children already in college and two more at home, could they pay for his education after he gave up his scholarship? How did he expect to pay for Katie's classes when she resumed her studies?

Hopefully, her parents would pay, but what if they didn't? Howard hadn't thought about how much it would cost for the delivery in eight months. He didn't even know if Katie had health insurance. He assumed that she was covered on her parents' policy, but what about the baby. Could they add a child to that insurance, or would they need their own coverage. Would a job at the mall include medical benefits? One thing was certain—if Howard didn't have insurance, he couldn't afford to keep getting bitten by Katie.

Then a horrid thought entered his head—*would she bite the baby?*

Howard realized that despite the euphoria of the past two weeks, he was not ready to become a father—not then. Possibly, not ever.

"We're not ready," Howard said, quietly.

"You're what!" Mr. Cooper asked cautiously.

"We're not ready," Howard repeated, looking Katie's father in the eye. The older man nodded sagely. Howard looked at Katie. Though her face was still covered in splotches, her eyes looked relieved, and Howard thought that he felt her jaw loosen minutely.

At the hospital, Katie received another muscle relaxant, and Howard cursed in blessed relief when his hand was finally free. It took forty-eight internal and external stitches to close the wound, and a transfusion to replace the two and a half pints of blood he'd lost.

The next day, Mrs. Cooper drove Katie and Howard to an abortion clinic and wrote a check for the operation. A nurse took Katie back to an examination room, while Mrs. Cooper and Howard sat in the waiting room making nervous small talk; they flinched every time the door opened or the nurse called another name. Howard's hand ached inside the heavy gauze, and he understood that in the future, he would have to be more careful about where he put all his appendages.

For months afterward, Howard wondered how he would avoid becoming an accidental father. If he continued to have sex, he might get Katie (or a future girlfriend) pregnant. It seemed that he had only four choices—none of which was realistic. He could abstain from sex for the rest of his life—a nonstarter. He could continue to leave birth control in the hands of his girlfriend(s), but that was obviously risky. He could use a condom every time, but he knew he was unlikely to maintain prophylactic discipline in a committed, monogamous relationship. Or, he could get a vasectomy, but that was too drastic for a man his age.

About a year after the abortion, Howard and Katie broke up. Their relationship wasn't torn apart by any major disputes, by the dark residue of the abortion, or by any fresh bites. They were just young college students who'd slowly grown bored with each other. It was a good thing they hadn't had a child together.

Howard continued to be haunted by the abortion, and he vowed that no other woman would have to endure that surgery because of him ever again.

# thirty-five

Howard woke up Tuesday morning, bleary eyed and queasy. He felt as if he'd gone binge drinking the night before, but he'd had only three beers at Hooters. With the chicken wings, hamburger, basket of fries and ice cream, that was hardly enough to give him a buzz, let alone a hangover. But his head was pounding and the face staring back at him in the mirror was ashen. Both eyes were swollen and red—even the healthy one.

He absently grabbed clothes out of the closet, and then stumbled down to the kitchen for a cup of coffee. He climbed into his SUV and started the hour-long trek to work. Howard looked at other drivers on the crowded Interstate, but no one looked back at him. He wondered what they would say if they knew about Sophia's affair. Would they accept Bob's theory that women were allowed to cheat? Would Sophia's desire for motherhood win their forgiveness? In the message, Sophia had said, "What did you expect?" Maybe Howard had been a fool to expect that his wife would give up children to spend her life with him—but that's exactly what he had expected and what she had agreed to do before they got married.

Sophia had known from their third date that Howard did not want to become a father. The subject had come up during lunch at the Washington Park Grill on a sunny Saturday afternoon when the patio was open, and a steady stream of pedestrians strolled by on their way to the park. After they placed their order, Howard had asked Sophia if the rubber band on her wrist was a fashion statement.

Sophia had looked down, noticing it for the first time and laughed. It wasn't a cute red or green rubber band of the type that were cyclically in style among teenage girls. It was wide and tan with dirty black smudges on it, and it looked as if it had come off a newspaper that had moldered in the rain for several days.

"I was cleaning up," Sophia explained, "and I found this on the floor. I put it on my wrist because it was the easiest way to hold it until I got to the trash can, but then I forgot."

"Well," Howard said, "it looks very nice with your watch."

She held her arm up in the sunlight. "Then maybe I'll leave it there." And she did. She wasn't embarrassed. She didn't seem to care if anyone else in the restaurant noticed the grungy rubber band on her wrist. She was at ease with herself, and Howard found that alluring.

After their meal, they sat at the table for a long time in companionable silence, sipping coffee and watching bikers, joggers and rollerbladers glide past on their way to Washington Park.

Eventually, Howard said, "I like you."

Sophia turned to look at him and smiled warmly. "I like you, too." She took his hand.

Howard smiled back, but his grin faltered as the rough texture of the rubber band grazed his wrist and reminded him that he had some moldering news that he needed to share. He took a long, slow breath and said, "Before things go much further. I need to tell you something important."

Sophia let go of his hand, stripped the rubber band off her wrist, and aimed it at his head. "You have a wife and three kids?" she guessed with a threatening glare.

Howard raised his hands defensively. "Nope. Never married, and no kids. You?"

Sophia shook her head and holstered the rubber band. "I got close once, but it didn't work out."

"Close to kids or to marriage?"

"Actually both," she said softly. "I had an abortion when I was twenty-one." She sounded as if she still regretted it. "And I almost got married a few years ago."

"Sorry about the abortion," Howard said, taking her hand again.

She shrugged. "I was young. It wasn't time for me to have a baby ... but sometimes I wonder about how that little guy or girl would have turned out."

Howard said, "I know what you mean. My girlfriend in college had an abortion, and even though I've always been pro-choice, and still am, I was uncomfortable having her go through that."

"I'm pro-choice, too," Sophia said, "and I know I made the right decision for me, but it wasn't easy."

Silence fell over them again.

"So you need to tell me something?" Sophia said.

"Yeah," Howard said.

Sophia said, "I have a feeling, you're going to try to ruin this whole thing."

Howard said, "I hope not."

"Well, I'm braced for the worst. Go ahead and give it to me."

Howard paused for another deliberate sip of coffee.

Watching him, waiting for him, Sophia said, "God! It seems so serious!"

Howard cleared his throat. Then, as matter-of-factly as he could, he said, "I'm going to have a vasectomy in two months."

Sophia sat back in her chair, staring at him. The waiter

came and asked if they needed anything else, and they shook their heads without taking their eyes off each other. After a moment, she said, "Just to be clear in my mind, a vasectomy is when they—." She scissored her fingers.

"Exactly."

"I thought men didn't do that until after they'd had a few kids."

"I'm unusual."

"You don't *like* kids?"

"I love kids," Howard said. "I just don't want to have any."

"Why not?"

*Why not?* was a question Howard hadn't quite figured out how to answer. Was it because he was selfish? Was it because he didn't believe he could handle children? Was it because he hated kids? Was it a fear of commitment? Was it an attempt to avoid responsibility? He'd been accused of all these motives by his previous girlfriends, family, friends, and even complete strangers.

"I've tried to explain," Howard said, "but no one understands."

"You mean no one *agrees*," Sophia said.

Howard paused to consider whether she might be right. "No," he said, eventually. "At this point, I don't expect agreement. I'd be happy if someone merely understood my point of view, or even just accepted it."

"Well," Sophia said, "it can be tough for people to understand or accept something that they disagree with."

Howard nodded.

"Listen," Sophia said, sitting forward and taking his hands in hers. "I appreciate your telling me this now. If you were a jerk, you could have waited until after we'd slept together or after I'd fallen in love with you. Or you could have not told me at all. You could have secretly had your vasectomy and then just led me on. The fact that you're telling me now is very respectful. So just explain yourself as best you can, and I'll try to listen with an open mind."

"Thank you." Howard raised one of her hands to his lips and kissed it gently. He thought for a moment. "Imagine," he said slowly, "a teacher takes ten kids to 7-11, and she tells them that they can have Slurpees."

"Is this part of your explanation?"

"I think it might help if I start off with an analogy."

"Okay, I'm imagining kids and Slurpees."

"Now imagine one of the kids—we'll call him Timmy—doesn't want one."

"Why not?" Sophia asked.

"My point, exactly," Howard said. "Why does Timmy have to explain himself?"

Sophia released his hands, and thought for a while, playing with the rubber band. "I see. Asking *why not* assumes that something is wrong with Timmy."

"Yes!" Howard said excitedly. He had never met anyone who understood him so quickly. "The other nine kids don't have to explain why they *want* Slurpees, and the teacher doesn't have to explain why she wants to buy them Slurpees. The only person who has to come up with an explanation is the kid who doesn't want one."

"Timmy *is* out of the norm," Sophia said.

"Why do *you* want to have children?" Howard asked, turning the question on her.

"How do you know that I do?"

Howard smiled. "You said you got an abortion because it wasn't *time* for you to have a baby. That suggests that eventually it will be time."

"Good point."

"So why do you want kids?"

She picked up her coffee cup and sipped from it slowly, studying Howard over the rim. "No one has ever asked me to explain." She took another moment to think. "How about this: I want to know what it feels like to make love when you're trying to make a baby. I want experience the physical and the emotional changes of pregnancy, and I want to anticipate the arrival of my child. I want to experience the bond that gets created between a man and a woman when they have a child together. I want to experience the unconditional love that parents and children feel toward each other. I want to watch my son or daughter grow up and learn to walk and talk, go to school, play sports, fall in love, get married and have families of their own. I want to teach them my values, and help them turn into the adults that they want to become. I want the special relationship and life-changing experience of raising children."

She paused for a long moment. "I guess that's it."

Howard gave her an approving nod. "That's a thoughtful answer."

"Thank you. So should I assume that you don't want those things?"

"It's not that I don't want the special relationship or the experiences," Howard said. "I just don't want the enormous responsibility. You gave a good answer, but you didn't list a single downside."

Sophia shrugged. "Maybe I believe the pluses outweigh the minuses."

"Maybe, but I'll bet that you don't actually think about the minuses."

"So you focus on the worst parts of parenthood, and you

believe that overall it will be a bad experience for you?"

"Not at all. Like you, I assume that I'll love the *best* parts of parenthood—who wouldn't? But the best parts are byproducts of the necessary parts. I've spent a lot of time with my nieces, nephews and other kids, and I love the wonderful energy that kids have and the special brand of love that they inspire. I agree with you that there doesn't seem to be anything that can compare to the love that parents feel toward their children. But I also see the challenges of parenthood. It's a 24-hour-a-day responsibility, and once you make the decision to have a child, you're in it for life. I admire people who take on the challenge, but I realized years ago, that I just wasn't sure if I wanted that for myself. And if I'm not absolutely sure, then I can't take the risk, because there's no turning back."

Sophia didn't respond for a while. "I can't argue with you," she said finally. "I guess it's very responsible of you to not have children if you don't think it's right for you."

"Thank you for understanding."

"I don't *agree* with you," Sophia said with a wink, "but I do *understand* you."

"Such rare grace," Howard smiled.

"But," Sophia said, "it's one thing for Timmy to decide that he doesn't want a Slurpee; it's another thing for him to dismantle the Slurpee machine. That's what you're doing with your vasectomy."

"Only for me," Howard said. "Everyone else can still have their Slurpees."

"Not anyone who stays with you."

Howard said, "That's why I'm telling you now." Each of his previous three serious relationships had ended, in part, because of his reluctance to become a father. After one girlfriend tearfully accused him of leading her on, Howard had made it a rule to share his feelings about parenthood no later than the third date. This policy had produced mixed results. Most women were turned off by this knowledge, and a few were even offended that he'd raised the issue.

"It's too soon to talk about anything like that," a date had said a few years ago. "Imagine how uncomfortable you might feel if I started talking about marriage on our third date. You're talking about children as if we're already serious."

They never had a fourth date.

Howard hadn't met many young women who were willing to surrender motherhood. And he didn't blame them. It was a lot to give up.

The waiter returned and refilled their coffee cups.

"So you're really going to go through with it?" Sophia asked.

"With what?"

"The vasectomy."

"It's the only way to ensure that I won't accidentally become a father."

"But why two months from now? Why not tomorrow? Or why not a year ago?"

"I finally found a urologist who will perform the surgery."

"*Finally*? You've been looking for a while?"

"I've spoken to several doctors, but they've all refused. They said that I was too young. They were convinced that I would change my mind. Even the doctor I'm scheduled with now is reluctant, so he advised me to think about it for three months. If I still feel the same way after the waiting period, then he'll give me a vasectomy."

"He told you this a month ago?"

"That's right."

"Then it looks like I've got two months to get you to fall

in love with me and change your mind," Sophia said with a smile. She said it in such a light and airy way that Howard thought she was joking. When they talked about the date years later, Sophia said she'd also believed that she was joking. But now, Howard finally understood that, Sophia had been quite serious that day. She had left lunch believing that if Howard loved *her* enough, he would have a child with her.

**********

Soon Howard and Sophia were spending nearly every night together. He was diligent in his use of condoms, and though Sophia occasionally commented about the cuteness of children that she saw when they were out in public, they didn't have another serious conversation about Howard's impending vasectomy until the day before the surgery.

"Just put it off for a few more months," Sophia had pleaded that day, her eyes wet with a desperate longing. "If you just wait a while you might want to have children with *me*."

Howard countered, "It's not about *who* I might want to have children with. It's about whether I want to be a parent at all."

"But we could do it together," she insisted. "It wouldn't be so hard if we did it together. It would be fun!"

Howard was baffled by this line of reasoning. He didn't think of parenthood as a project that two people took on because it would be *fun* or some sort of mutual challenge. He didn't doubt that it was logistically and emotionally easier for two committed people to raise a child than for one, but he saw parenthood as an experience that each partner had to desire solely for the independent relationship that he or she would have with the child. Especially given the high divorce rate, it seemed foolish to think of parenthood primarily as an experience that a couple would share.

"Parenthood is like skydiving," Howard said, reaching for another analogy. "In my case, I don't want to experience the sensation of freefall, so even if you were next to me when I jumped out of the plane it wouldn't change what I was experiencing." He felt that he owed it to both of them to make it absolutely clear that he was not going to change his mind. "I just don't want children," he said bluntly.

# thirty-six

The next morning, Howard drove himself to the doctor's office and walked into the surgical room without a single pang of doubt. He knew that he might push Sophia away, but he was willing to risk losing her to ensure that he wouldn't become a parent by accident.

He lay back on the examination table and placed his legs in the stirrups, and the doctor raised a sheet at Howard's waist, so Howard couldn't see anything on the other end of the table. The surgery marked the only time that a man had ever caressed Howard's balls. A nurse named Rachel was standing at Howard's side watching the action on the other side of the sheet. She was cute, with short sandy hair and blue eyes. Howard was getting turned on watching Rachel watching him, but he had to remind himself that it was the white-haired doctor—*not Rachel!*—rubbing warm soapy water onto his testicles. Howard dove deep into his imagination, searching for a vile and disgusting thought on which to concentrate. He envisioned himself strapped to a medieval torture table, about to be savagely castrated with a pair of rusty shears, and, thankfully, this gruesome image kept his penis from responding to the doctor's too light touch.

The procedure—from soaping, shaving, local injection, incision, snipping, cauterization and suture—took only twenty minutes. Howard was admonished to avoid exercise for several weeks, to call if he had inflammation or pain, and to have sex when he felt up to it (no pun intended). He had to produce a semen sample in one month so the doctor could make sure there were no lingering sperm. All in all, Howard's vasectomy was quick and painless. He and Sophia had sex two days later—with a condom—and Howard never had any medical complications from the surgery. But now that his wife was auditioning Davis Delaney as a potential father for her children, he could see that their relationship had become infected the moment the doctor closed the incision.

Initially, Sophia had refused to talk about the vasectomy except to ask Howard how he was feeling, physically. They'd kept dating for about six weeks, but it was clear to Howard that she felt pressed to make up her mind about children. Now that she couldn't entertain the possibility that Howard would love *her* enough to want children, she had to decide whether she loved *him* enough to live without kids. Eventually, he lost that competition.

"What's the point?" she asked, sobbing. "I love you, and I really believe that you're the man that I'm supposed to marry, but if you don't want children, what's the point?"

Howard, crying too, had agreed with her. There was no chance that he was going to get his vasectomy reversed, and there seemed to be no chance that she would give up on children. It was a sad parting for both of them, but they both believed it was for the best.

After they separated, Howard started dating J-Lo, and Sophia dated a commercial real estate broker. But they'd both been miserable. Eventually, they realized that, despite their incompatibility about children, they loved each other. So they'd reunited, but rarely talked about kids.

Now Howard could see that they'd made assumptions about each other that had been completely off the mark. Because Howard was stable, conservative, seemed to enjoy interacting with children, and was totally in love with Sophia, she had concluded that he would eventually reverse the vasectomy.

Howard had erroneously concluded that Sophia would grow to embrace a life without children of her own, because her wildest fantasies always seemed to involve being untethered from responsibility. She dreamed of leaving her gallery and traveling through Central and South America sampling the rustic beauty of indigenous art while carrying nothing more than the possessions she could stuff into her backpack. She wanted to move to a remote Indian village and study yoga for a year. None of these exotic dreams was compatible with having a baby, because they reflected Sophia's desire to improvise rather than plan.

Howard thought Sophia's desire for complete flexibility demonstrated that, deep down, she didn't want to have children, and eventually, she seemed to realize that, too.

That was when she started calling him *Mounds*.

At first he had simply laughed at this enigmatic nickname without asking for an explanation, but after a few days, he'd had to ask Sophia what it meant.

"'Cause Almond Joy's got *nuts!*" Sophia exclaimed, showing him her wickedest smile. He couldn't help laughing with her. Soon, Howard understood that this was her way of telling him that she accepted him as he was, with no warranty, no guarantees, and no nuts, as it were.

A month later, he proposed to her on the conveyor belt at Denver International Airport. While he was hugging her and the crowd was cheering, he reminded her that marrying him would mean giving up on children.

"So even though you said yes right now," he whispered, "you should think about it for a few days."

"Watch out!" several people yelled.

"I don't need to think about it, Mounds," she said, squeezing him tight. "I love you, and I want to be your wife."

They had tumbled off the conveyor belt into a marriage that now seemed doomed.

# thirty-seven

"Lord, have mercy!" Bob Carson exclaimed. "Did you get dressed in the dark?"

Howard looked down at his suit and realized that his pants and jacket didn't match. The pants were navy blue with narrow pinstripes. The jacket was black. Somehow, he had grabbed pieces of two different suits as he'd stumbled out of the house.

"I didn't notice," Howard said, absently slipping off the jacket and laying it over the back of a chair.

"That's barely an improvement," Bob said. "That shirt … and that tie …" He shook his head. The shirt was white with red vertical stripes. The tie had red and white horizontal stripes. Even though the current fashion permitted patterns on patterns, these two items simply didn't belong together.

"And your hair is uncombed," Bob said. "Your breath smells like a West African steam bath, and you generally look like shit."

"Thank you," Howard said.

"You've got to pull yourself together," Bob said. "I talked to Ah-zoon-tit and Kinky today, and they want to get together with us tonight."

"Aziza and Keiko."

"That's them. They're hot for me and you, amigo, and since your wife has clearly decided that marriage isn't her cup of tea, I think you need to put these girls on the front burner."

"I can't do that," Howard said.

"Sure you can," Bob insisted. "I've been through this a few

255

times myself. It's like the old saying, when *wife* knocks you down, you've got to get back up. You never know, Ah-zun-tite or Kinko could become your next ex-wife."

"Not tonight," Howard said. "I have to go to an HOA meeting."

"Are you out of your mind? You'd rather deal with that domestic shit rather than go out with two hot chicks?"

"I got a summons. I have to go."

"How can you stand living in a place where the HOA is so far up your ass they get to tell you what brand of toilet paper to use?"

"It's not that bad," Howard said. Although he often complained about the HOA Nazis, he got defensive when Bob did it. "They help keep the neighborhood looking orderly."

"Yeah? Prisons are orderly too. You ever think of that?"

# thirty-eight

The rest of the day dragged on. Howard worked lethargically, ignored his phone, and snuck out before 3 p.m. without saying goodbye to Bob or anyone else.

Even in lighter, mid-afternoon traffic, it still took forty-five minutes to get back to Highlands Ranch. As he pulled into his driveway, Howard noticed Mrs. Stephenson watching him as always, but for a moment in the glare of the descending sun, she looked different. She looked younger, livelier, more like a normal neighbor. He waved, and amazingly, she waved back. Howard was startled. In the three years he'd lived across the street, she'd never waved back. After Howard parked, he stepped back out of the garage and looked up at her again. The glare was still reflecting off her windows, making it tough to see, but, eventually, Howard concluded that she was gone. He walked down to the mailbox, wondering if Mrs. Stephenson was still angry about the landscaping he'd damaged over the weekend. Her yard looked almost as good as new. The sod that Gene and Jean had replaced looked healthy.

Howard retrieved the mail and shuffled into the house. He threw a frozen dinner into the microwave, and then sat in his recliner with his eyes closed, waiting for the microwave timer to go off.

He was sinking again. Navy blue pinstriped trousers, black jacket, red-and-white-striped shirt, red-and-white-striped tie, and his black leather briefcase. Everything was mismatched, and everything around him seemed incongruous. He was in the middle of a forest that was in the middle of a city. Monkeys, dressed like people, walked right past him, but no one saw him. The murky substance slowly climbed up his body, but rather than waiting impassively, Howard looked around for something to grab onto. He twisted his head from side to side, searching, and finally, he saw a single, tall rose behind him. It was brilliant red, with thick, leafy petals. He reached back slowly, and wrapped his fingers around the stalk just below the bloom. He knew the flower's roots weren't strong enough to anchor him to pull himself out of the bog, but he hoped he could use it to change his position. If he could just move closer to the edge, he could grab something else. He pulled as carefully as he could. Slowly. Slowly. Suddenly the flower tore out of the soil. Howard looked at it helplessly for a long moment as he continued to sink. He looked down and saw the warm glow, and again felt that if he could just get to it, he would be saved. But he knew that it was deep below the surface, and he couldn't possibly hold his breath long enough to reach it. Soon his head was submerged. He kept one arm extended, holding the rose aloft, as if he could save it, but eventually, it too was consumed.

Howard woke up instantly. *I sent her roses,* he realized.

He saw Davis Delaney's face floating eight feet off the ground. Howard blinked twice, but the image didn't disappear. When Howard had been drunk Saturday night, he'd seen Davis' face. Now he was seeing it again, but this time he realized that Davis wasn't hovering *outside* the window. The artist was *inside* the house, hanging over the mantle. The image hidden in the green squiggles of Cynthia's painting, *Hidden Treasure,* was a picture of Davis Delaney with long hair, eyes looking straight ahead, and a smug victorious smile creasing his face. Howard stared at the painting, stunned. He could not believe that Sophia had hung a picture of her boyfriend in plain sight, where all of their visiting friends could see it, but where her husband, until now, could not.

Howard couldn't tear his eyes away from the painting. For the hundredth time, he wondered if he knew a single thing about Sophia. He never would have believed that she was capable of such malice.

Howard leaped to his feet and tried to snatch the picture off the wall. He yanked the bottom of the frame, but the painting was held in place by a pair of hooks that had been drilled into the studs. Howard needed to lift *up*, then *out* to get the painting off its moorings, but he just kept pulling down, trying to tear the picture off the wall with brute force. Finally, he heard something crack. He gave it one more yank, and the picture snapped off the hooks. The bottom edge slammed into Howard's mouth, gashing his lip. A thin mist of blood sprayed everywhere. He stumbled backward and fell heavily onto the coffee table. It creaked ominously under his weight. He sat up and delicately probed his mouth. The painting was at his feet, and Davis was still staring up at him smugly, as if the artist had deliberately punched Howard in the mouth. Howard grabbed the painting and flung it at the wall, intending to smash it into pieces. Instead, the big wooden frame sailed through the living room window with a loud crash. Glass cascaded onto the sill, and the painting tumbled several times before coming to rest halfway to the street.

Howard, breathing hard and bleeding, finally realized that throwing Davis out of the house was a good idea, but it was a couple of months too late. He marched into the kitchen and grabbed a hammer out of a drawer. Then he climbed through the shattered window recklessly, dislodging shards of glass with his shoulders and crunching them under his feet. He flipped the painting over and saw that the frame was secured by sixteen gleaming nails. He stabbed the claw end of the hammer into the wood and retracted the nails one at a time, grunting loudly. The nails squealed against the wood as if they were in pain, but they came out and fell impotently into the grass.

Several of his neighbors nervously peered out of their windows, but they snapped their drapes closed quickly whenever Howard's bloody, manic face rose in their direction. Once the nails were removed, the frame flopped open, but it still retained its basic shape, because the canvas was stapled to the wood at three-inch intervals. Howard dropped the picture, scooped up the nails, and walked to Davis' van. He pounded the nails, methodically, into the hard rubber sidewalls of Davis' tires. The wheels sighed dramatically and melted into the pavement.

Howard couldn't believe that Sophia had been sleeping with Davis, had taken him to *their* favorite places, and had hung a picture of him inside the house. How many more clues did Howard need? He stepped back from the van and let the cool wind blow through his hair. How many clues he *needed* was a good question, he realized, but a better question might be *how many clues were there?* He scowled, thinking about Sophia's credit card statement in the folder on her desk. Had she left it out deliberately, knowing that he would find it? Was there something else that he was supposed to see?

He marched back into the house—through the front door this time—and approached the stairs. He walked into Sophia's office and sat down at her desk. He pulled out her American Express statement and dragged his fingers down the page. Aside from the charges for the watch, Panzano's and the Hotel Monaco, everything looked mundane.

Movement across the street caught his eye. Mrs. Stephenson

was not at the window with her binoculars, which was surprising given the excitement of his wild behavior on the front lawn. She was on her knees pulling on something, and in the dim light of the setting sun, Howard could just see the top of her head and her back each time she yanked up. He realized that he'd never seen her window from this perspective because Sophia's home office had the only second-story window in the house with a view of Mrs. Stephenson's house.

But what was she doing over there?

*Binoculars!*

Howard ran to the master bedroom and rooted through the big walk-in closet, searching for a set of binoculars he hadn't used since he attended a Rockies game a year ago. It took a few minutes, but he finally located them. He pulled them out of the case and ran back down the hall. When he reached the window, Mrs. Stephenson was still on the floor, pulling back and forth. Howard trained the binoculars just above the window ledge.

From what little he could see, Mrs. Stephenson was younger and more active than he had expected. He'd only seen her standing nearly motionless in the window, spying with her high-powered binoculars, and he'd always thought she looked matronly. But now he could see that her hair was brown with blonde highlights. She was wearing a fashionable black coat with the collar turned up, and judging by her shoulders and back, she was thin—not at all what he had imagined.

Then she sat up, breathing hard, and Howard saw her face in profile.

*It was J-Lo!*

She took a deep breath and bent over again. He realized that she wasn't pulling—she was pumping! Mrs. Stephenson must have had a heart attack! Howard dropped the binoculars, ran

261

down the stairs, and barreled out of the house. He sprinted across the street and tried Mrs. Stephenson's front door; it was locked. He ran around to the back door, which was unlocked. He entered through her kitchen and took the stairs two at a time.

Gasping after the long sprint, Howard crested the top step and came to a complete stop, dumbfounded. He bent over, hands on knees, breathing heavily as he stared at three computer stations surrounded by several dozen closed-circuit TV screens. Wires ran everywhere—strapped together in bundles of ten or so, racing across the floor in every direction, and stereo speakers were mounted in opposing corners.

"Tim? Is that you?" J-Lo called from the front of the house.

Howard's breathing finally started to slow down. The entire upstairs area was an electronic command center that roughly resembled the bridge of an ocean liner. *Or the Star Trek Enterprise*, Howard thought. Three recliners faced the big wall of monitors. The middle chair had armrests packed with controls, and the other seats were set back a couple of feet, flanking the middle chair like fighter jets in formation. Off to his right he saw a table with a coffee machine and a selection of donuts and bagels. A huge marker board on his left was covered with handwritten notes—

10/12 – 12135 Pen. Dr. – wheel barrel f. yard

10/12 – 12120 Pen. Dr. – bulb out f. porch

10/13 – 12148 Pen. Dr. – garage door open

And on and on down the board. Howard recognized the citations as references to houses on his street—Pendleton Drive.

"Tim?" J-Lo called. "I could use some help in here."

Howard walked slowly toward her voice. As he passed each doorway, he saw a pair of railroad tracks near the windows. They seemed to encircle the entire top floor.

"Goddamnit!" J-Lo cursed. "This stupid thing!"

Finally, Howard stepped into the front room and saw J-Lo hunched over Mrs. Stephenson's inert form, trying to pull the old lady up. Mrs. Stephenson was lying on her right side, propped up on her right elbow. Her left elbow was extended toward the ceiling, and Howard knew from the position that her hands were wrapped around a set of binoculars in front of her eyes. He looked down and discovered that her body ended about mid-thigh; she was connected by a narrow pole to a trolley on train tracks.

J-Lo screamed, "Tim! I need your—" She stopped abruptly when she saw Howard standing in the doorway.

They stared at each other for several long beats, as the shock of meeting in this room, under these circumstances, stilled both of their tongues. J-Lo recovered first. She stood and shook her brown hair out sensually, fluffing it with both hands. Her black pea-coat was unbuttoned, revealing a multicolored silk shirt. She wore blue jeans with six-inch cuffs, and a pair of open-toed black Enzos.

"What happened to you?" she asked. She looked at his mismatched shirt and tie, his cut swollen bottom lip, and his bloody teeth.

"What are you doing?" he asked.

"What are *you* doing?" J-Lo countered, walking toward him slowly, as if stalking him. "Coming in here without knocking. Shame on you, Howard!"

"I saw you through the window," Howard said numbly.

"And?" J-Lo asked suggestively, taking a couple more steps forward.

"I thought Mrs. Stephenson was having a heart attack."

J-Lo laughed. "Not much chance of that."

"All this time, she's just been a mannequin?"

"Not always," J-Lo said, glancing back at the dummy on the floor. "The real Mrs. Stephenson spent most of her time standing in the window with her binoculars. When she died three years ago, she donated her house to the homeowners association."

"She died?"

J-Lo shrugged and inched closer. "She left instructions to turn her house into an HOA listening station."

Howard shook his head, still trying to comprehend all of this. "She's a mannequin?"

"On tracks and on a motion detector. It's pretty amazing actually. This thing can scoot from window to window, and from up here, you can physically see part or all of forty-seven houses—especially with the magnification, and the microphones are incredible. They can pick up sound from over two hundred feet away."

"You can't spy on people like this!"

She stopped in front of him. "I have to make sure the residents are abiding by the covenants." They stared at each other for a moment. "Are you abiding, Howard?" She took another step forward, getting so close that her breasts touched his abdomen. They hadn't been alone together, inside, in years, and J-Lo seemed to sense that Howard's willpower was weakening. "Or are you breaking the rules?" Her voice was sultry, but her botoxed face didn't betray any emotion. She took his hands and placed them on her hips, and then wrapped her arms around his neck, laying her head in the hollow of his shoulder.

The softness of her body instantly aroused Howard.

J-Lo smiled and softly kissed the corner of his mouth. She kissed his cheek and sucked on his neck. She paused to take off her jacket, holding Howard's eyes as she unbuttoned her shirt and let it slide off her shoulders. She stood in front of him in blue jeans and a push-up bra, her huge breasts bulging up obscenely. She hugged him again, pressing against him and slowly weaving back and forth like a snake charmer wooing a cobra.

"Does that feel good, baby?" she whispered.

Howard's eyes were closed, and his hands dropped to his sides. She dragged her tongue sensually up his neck. The whole situation was surreal to Howard. He was standing over a mannequin of the late Mrs. Stephenson, inside a house that had been turned into a high-tech surveillance post, looking out the window at his own house, where his wife had been fucking Davis Delaney for weeks, and now he was being seduced by J-Lo—who would probably levy an assessment against him if he didn't fuck her according to the rigid mandates of the RIGs.

Outside, Howard saw Bob's Range Rover limousine pull up in front of his house. Bob, Aziza and Keiko climbed out.

"Hey," Howard said.

"Oh? You like that?" J-Lo asked, nibbling on his earlobe. He looked at her face, but it was as expression-less as the mannequin on the floor.

Aziza and Keiko shuffled quickly toward the door. Their long heavy coats were cinched up against the cold. Bob walked into the yard and picked up the wobbly painting of Davis Delaney.

Suddenly, Howard heard a male voice behind him say, "What the heck is going on?"

Howard and J-Lo turned to see Tim Gorman, one of the HOA board members, staring at them. He was a slim, gray-haired accountant with perpetually raised eyebrows that gave him the appearance of being startled. Howard knew that at the moment, Tim was genuinely surprised.

J-Lo shrieked and covered herself. "Get out of here, Tim!" She squatted down to grab her shirt.

"I was just … coming … over to …," Tim sputtered, his eyes locked on J-Lo's nearly naked upper body.

"Get the fuck out of here!" she screamed, holding her shirt up in front of her.

The F-word seemed to jolt both Tim and Howard out of a trance. Tim, looking even more startled than usual, turned and ran down the hall. Howard heard him clump down the stairs.

Howard started to leave.

"Don't go—" J-Lo started, reaching out to grab his arm. "Listen, we should—"

Howard said, "I can't," and walked out of the room.

When Howard left Mrs. Stephenson's house, Bob Carson was across the street, yelling into the broken window.

"Hooooow-waaaaaard!"

Howard trotted over and said, "What are you guys doing here?"

Bob jumped and they all turned to him. "We wanted to see you before we leave town tomorrow," Keiko said.

"What we're doing is freezing our asses off," Bob said. He saw Howard's bloody mouth and said, "Looks like you lost the fight. Is the boyfriend back?"

Howard shook his head and opened the door for them.

"What are you wearing?" Keiko asked gently. Both women stamped their feet as they came into the foyer, trying to warm up.

Bob held up the painting and asked, "Who threw this out?" Howard looked at the picture, but he could no longer make out Davis' face. Now it looked like the rest of Cynthia's paintings—just rows of meaningless green squiggles.

"It's a man," Aziza said, after a moment.

"Isn't that the guy who came to the restaurant with your wife on Friday night?" Keiko asked.

"It was hanging up there?" Aziza asked, pointing to the empty spot over the mantle.

"Why would you have a picture of your wife's boyfriend in your house?" Bob asked.

Howard didn't have the voice to answer any of these questions. He stared at his hands for a long moment as a memory came back to him. He said, "I dreamed that I had a rose."

Aziza tiptoed through broken glass to examine the shattered front window. She turned back toward Howard and said, "There's a woman across the street, watching us with binoculars."

"Are you okay, Howard?" Keiko asked, scowling fearfully. She examined the aging bruise around his eye, the long cut on his bottom lip, the fresh blood in his mouth and the haunted look in his eyes.

Staring at the picture, Howard recalled the dream he had had just before waking up and seeing Davis Delaney's face. "Sophia …," he said, blotting his lips with the back of his hand, "is *not* in New York."

"She's here?" Bob whispered, looking around guiltily.

Aziza whispered, "I thought you said she left for a conference?"

"Should we leave?" Keiko wondered quietly.

Howard had had a rose in his hands, but it hadn't been strong enough to save him from the bog. The flower told him something that he should have realized days ago. He picked up the phone and dialed directory assistance. Once he was connected to Sophia's hotel in New York, he asked the operator if the hotel was hosting a Contemporary Art Convention.

"Yes, sir, we certainly are," she said, proudly. "The exhibits are on display in our conference center, and they're open to the public daily from 8 a.m. to 9 p.m. through Saturday."

At least Sophia hadn't lied about that. Howard asked the operator to put him through to her room. He heard fingers clicking on a computer keyboard.

"I'm sorry, sir. We have the reservation, but that guest never checked in."

"Never checked in?" Howard repeated dully.

"No, sir."

He turned off the phone and stood still with his eyes closed.

Bob snapped his fingers. "Wake up, Howard!"

"Howard?" Keiko reached out carefully to touch his arm, and his eyes flew open. She jerked her hand back. "Are you okay?" she asked.

He looked at her for a long moment as if he didn't recognize her. Then he said, "I sent flowers."

"To me?" Keiko asked, blushing.

"To Sophia," Howard said. "Roses. Saturday."

"Ah, that's right," Bob said. "I tried to talk him out of it. I told him that a man can't surprise a woman with flowers, because she'll think he's cheating on her."

Aziza put a hand to her forehead as if she had a headache. "Bob, what the hell are you talking about?"

"Women aren't innately romantic," Bob said, "so when a man tries to surprise her, she thinks he must be apologizing for something."

She put up a hand to stop Bob and turned back to Howard. "You sent your wife flowers and then what happened?"

"She never said 'thank you.'"

Aziza said, "Maybe she's been busy."

Keiko said, "Maybe she left you a message."

Howard laughed abruptly, baring his ghoulish, bloody teeth. "She left me a hundred messages," he said derisively, "but she never mentioned the flowers."

Howard knew that if Sophia had received the flowers—with the note *"Bassiff, have fun in New York! Mounds"*—she would have assumed that he'd sent them *after* learning of her affair. She would have seen them as a gesture of forgiveness, and she would have acknowledged them in one of her messages. Instead, she had berated him for not contacting her.

Brisk October wind blew through the broken window, causing the drapes to billow up in delicate waves. Aziza and Keiko shivered, but Howard, wearing just the mismatched dress shirt and tie, didn't notice the chill.

"Bob," Aziza said, "why don't you check in the garage and see if you can find something to cover this window."

Bob groused for a moment, but Aziza's intense glare propelled him into the garage.

Howard said, "Bob says that women are allowed to cheat."

"Howard, honey," Keiko said. "I'm worried about you. Things seem to be falling apart."

*"Allowed* to cheat?" Aziza asked. "In what way?"

"If they have a good reason," Howard said.

Bob walked back into the house with a nail gun in one hand, and a tarp in the other. "I found this," he said proudly. "We can nail it up over the window."

Keiko grabbed part of the tarp and helped pull it to the front window. "How will we get it all the way up there?" she asked, pointing toward the top.

"I saw a ladder," Bob said. He darted back into the garage and returned a minute later, easing a six-foot A-frame ladder through the door.

Like a school teacher addressing an eighth grader, Aziza said, "Bob, did you tell Howard that women are *allowed* to cheat?"

Everyone stared a Bob, who looked back defensively. He shrugged and set the ladder up near the window. "I was just making an observation." He grabbed the nail gun and climbed up onto the first rung.

"What observation?" Aziza insisted.

Bob glared at Howard, resenting that he had told the women about their Hooters conversation. What happened at Hooters was supposed to stay at Hooters.

"Look," Bob said, climbing as high as he could on the ladder, "in the movies the set-up is always the same. A man who cheats is portrayed as a dirty dog." He positioned the top corner of the tarp near the edge of the window and pressed the nail gun against it. When he pulled the trigger, the nail shot into the wood with a hard *thump*, and the gun jumped in his hand. Bob issued a satisfying grunt and pressed the gun to the wood again a foot farther along—*thump*. "But when a woman cheats"—he climbed down the ladder and repositioned it in the middle of the window so that he could reach both sides—"they show you a lot of scenes of her being abused"—*thump*—"or neglected"—*thump*—"or unappreciated"—*thump thump*—"or suffering in some other way that's supposed to make her affair seem legitimate." *thump thump thump*. "If you pay attention, it's pretty obvious that society is biased and women are allowed to cheat if they have a good reason." *Thump thump thump thump thump*. The tarp was a perfect fit for the window, and the room was instantly warmer without the harsh wind blowing in.

Aziza said, "Howard, even though Bob is your boss, you should ignore just about every word that comes out of his mouth."

"Do we have to stay in this room?" Keiko asked, her arms folded tightly across her chest. "I'm freezing."

"The basement's probably the warmest spot in the house," Bob said.

Before Howard could object, Bob and the women had

moved into the kitchen. "You're gonna *love* what Howard and Sophia have done down there," Bob promised. "It's plush!" They opened the door and started down the stairs.

Howard stayed rooted in place.

"You coming, Howard?" Bob called as they descended.

*Was he?*

"It's so dark!" Keiko exclaimed.

"We don't go down there when we have a guest," Howard said softly. He meant to say it loud enough for them to hear, but his throat was constricted and a low whisper was all he could manage. He and Sophia had generally protected the privacy of their artists by staying out of the basement—but clearly Sophia had broken that rule in spades.

The phone rang, and Howard picked it up automatically.

"Why did you cover the window?" a female voice asked fiercely.

"What is it, J-Lo?" Howard said.

"What's going on?" she demanded.

"What do you want?" Howard asked. He was preparing himself to descend into the cozy basement suite that had become a lover's nest.

J-Lo paused before answering, as if his query were more than just a perfunctory question. She seemed to be contemplating her deepest desires.

Eventually, she asked, "Who are those women?"

"Friends," Howard said.

"They didn't look like *friends*." She was breathing hard. "I hope you're not going to do something you'll regret."

Howard laughed mirthlessly. "At this point, I'm not sure it's possible for me to regret *anything* that I do."

J-Lo said, "Uncover the window so I can see!"

He hung up and walked toward the basement door. He stood

at the top of the stairs, looking down into the gloom for several minutes. He could hear Bob in the distance, describing the various rooms as if he were a tour guide. The stairs were dark. He reached out to the light switch, but when he flipped it nothing happened. He toggled the switch several times, but the bulb had burned out. The steps remained shrouded in darkness.

The phone rang again. Howard hadn't realized that he was still holding it.

"*What*, J-Lo?" Howard asked impatiently. He cocked his head as he studied the stairwell. He could only see the first seven steps, because the flight hit a small angled landing and made a ninety-degree turn. He knew that there were six more steps, before the staircase made another thirty-degree turn for the final three steps. Lights farther in the basement illuminated the first landing with a faint glow that perplexed Howard because it looked so familiar. Of course, he'd been down these stairs many times in the past three years, but the light wasn't normally burned out and the stairwell wasn't gloomy. Something about this scene reminded him of something he'd seen recently.

J-Lo said, "You need to get those goddamned hoochie-mamas out of your house, Howard!"

"What difference does it make to you?"

J-Lo said, "I just don't want you to do anything stupid."

"Weren't you just encouraging me to do something stupid with *you* in Mrs. Stephenson's house?"

"That was different," she said.

Howard could smell Sophia. His nose picked up a light jasmine scent that seemed to be emanating from the warm glow on the landing.

J-Lo said softly, "Don't you sometimes wonder if we quit too soon? Like we might have had something special if we'd just given it a chance?" She sounded sweet and innocent—

nothing like the woman who bellowed at her neighbors through a bullhorn on Saturday mornings. Howard hadn't heard this voice in years, and it caught his attention. He was not surprised that J-Lo still fantasized about what their relationship *could* have been. She never seemed to recover from any emotional pain. When her feelings got hurt, she'd escape by putting her emotions into a mental zip-lock bag, labeling it, and placing it in her mind's freezer, where it would lay dormant for years without spoiling. Every now and then, she would rummage through her mind, yank out a bag, pop it into her mental microwave, and minutes later, the odor of old hurt would swirl around her and she would feel anguish or regret as fresh as the day she'd put it away.

"I really care about you, Howard," J-Lo said in her pillow talk voice. "Alan and I have been on the outs for years, and this time I think we're separated for good." Her voice drifted off. "Things seem to be winding down for you and Sophia, too, and I just thought—"

Howard, still standing at the top of the basement stairs, suddenly recalled where he had seen this pale glow.

"My dream!" he exclaimed.

"What?" J-Lo asked, confused but hopeful. "I'm your ... your dream?"

Every time the thick substance had swallowed Howard, he'd seen muted light far below him.

"I've gotta go," he said.

"Howard, wait!" J-Lo said. "I've dreamed about you, too! I've—"

He dropped the phone on the floor and lowered his right foot onto the first step; the unseen wet concrete wrapped around his ankle. It was neither warm nor cool, but it was remarkably familiar. Its grip was firm. He took another step and his leg was immersed up to the knee. After two more steps, the substance was past his waist. He continued down and took a deep breath just before his head sank below the surface. He kept his eyes on the warm light that grew brighter as he approached. The scent of Sophia was stronger down here. Lingering tendrils of her perfume floated to him, and he detected the gentle fragrance of her body lotion, her Aveda hair conditioner, and the sweet scent of her sweat. He smelled Davis Delaney, too. The artist's scent clung to the walls and rose up from the carpet like the stench of raw sewage.

When Howard finally reached the bottom of the staircase, he paused for a long moment, and then inhaled dramatically. After holding his breath all the way down, he was relieved to discover that he could breathe.

On his right was an art niche carved into the wall; a small spotlight in the ceiling was trained on a Davis Delaney's painting titled *Are you sure you want to shut down?* It was a picture of a laptop computer, closed, sitting on a desktop with a huge nail hammered through it. The point of the nail was visible on the underside of the desk.

Howard heard Bob and Aziza arguing. He continued down a hallway, past a small laundry room, and past an artist's studio with one painting on an easel covered by a white sheet, and several completed and half-finished canvases leaning against the walls. He passed a workout room, where a treadmill, an elliptical machine, and a small cluster of free weights were arrayed on foam rubber mats. He finally walked into a wide sitting area that had two leather couches, a honey-oak coffee table and a flat-screen television. Bob and the women were just coming out of the bedroom.

"There he is!" Bob said.

"Howard," Aziza said, "please tell me that you don't believe that women are *allowed* to cheat."

The smell of Sophia was overwhelming. Howard wondered how much time his wife had spent down here.

"Sophia wants children," he said matter-of-factly. "Doesn't that somehow make her affair seem justified?"

"*Justified* is the wrong word," Aziza said. "There's no justification for having an affair."

Bob snorted.

Aziza continued, "Despite what Bob says, women do not have a free pass."

Bob asked, "Then why is it that a woman cheating can be a love story, but a story about a man cheating can't?"

"That's the wrong question," Aziza said. "A better question would be why a movie about a woman cheating *has* to be a love story."

Howard scowled. "What do you mean?"

Aziza said, "This is a very paternalistic, patriarchal society. Men control all of the major institutions, define everything to their advantage, and, most importantly, they shape the way that women are judged."

"Pu-leeze," Bob said. "This women's lib shit is so yesterday. Look at you two. You've got great jobs. You make a lot of money. All kinds of women are going off to college, buying houses, getting divorces, getting custody of the kids, extorting child support and alimony from men and getting pretty much everything else they want. So don't give us this crap about men having all the power."

Aziza paused for a long moment, and Bob preened, thinking that he had stumped her. Then, in a long-suffering tone, she said, "Bob, there's so much in that little sound-bite that I hardly know where to start."

"I'll bet," Bob said proudly.

"For the moment, let's just focus on sex."

Sophia's scent swirled around Howard and made him feel lightheaded.

Bob said, "*That's* what I like. Let's talk about *sex*, baby!" He rubbed his hands together, leering at her.

"Suppose a sixteen-year-old girl goes to a party, gets drunk and has sex with three of her male classmates. What would you call her?"

"A ho!" Bob exclaimed.

"Yes, most of society—even other women—would call her a whore or a slut. Everyone in her school would hear about it, and for the rest of her high school career, she would be known as a slut. Ten years later, when everyone came back for their reunion, they would still refer to her as a slut. Twenty years later, she would be a slut. She would never escape the label from that one night of sexual experimentation."

Howard could detect his wife's odor everywhere in the basement, but it was strongest behind him.

Bob said, "Jesus, Ah-zee-za, did you do something in high school that you regret?" He poked his index finger against his temple. "Sounds like you're battling some demons in there."

Aziza continued, "Now suppose a sixteen-year-old boy went to a party, got drunk and slept with three girls. He wouldn't be a slut. He'd be a stud. The next day everyone in the school would hear about it, and he would be known as a stud for the rest of his high school career. At every reunion he'd be a stud, and no matter how old he got, whenever he told his male peers about his high school conquests, he would be congratulated as a stud."

"That's right!" Bob crowed. "Any guy who can talk three girls into giving up the panties on the same night would be a stud for life."

Howard turned around and stared back down the hall. All week, he'd been terrified of coming down to the basement, afraid of the way he'd feel if he saw the rumpled sheets on Davis' bed. But now it wasn't the *bedroom* that was bombarding his olfactory membrane with illicit scents.

"The interesting thing is that even though the boy is the one who had sex with multiple partners, it's the three girls who would be called sluts for sleeping with him all on the same night."

"What's the point of all this?" Bob asked impatiently.

"The point is that our society is very uncharitable toward women who have sex. If a woman has sex too soon in a relationship, she's a whore. If she has too many partners she's a whore. If she's into anything freaky—even if it's with her husband—she's a whore. If she has an affair after she's married, she's an adulterous whore. If she's sleeping with a married man, she's a home-wrecking whore. If she does anything outside of a very narrow bandwidth of approved sexual activity, she's a whore. So the director of any movie knows that if he shows a woman having sex, the audience will judge her very harshly. The lengthy process of presenting a 'rationale' doesn't prove that it's okay for a woman to cheat. It proves the opposite. It's so wrong for a woman to *have sex*, that the director has to devote ten or twenty percent of the movie to making her a sympathetic character, so that when she *does* have sex, the audience can see her as something other than a whore. This isn't necessary for men, because audiences of both sexes are already sympathetic toward philandering men."

"Puh-leeze," Bob said again.

Howard slowly walked out of the room and down the hall.

"Howard?" Keiko called, running after him. Bob and Aziza followed.

Howard stood in the doorway of the artists' studio; Sophia's scent wrapped around him in a suffocating embrace. He stared at the sheet draped over the easel. He recalled the night last week when he'd gone looking for Sophia and had found her in the kitchen eating ice cream. He had wondered if she was naked under her robe; now he was certain that she had been. Somehow, Howard knew that she'd been posing for Davis Delaney.

He walked forward slowly and pulled the sheet off the easel. He uncovered a painting of Sophia lying naked on a cross with a giant nail through her pelvis. Although Howard recognized the cross and nail as Davis' signature combination, he'd never known the artist to actually mount anyone on one of his crosses.

Sophia was lying on her back with her arms extended along the horizontal plank of the cross, and her legs stretched out straight. Her breasts were slightly flattened in this pose, but her pink nipples were erect. Davis had accurately rendered the shape of her body—the definition of her stomach, the subtle musculature in her arms, the sculpted patch of hair just above her vagina, and the way that her knee-caps were slightly out of line. A small piece of jewelry dangled from her belly button.

Aziza groaned dramatically and said, "Only a man would take a beautiful woman and present her naked with a nail through her crotch."

"It means he *nailed* her," Bob explained. "As in, *got some action.*"

"Trust me," Aziza said, "I get it." She glared at the painting. "In a man's eyes a woman exists only to be objectified, to get *nailed*, or to be the victim of violence. This artist has committed all three acts."

"Isn't that your wife?" Keiko asked.

Howard's eyes were locked on Sophia's face. She wore an enigmatic expression. Her face wasn't colored with regret about the affair, or embarrassment at posing nude, or pain from the nail that had been driven through her middle. Satisfaction seemed to shimmer in her eyes and tug at the corners of her mouth. He recalled his conversation with Adam on Sunday, *"She calls him 'The Big O.' Did you know that?"* Davis seemed to have captured Sophia's expression in a moment of post-orgasmic bliss.

The doorbell rang several times in quick succession. They all looked up as footsteps clattered on the main floor. Someone came barreling down the basement stairs.

"How-ward?" J-Lo called. "How-ward? … How-ward? … Oh, there you are!" she exclaimed, gruffly pushing past Bob and the women.

"Holy shit!" Bob said, gawking at her breasts. They swayed obscenely under the thin fabric of her silk shirt.

"Thank God you're okay!" J-Lo said. She was breathing hard, but smiling with relief.

Howard challenged, "You can't just walk into my house."

"Silly," J-Lo said, smiling sweetly, "I came to remind you about the meeting tonight."

"He said you can't come into his house," Aziza said, sounding surprisingly jealous and defensive.

J-Lo turned to glare at her. "Not that it's any of your business, but Article 9.1 of the Community Declaration gives me the right to enter any home in the neighborhood if I believe there's an emergency."

Aziza said, "There's no emergency here."

"The front window of the house is busted, and when I was talking to Howard on the phone a few minutes ago, the line went dead. I tried to call back, but the phone was off the

279

hook. I naturally assumed that something was wrong." J-Lo stroked Howard's arm lovingly and cooed, "Let me help you get cleaned up."

Howard said coldly, "Get out of my house."

J-Lo stared at him for a long moment. "But, Howard, I thought—"

He shrugged off her hands. "I'm serious, J-Lo," he said. "Get the fuck out of my house."

J-Lo gaped at him and turned red—the only hint of embarrassment on her Botoxed face. Aziza and Keiko snickered.

"You're going to regret this," J-Lo warned, her eyes watery as she started to leave the room.

"Let me help you," Bob offered, reaching out. J-Lo slapped his hands away as they veered toward her breasts. She raced up the stairs and out of the house.

"You want me to go after her, Howard?" Bob begged "Smooth things over for you?"

Howard stared at the picture of his wife, wondering if he had ever given her the satisfied expression she had in the painting.

"I need to take a shower," he said, glancing at his watch.

"Good idea," Bob said. "Get cleaned up and change out of that ridiculous outfit. We'll grab some dinner when you're done."

# thirty-nine

Howard took his time in the shower, even though the HOA meeting would start in half an hour. He stood still under the stream of water for a long time, replaying the events of the past week, wondering if the water sluicing down the drain was a metaphor for his doomed marriage. He had been honest with Sophia from the start, telling her that he didn't want children. When he'd proposed he'd asked if she was still comfortable about not having children; she had assured him that she was. Had she been *lying* from the start? *Maybe she just changed her mind*, Howard thought charitably. Maybe she had truly believed that she could live without children, but later decided that she couldn't. *But why didn't she tell me? Why have an affair, and why be so deliberately spiteful?*

When he finally stepped out of the shower, Andrew Metcalf's eighty-seven eyes were dripping wet and mournful. Howard stared at them for a long moment, wondering if they were merely reflecting his mood or if, somehow, they knew what was happening to his marriage.

He wiped mist off the mirror and spread shaving cream on his face. Sophia had attacked the sanctity of their marriage physically, spiritually, and emotionally, and Howard doubted that they could ever restore what they'd had previously. He dragged the blade down his face slowly, scraping away his five-o'clock shadow. Why had she called incessantly and apologized repeatedly? If she didn't want to be married anymore (at least not to Howard), why make such an effort? He rubbed peroxide

281

on the cut on his lip and placed a flesh-colored butterfly Band-Aid over the wound. He realized that her phone calls and apologies didn't necessarily reveal regret. He combed his hair, pulled on a pair of boxer shorts, and walked into the closet to grab a starched white dress shirt, a blue-and-red striped tie, and a navy Brooks Brothers' suit. It was more likely that Sophia was just hedging her bets. She wanted things to work out with Davis, but until they did, she was keeping her options open with *boring* Howard. He slipped on a pair of Italian loafers and checked his appearance in the bathroom mirror. The steam had dissipated by then. He looked at the eighty-seven eyes. They stared back at him, resolute.

Howard recalled Officer's Schleiden's question Saturday morning: *"You gonna divorce her?"* He pulled out his wallet, looking for the cop's business card. He studied the embossed Denver Police Department logo for a moment, and then dialed the number. When he got the officer's voice mail, he identified himself as "Howard Marshall, the cuckhold with the trash blowing out of his SUV last Saturday," and then said, "I have a tip about a crime you might want to investigate." He left his cell phone number.

Howard marched down the stairs, past all of Geraldine Crawford's star paintings. At the bottom, he paused to study the star with the single point extended across the canvas. The tip looked more strained than usual. It was thinner, on the verge of bursting. *You're almost there*, he thought, tracing a finger over the tiny point, encouraging the trapped spirit to keep pushing. *Almost there.*

"Whoa! You got cleaned up!" Bob said, when Howard stepped into the living room.

Howard barely noticed his boss. He stared at the walls in disbelief. Every one of Cynthia Mason's hidden images was visible to him. Now he clearly saw Davis Delaney's face in the painting that Bob had propped against the wall. In *Whoa Nellie!*, he saw Bill Clinton holding an iPod, standing next to an enormous seashell. *Guppies on the Move* was a picture of a huge stampede of cats, storming over a snow-covered mountain peak. In *Waterlogged*, he saw the dried husk of a camel's skull half-submerged in a mound of sand.

"I've got to go." Howard started toward the garage.

Bob said, "Hey, ride with us in the limo."

# forty

At least fifty people were seated in the meeting room at the Highlands Ranch Special Districts building. The room was designed like a courthouse with the seven HOA board members sitting behind a raised, crescent-shaped table while witnesses testified from low tables facing the exalted board.

"Howard's here!" someone in the crowd exclaimed.

Howard walked into the room regally, head held high. Aziza and Keiko followed him, side-by-side, beautiful and confident. Bob brought up the rear, strutting with his arms crossed behind his back.

Howard marched down the center aisle without looking around for a seat. He appeared to be heading straight for J-Lo, as if he were going to climb over the raised dias and throttle her.

"Mr. Marshall, please take a seat," J-Lo said, from her high perch. She glanced self-consciously at Tim Gorman, whose face still looked extra-shocked by the memory of her nearly naked breasts.

Howard continued toward her. "Mr. Marshall! Take a seat!" she screeched. A pair of oversized security guards stepped forward to block Howard's path, and he stopped, finally, looking at them curiously. The crowd started to murmur.

"Right here," Aziza said, grabbing Howard's arm and leading him into a mostly vacant row near the front.

J-Lo banged her gavel several times, staring angrily at Aziza and Keiko.

"This meeting is for residents of Highlands Ranch only," she said.

Howard didn't react to this announcement, but Bob and the women looked at him expectantly.

Bob leaped to his feet. "Ma'am, we're here with Howard Marshall. You summoned him to talk about the van in his driveway. Well, I'm the owner of the van … and these are my … nieces."

"Your nieces?" J-Lo asked doubtfully. She looked at them as if she wanted to set them on fire.

"That's right," Bob said. He leaned over to kiss Aziza on the cheek, but she shoved his face away.

"The van doesn't belong to you," J-Lo said, reaching for a piece of paper on her desk. "It belongs to Davis De—"

"The meeting is open to the public," Howard said in a dead-flat tone that caused everyone to stop and stare at him.

"Just the members of the public who *live* here," J-Lo insisted.

"There's nothing in the RIGs or the CD about that," Howard continued. "If residency were a requirement, you'd have someone at the door checking IDs."

Bob, who was still standing, turned to the room and said, "Did anyone have to show a driver's license to get in tonight?" Everyone in the crowd shook their heads and started to murmur.

J-Lo banged her gavel again fiercely and decided to change the subject. "I shouldn't have to remind you that Jan Hardeman is currently arguing her case."

Bob sat back down, and the crowd grew quiet.

The HOA had levied a five hundred dollar fine against Jan Hardeman for replacing the small flower garden in her front yard with a larger, and more attractive, rock and cactus garden.

Jan argued, "Colorado has been hit with summer droughts

for four of the last five years, and everyone from the governor to the legislature to mayors to various water boards has urged us to conserve water. So our garden will help conserve our state's most precious resource, plus it's—"

"You didn't have permission," J-Lo interrupted.

"I submitted a proposal—"

"But it was rejected."

"Yes," Jan conceded, "but it shouldn't have been. My xeriscaping plan is identical to designs that you've approved for other people in the neighborhood."

"The other homes were in different parts of Highlands Ranch."

"Even if they were in different parts of the neighborhood, the fact that the plan was approved shows that it's an acceptable design," Jan said. "So there was no reason for you to disallow my garden."

"As board president," J-Lo said officiously, "I'm not required to explain why your request was denied, but in this instance, I'll tell you. It'll help educate you and everyone else about our process. As you know, Highlands Ranch is divided into five metro districts, and further subdivided into 'pods' of about forty lots each. Homes in each pod are supposed to maintain similar appearances to preserve property values. We approved xeriscaping plans in other pods, because there were several homes in the pod that were already xeriscaped. But no homes in your pod have this type of landscaping, so we rejected your application."

"So I'm the *first*," Jan shrugged. "Other people are probably as interested in conservation as I am, so I'm sure that some of them will xeriscape, too."

J-Lo shook her head. "That's not how we do things. You can't be different from your neighbors."

"But how can my pod ever become eligible for xeriscaping if you don't allow someone to be the *first* home to make the change?"

"You have to match your neighbors," J-Lo said simply. "So now you have thirty days to restore your yard to its previous condition, plus pay the five hundred dollar fine. If you fail to comply, we will begin enforcement proceedings against you."

"Are you crazy?" Jan demanded, her face turning bright red. "It'll cost me thousands to rip out the rocks and reinstall flowers and sod! Then I'll be wasting precious water all because you want to make sure no one in my pod gets xeriscaping!"

"Next time, if you want to get your project approved, you'll obey the rules."

"I tried to obey the rules, but the rules are idiotic!"

"Bailiffs, please remove her from the witness table," J-Lo said. The burly men in uniforms were actually just security guards making fifteen dollars an hour, but J-Lo referred to them as bailiffs because she thought of herself as a judge. Jan screamed at the men to keep their filthy hands off her as she stood up and stormed back to her seat in the audience.

"Next case," J-Lo said, "is Highlands Ranch Community Association versus Richard and Janet Kelmer."

During the next half hour, the board upheld assessments against the Kelmers for putting a portable basketball goal in their driveway (RIGs Article 2.9), the Olsons for not acting quickly enough in getting their landscaping installed after they moved in (RIGs Article 2.41), the Johnsons for letting their daughter set up a table in front of their house to sell lemonade (RIGs Article 2.13), the Mercers for parking a Ford F-350 dually pickup truck in their driveway (RIGs Article 2.48), and the Andersons for not replacing a sun-faded section of wood in their fence ((RIGs Article 2.28).

J-Lo sailed through the hearings, rejecting every appeal for leniency. Each time, the crowd murmured its disapproval, and she banged her gavel to regain control of the room.

"If we make an exception," J-Lo admonished repeatedly, "then we'll be setting a dangerous precedent." She looked down at her docket and announced that the next case would be, "Highlands Ranch Community Association versus Sophia and Howard Marshall."

"Good luck," Keiko whispered, patting Howard's back.

J-Lo glared at Aziza and Keiko as Howard walked forward and took a seat at the defendant's table.

"Good evening, Mr. Marshall," J-Lo said formally.

"J-Lo," he replied.

"You will refer to me as Chairwoman Meagert-Logan."

Howard didn't respond.

J-Lo cleared her throat and read the charge against him. "Two months ago, you were advised that the commercial van parked in your driveway was in violation of Article 2.18 of the Residential Improvement Guidelines. You were advised to remove it or file for an exception. You failed to respond to the notice or to remove the vehicle, so a fine was imposed and a second notice was issued. You were advised that this hearing would be your final opportunity to plead—"

Howard asked, "Who wrote the RIGs?"

J-Lo glared at him for a moment, and said, "We're not going to get sidetracked. We're here to discuss the commercial vehicle parked in your driveway. As of this evening, your fine is increased to one thousand dollars, and you have until 8 a.m. tomorrow to remove the van."

Howard said, "If Highlands Ranch is divided into pods, why can't Jan ask her immediate neighbors how they feel about her landscaping? If the majority of them approve, then she ought to able to keep it, and the board should remove the assessments against her."

"Yeah!" someone in the crowd yelled.

J-Lo slammed an open palm on the table, and her wedding band clicked hard against the walnut surface.

"We're discussing *your* case at the moment," she said.

Howard asked, "Why can't someone back a truck into their driveway just to load it? Why can't someone put up a basketball hoop or let their kids set up a lemonade stand on the sidewalk? Why should a central board of *seven* people decide all these issues for the 80,000 people who live here? Why shouldn't this authority be delegated out to the people who live in each pod?"

"Get her, Howard!" someone yelled, and the audience broke into applause. J-Lo banged her gavel.

"We ... are ... discussing ... *your* ... case," she hissed, "All these other people have already had their hearings."

"They didn't have *hearings*," Howard said. "The word *hearing* suggests that an impartial arbiter is *listening* and trying to make a fair decision."

"She wouldn't recognize a fair decision if it bit her on the tit!" someone screamed, getting a laugh from the audience.

Howard continued, "You're the one who *issues* the assessment, and when they appeal, you ignore every argument, and impose a penalty. You get to be judge, jury and executioner, but you don't even do it in a thoughtful manner. You just read the relevant line in the RIGs as if it were the divine word of God. But if we're going to rely so completely on the RIGs without using common sense, then shouldn't we know who wrote the RIGs?"

"Now is not the time for—"

"I think it *is* the time," Howard continued. "*You* didn't

write the RIGs. The board didn't write them. The residents of Highlands Ranch didn't write them. No government agency wrote them. So who wrote these rules that intrude into our lives and impede our ability to use our common sense?"

"Get her, Howard!" someone yelled again.

Howard said, "The *developers* wrote the RIGs. The developers wrote them before they built the first house. They wrote them before the first resident moved in. Their goal was to ensure that when they sold the *last* house in Highlands Ranch, twenty or thirty years down the road, the neighborhood would still look the way *they* envisioned it."

"What they envisioned is a neighborhood that would be attractive and desirable," J-Lo snapped. "That's not a bad thing."

"True, but the definitions of *attractive* and *desirable* change over time. We're a neighborhood full of upper-middle class professionals who are capable of using our own judgment to keep the neighborhood looking nice. The RIGs and the CD serve to merely preserve the developers' vision, at the expense of ours."

J-Lo said, "The rules exist to protect all of our—"

"Property values," Howard finished for her. "I know. We've all heard the spiel. But in Jan's case, you've approved the same xeriscaping plan for other homes, so clearly it's attractive. And if Jan's neighbors don't believe that their property values have been harmed, then how do you know that this change will downgrade the neighborhood? In fact, attractive xeriscaping has *improved* home values throughout the metro area, so it would likely do the same in Jan's case. If a majority of families in a pod agree that a particular change enhances the neighborhood, why shouldn't we trust their judgment? The residents are doctors, lawyers, politicians, engineers, architects—successful business people in every field. Do we really think that this group is incapable of using a democratic process to maintain a beautiful neighborhood?"

The crowd erupted again, clapping, cheering, and whistling. It took several minutes for the board and the bailiffs to restore order.

"We're talking about *your* case," J-Lo said, exasperated. "You're about to get another assessment for un-repaired hail damage on the vehicle"—she held up pictures of three spider-webbed impact marks in the windshield of the van from the hail storm Friday night—"and the front window of your house has been destroyed and must be replaced immediately. So your problems seem to be getting worse, Mr. Marshall. This is your final warning about the van. Either you remove it, or we will!"

"How do you think people would feel if they knew that Mrs. Stephenson's house on Pendleton Drive had been turned into a high-tech surveillance station?" Howard asked.

J-Lo blanched and watched him nervously as a low murmur spread through the room.

Howard turned toward the audience. "I went over there this afternoon, thinking that Mrs. Stephenson was ill. But when I got into her house, I found out that she's been dead for three years."

The crowd gasped.

"The homeowners association has erected a Mrs. Stephenson mannequin to patrol the windows and spy on us," he explained. "They've got dozens of closed-circuit TV monitors and VCRs set up to record our every move."

J-Lo banged her gavel. "Mr. Marshall!" She screamed over the grumbling audience. "Mr. Marshall! Mr. Marshall!"

"And this is just one house," Howard yelled. "How many more surveillance stations do they have?" To the crowd, he asked, "Is there a house in your pod where someone always seems to be staring at you with binoculars?"

A look of recognition spread through the audience. Howard saw dozens of people nodding their heads.

"Mr. Johnson is *always* in his window, even when I come home in the middle of the night," a male voice called out.

"Mrs. Antonopolus on my street," someone else said.

"Yeah!" someone agreed. "She's always watching!"

All of the board members looked nervous. J-Lo banged her gavel so hard that the hammer popped off the handle and skittered onto the floor. "Bailiffs!" she screamed.

Howard stood as the guards approached. He marched out of the room with Bob, Aziza and Keiko on his heels. The crowd chanted his name.

# forty-one

"You were terrific!" Aziza said in the limo.

Bob said, "Howard's studying for the bar exam. He's gonna be a great lawyer!"

"You ought to run for board president," Keiko suggested. "You know everyone would vote for you."

Howard shrugged indifferently.

"I'm starving," Bob said. "Hey, Edward," he called to the driver. "Take us to Claim Jumper over by Park Meadows."

"What's Claim Jumper?" Keiko asked.

"It's a restaurant. You'll like it," Bob promised.

Howard pulled out his cell phone and dialed Sophia's number.

When she answered, he said, "Let me talk to Davis."

"What do you mean?" Sophia hesitated. "You want his cell number?"

"I mean, hand him the phone."

"Mounds, I told you that he wasn't coming to New York."

"I know," Howard said. "He didn't go to New York, because *you* didn't go to New York. Where are you? In Santa Fe with him?"

She didn't speak for a few beats. "Honey," she said slowly, "what are you talking about?"

Howard said, "Let's stop playing games. I know that you've been sleeping with him for quite a while. I know that you posed nude for him. I know that you took him to Panzano and the Hotel Monaco, I know that you never checked into your hotel in New York, and—" Howard stopped suddenly, an image coming back to him. He couldn't speak for a moment. "And even though you told me on Sunday that you'd broken up with Davis, you didn't come home immediately to try to fix our marriage. You continued your trip. So now you've been with him for four days, and I can only guess that you planned to stay with him until Saturday so that you could maintain the lie about going to New York."

Sophia said, "This situation is complicated."

"Let me talk to him," Howard said numbly. The painting of Sophia replayed in his mind.

"This isn't *Davis'* fault."

"Trust me," Howard said, laughing acidly, "I don't blame *him*." He saw her lying on the cross, enigmatic smile on her face, huge stake nailed through her pelvis.

"What do you want to talk to him about?"

"Man stuff."

"Like what?"

"Sophia, put him on the goddamned phone!" Howard saw the curve of her legs, the patch of hair over her vagina, the small piece of jewelry hanging from her belly button, and her hard, pink nipples.

The line went silent, and Howard thought that she had hung up on him. Then Davis said, "What's up, Money?"

Howard wanted to ask him how many times Sophia had posed for him, but instead, he said, "Your van is going to get towed in the morning."

"What the fuck?" Davis said. "Come on, Howard! Your wife chose me, dog. Don't take it out on my van!"

Howard chuckled mirthlessly. "It's not me. It's the HOA."

"The who?"

"The homeowners association. They're going to tow your van."

"Move it for me, dog? The keys are in the basement."

"You know," Howard said, slowly, "the *energy* of that doesn't feel right to me." He hung up.

"Way to go, Howard!" Bob said. "Fuck him *and* his van."

Howard closed his eyes and said, "I need to go back to the house."

"You're not hungry?" Bob asked, disappointed.

Howard shook his head. "Sophia's pregnant."

No one spoke for several moments.

"Is it your baby?" Keiko asked gently.

Howard laughed mirthlessly. It would have taken divine intervention for it to be his baby.

"She just told you about it on the phone?" Aziza asked.

Howard shook his head again. "I'll know for sure when we get home."

"So you don't want to eat?" Bob groused.

**\*\*\*\*\*\*\*\*\*\***

When they got back to the house, Howard marched straight into the basement. Bob and the women chased after him. He was no longer haunted by his sinking dream. He didn't experience the sensation of suffocating. He went directly into the artist's studio, where Sophia was still nailed to the cross with a contented expression on her face. Though he'd studied the painting intently earlier, he hadn't detected its hidden meaning—at least not consciously. Now, he could see that the piece of jewelry dangling from his wife's belly button was a gleaming nail—curved into the fetal position.

# forty-two

Howard, Aziza, Keiko and Bob sat on the chairs and sofa in the spacious master bedroom eating pizza. Bob had given Edward the rest of the night off with instructions to return for them with the limo in the morning. He'd ordered two large pizzas from Pizza Hut, but the delivery boy had gotten hopelessly lost in the maze of Highlands Ranch.

"He's lost," Bob said, when the restaurant called to report the problem.

"Tell him to knock on any door," Howard said. "Ask the residents to use the Directory to look us up."

"Any door?" Bob had asked suspiciously. "What Directory?"

Howard said, "Just tell him."

Bob repeated the instructions into the phone, and ten minutes later, the pizzas arrived.

"God, I was starving!" Bob said, stuffing his mouth. They were in the master bedroom because the main floor was still too cold. The tarp over the broken window stopped the main force of the wind, but it didn't keep the chilly air completely out.

Aziza studied Howard with real interest. "Do you have a passport?"

Howard nodded, nibbling on a slice of pizza.

"Come to Mexico with us," Aziza said.

Bob perked up. "Really?"

"Not you, Chief," Aziza said, with no hint of apology in her voice. "Howard, we're leaving for Cabo tomorrow. We'll be there for ten days. You should come with us."

"That's tempting," Howard said, chewing slowly.

Aziza said, "We've got a two-bedroom cabana on the beach."

"You can stay in my room," Keiko offered.

"No," Aziza said a little possessively, "you can have a room to *yourself*. Keiko and I will share the other one."

"I'd have to get time off from my boss," Howard said. He and the women turned to stare at Bob.

Bob looked jealous, but he said, "Of course, Howard. I've been through three divorces myself. I know how tough it can be."

# forty-three

Howard was lying on a deserted white sand beach with a sombrero over his face. He hadn't had a beach vacation since the Costa Rica trip a few years ago, and he'd forgotten how good it felt to just lie in the sun and do nothing. A guide at the resort in Cabo San Lucas had driven Howard, Aziza and Keiko about an hour down the coast and dropped them off at the top of a cliff that offered an amazing view of the Pacific Ocean.

"To jor right," the guide said in heavily accented English, "ees a path, tha weel lead to tha beash. Es berry priveet. Jew weel hab tha beash to jorself. I weel come back for jew beefore tha sun set, okay?"

They hiked down a narrow path that had been cut through heavy foliage, and, eventually, reached a crescent-shaped beach, half a mile long and bordered on each end by sheer cliffs that jutted out into the sea. They slathered sun-tan lotion on their bodies, and then plopped down to enjoy the warmth and solitude. Howard had an Elmore Leonard novel and an iPod in his bag, but, so far, he hadn't been tempted to do much more than doze.

"Someone's here," he heard Keiko say, but he didn't open his eyes.

"Are you sure?" Aziza asked.

Howard kept the sombrero over his face. It didn't matter to him if someone was coming. If they had to share the beach with ten or even a hundred people, it would still be more peaceful than the tourist-infested shore behind their hotel.

"Can't you hear them?" Keiko asked.

"Yeah," Aziza said. "We should get dressed."

Howard recalled that they were both topless.

"What the fuck is going on here?" a female voice said from about ten feet away. Howard scowled under the sombrero; the voice was familiar but totally out of place on this Mexican beach.

He lifted the hat and sat up, blinking in the bright light. Sophia and Davis were staring at him. Howard cleared his throat and rubbed his eyes, looking around, disoriented. There was no hot sun, no secluded beach and no hidden path. He was sitting on the couch in the master bedroom, and his back ached from sleeping on the soft cushions. A few feet away, Bob was still out cold in an arm chair. His mouth was wide open, revealing the glistening Chicklets. Drool dribbled down his chin.

Sophia and Davis were standing just inside the bedroom door, wearing full leather motorcycling outfits that were splattered with tiny dots of color. They must have ridden all night to make it from Santa Fe to Denver by—Howard looked at his watch—8:17 a.m.

"You made good time," he said.

"Looks like *you've* been making good time, too," Sophia fumed. "You want to tell me why there are two women in our bed?"

Howard looked over at Aziza and Keiko, who were sitting up with the sheet bunched under their chins.

"It's not what you think," he said.

"These are the girls from The Palm Friday night!" Sophia realized.

Keiko waved and smiled sheepishly. "It's good to see you again."

"Howard, what the hell is going on?" Sophia asked, scowling.

"Where's my van, dog?" Davis demanded, marching forward.

Howard rubbed his face and groaned. J-Lo must have sent a tow truck at first light.

"They took it," Howard said indifferently. He stood, intending to go into the restroom.

Davis shoved him. "Dog, you're gonna get my van back!"

Howard regained his balance and looked at Davis curiously. "No, *dog*, I'm not."

Davis snarled and threw a fierce round-house punch at Howard. Aziza and Keiko gasped, but Howard barely reacted. His long-dormant Golden Gloves reflexes kicked in and he leaned back about four inches. Davis' fist flew past harmlessly. The artist grunted and swung again, this time driving a straight left at Howard's nose, but Howard slid his head a few inches to the right and the blow missed. Davis gathered himself to launch another right, but before he could get the punch uncorked, Howard threw a short, left uppercut that caught Davis under the chin and dropped him gracelessly. The artist crumpled into Bob's lap, waking the boss with a start.

"What?" Bob asked, groggily, wiping his mouth.

Sophia looked down at Davis, but made no move to attend to him.

Howard asked, "How far along are you?"

Sophia said, "How *what*?"

"The pregnancy," he said. "How far along are you?"

That brought things to a halt. They stared at each other for a long moment. Bob, Aziza and Keiko watched intently. Davis groaned, just starting to come around.

"How do you know that?" Sophia asked defensively.

"I know a lot of things," Howard said.

"Well, here's something you probably don't know," she said. "I'm leaving Davis." She stepped closer to Howard, her eyes moist.

"Yeah, that's what you said on Sunday."

"It's true."

"So why didn't you come home?"

Sophia was quiet for a moment. "I just didn't know what to do," she said softly.

"Funny, Davis raced back here to rescue his van, but you were in no hurry to rescue your marriage." Howard studied her leather outfit. It looked as if she'd been standing too close to someone using a paint sprayer. "Is that paint?"

"Bugs," Sophia said. "There were swarms everywhere." She stopped just in front of him. "Mounds, I made a terrible mistake. I hope you can forgive me."

Who knew that bugs were so active at night? A squished dragonfly was plastered on her shoulder. "They must be drawn to the headlight," Howard observed.

"What?" Sophia asked.

"You were drawn to the Big O, but now that you've caught him, you feel a little splattered, huh?"

Davis sat up, and worked his jaw back and forth, "Don't get it twisted, dog," he slurred. "I kicked *her* to the curb. I nail 'em, but I ain't down for raisin' no babies. That's not how I roll."

"Of course not," Howard said.

Sophia's eyes darted between the two men desperately. "Honey, that's not true. I want to save our marriage. I love you so much."

"Ladies?" Howard said, turning to Aziza and Keiko. "We need to get to the airport, right?"

They smiled and climbed out of bed, holding the thin sheet

tightly around themselves. Sunlight coming through the window silhouetted their bodies, revealing that they were naked.

"God damn!" Bob said, appreciatively.

They grabbed their clothes and shuffled into the bathroom, giggling.

Sophia turned back to Howard, and asked in alarm, "The *airport*? Where are you going?"

He studied her for a moment, as if committing her face to memory. "How did you get in here? When you left on Saturday, you said you didn't have your keys with you."

"We came through the window, dog," Davis said.

"Don't change the subject, Howard," Sophia demanded. "*Where* are you going?"

Howard chuckled. "That's the second time in twelve hours that Davis has gone through that window." First the painting, then the artist himself. Howard didn't feel the need to throw him out again. For all he cared, Davis could stay forever. Howard started toward the closet.

"*Where* are you going?" Sophia screamed.

"I'll tell you where I'm *not* going," Howard said, "I'm not going to stay *here*."

# forty-four

When Howard, Bob, Aziza, and Keiko walked out of the front door, the sun was shining brightly and the air was much warmer than it had been in weeks. Sophia and Davis trailed behind them. Davis was still working his jaw from side to side, and he was wobbly on his feet. Howard was rolling a suitcase that he'd hurriedly packed with shorts, T-shirts, toiletries and a couple of novels. He had his cell phone and passport in his hand.

Edward was standing at the back door of the Range Rover limo in a smart, navy chauffeur's suit.

"I can't believe you're leaving with them," Sophia said. "You barely know them!"

"No," Howard said softly. "I barely know *you*. I'll get the rest of my things when I come back."

Off to their right, J-Lo was in the front yard, hammering a bright orange sign into the turf.

"What are you doing on my property?" Sophia demanded.

"This is a notice of foreclosure," J-Lo said, her eyes locked on Howard. "Don't leave," she begged.

Howard continued toward the limo.

"Foreclosure?" Sophia asked. "What are you talking about?"

J-Lo walked toward Howard, and said distractedly, "Article 8.35 of the CD. We can foreclose on the property to collect overdue assessments." To Howard, she said, "Don't you want to finish what we started?"

"What you *started*?" Sophia asked, alarmed. "What the hell is she talking about Howard?"

"Last night we picked up where we left off years ago," J-Lo bragged.

Sophia slapped J-Lo hard across the mouth. The smack reverberated in the air for several seconds. It was hard to tell if J-Lo was surprised, because the Botox smothered her reaction. But then she screamed like a Karate student and kicked Sophia in the shin with the sharp point of one of her Manolo Blahnik Curcia mules. Sophia screamed and doubled over, grabbing her leg. When J-Lo swung again, aiming for the other shin, Sophia caught her ankle and tried to throw the smaller woman onto the lawn. J-Lo grabbed Sophia's hair, and they tumbled onto the ground together, screeching.

Howard climbed into the limo.

"Are you sad?" Keiko asked as they watched his wife and ex-girlfriend wrestling in the damp grass.

"Damn, they look good together," Bob said appreciatively.

Howard felt like a spirit that had just escaped from a star prison. "No," he said to Keiko softly. "Not any more—I'm glad to be out."

His cell phone rang. Howard answered and was pleasantly surprised to hear Officer's Schleiden's voice.

"Your timing couldn't be better," Howard said.

"You decided to leave her, huh?"

"Yes, I did," Howard said.

"Smart man! Trust me. In the long run, it's better than shooting her."

Howard laughed. "I'm sure that's true."

"You said you have a tip for me?"

Howard said, "I believe I've discovered a criminal network."

"Where? In Highlands Ranch?"

"Yes."

"That's out of my jurisdiction, but you can tell me what you know, and I'll pass it on to the Douglas County Sheriff's Office."

Howard said, "On Saturday, you told me that my neighbor Edith Stephenson had filed a complaint against me."

"Uh … I don't remember the name, but yeah, there was a hit-and-run."

"I just learned last night that the complainant has been dead for three years."

Officer Schleiden didn't speak for a moment. "Let me look this up." He typed on his keyboard for a moment and retrieved the file. "Yeah … Edith Stephenson, age seventy-three, at 12135 Pendleton Drive."

"Someone filed a false report," Howard said.

"Why would anyone pretend to be a dead lady just to file on you for driving into the yard?"

"After Mrs. Stephenson died, the HOA turned her house into a high-tech surveillance post, including a Mrs. Stephenson mannequin to patrol the windows. The HOA makes video and audio recordings of the residents' activities. They probably didn't want the cops to knock on the door and try to talk to the homeowner, so they hustled someone out to pretend to be Mrs. Stephenson."

"If they're recording video *and* audio, then filing a false report is the least of their problems," Officer Schleiden said.

"The problem is the audio," Howard said.

"You're damned right it is! They can't secretly record private conversations. That's against the law!"

"I thought I should let you know."

"Trust me, the sheriff's gonna be real interested."